WAITING IN THE SILENCE

Additional Books by Rosalyn W. Berne

Creating Life from Life: Biotechnology and Science Fiction
Pan Stanford Press, 2014

When the Horses Whisper
Rainbow Ridge Books, 2013

Nanotalk: Conversations with Engineers and Scientists about Ethics, Meaning and Belief in the Development of Nanotechnology
CRC Press, 2005

WAITING IN THE SILENCE

Rosalyn W. Berne

WAITING IN THE SILENCE
Rosalyn W. Berne
Copyright © Rosalyn W. Berne 2012

ISBN-13: 978-1511851954

ISBN-10: 1511851953

PRINTING HISTORY

Spore Press, LLC / September 2012
Spore Press Ebook / September2012
Create Space / May 2015

For information use contact link at:
http://RosalynBerne.com

Cover design by Kaia Otstak

In Loving Memory of Zoe

ACKNOWLEDGEMENTS

My heartfelt appreciation to all those who supported, encouraged, and assisted me with this endeavor: Hedgebrook (Women Authoring Change); research assistants Priya Curtis and Kate Howling; Rochelle Hollander and the National Science Foundation; Gordon D. Berne; Pamela Friedman; Linn Prentis; Claudia Sencer; Kinnaird Fox; Darcy Galluccio; Lou Anders; and William Prindle. A special thanks goes to Kathleen Manuel for her editorial work.

" . . . O breaking heart that will not break,
    Oriana!
O pale, pale face so sweet and meek,
    Oriana!
Thou smilest, but thou dost not speak,
And then the tears run down my cheek,
    Oriana.
What wantest thou? whom dost thou seek,
    Oriana?
I cry aloud; none hear my cries,
    Oriana.
Thou comest atween me and the skies,
Oriana.
I feel the tears of blood arise
Up from my heart unto my eyes,
    Oriana.
Within thy heart my arrow lies,
    Oriana.
O cursed hand! O cursed blow!
    Oriana!
O happy thou that liest low,
    Oriana!
All night the silence seems to flow
Beside me in my utter woe,
    Oriana.
A weary, weary way I go,
    Oriana!"

        From The Ballad Of Oriana, by Lord Alfred Tennyson

CONTENTS

PROLOGUE

When the Virtual Information System for Human Noetic Evolution and Welfare emerged, it was detected in very few localities on Earth. Exquisitely intelligent, it appears to have formed independently of human design. Discretely linked in time and space to the global circuitry of ubiquitous nano-systems, by all accounts it appears to garner its power and knowledge from the hundreds of thousands of satellites that orbit close to the Earth's atmosphere.

One theory suggests that its emergence is the first phase of the long predicted "synchronicity," an evolutionary outgrowth of converging human and machine intelligences. Another view suspects it to be a cleverly orchestrated system of social manipulation; but by whom, no one can say. Then, of course, there are the Seekers, those who believe VISHNEW to be a technological incarnation of God. Desperate to connect, they travel the world to the edge of the VISHNEW communities, hoping to gain access somehow.

Whatever it is, VISHNEW is both venerated and abhorred. Jealousy and resentment are harbored against those who have access, by those who do not. Those who are connected prosper and thrive, but the criteria for access to VISHEW are not known. Seven localities to date have succeeded in making the connection, each striving to protect itself against the envy and rage of an otherwise hard-suffering world: the Scottish Isles, Patagonia, Iceland, Yemen, Sri Lanka, the Monkey Bay region of Malawi, and Nantucket.

PART ONE.
VIRGINITY

NANTUCKET

"What have I done now?" Oriana whispers, as if to someone near. She purses her lips and lifts her chin. Inhaling deeply, she releases the breath with a sigh. The day is Sunday, December 12, and the time is 5:22 p.m. Eighteen hours and thirty-eight minutes remain until the court-ordered retrieval of the child from her womb.

She steps out of the white-clapboard saltbox house, closing the door behind her as quietly as she is able, and a frigid blast slams against her face. She blinks, tears forming, and heads out into the dreary gloaming.

Gray and white clouds rush across the sky in rapidly changing formations. The billowy puffs form a pregnant woman, and then change into a newborn child waving her arms in distress.

Oriana reaches the end of Copper Lane, looking over her shoulder a last time to the structure she once knew as home. At that moment, the window shutters close tight, precisely as they have been programmed to do when their sensors detect diminishing

3

daylight. Oriana's hopefulness fades into remorse, as the sense of loss pulls down on her heart.

Overhead, the clouds disperse into a hundred newborn spiders released from a dissipating web.

Along Quaker Road toward Milk Street, Oriana moves onward, with no sense of direction or purpose. She knows only that she has left home, and that going back is not an option.

Naked branches of a sycamore crackle in the grip of winter, and the last wisps of clouds form into a dark mass, moving northeast over the sea. A gray mist settles over Nantucket Town, dampening the night. The evening is far colder than she had anticipated.

Silent shadows of days long gone fall in ebony shades along the empty streets. An upward gust lifts a cluster of decaying leaves across the stones of the sidewalk. *My feet are cold*, Oriana notices, glancing down at her bare toes.

Oriana crosses onto Main Street, reminding herself that she had no choice but to leave her shoes behind, so that her movements will remain undetected. She pushes on, though walking barefoot on the cobblestones is awkward. North Church comes into view. She lifts her gaze, considering how its steeple seems to reach for something that isn't there. *What a strange relic*, she muses.

"Good evening, Oriana."

She jerks her head in the direction of the voice; startled that someone is suddenly standing so near. The eyes of a man smile through a scarf covering the rest of his face. She finds it odd that he's wearing a scarf, odder still that it seems to be made of actual wool. Baffled that his hands are gloved, she wonders why he's not wearing the warming cream made for protecting extremities. She wonders where this man is from, half afraid to learn the real answer.

"Good evening," she replies, anxious at his presence, and more so at the fact that he knows her name.

"Chilly this evening," he says in a raspy tone like the sound of laryngitis. The voice is nearly recognizable, only she can't fathom why.

"Yes, I would say so," she returns, trying to identify the source of the voice whose timbre and cadence is so hauntingly familiar. "Brrrrr!" he shudders. The man seems to be trying to put Oriana at ease, which only serves to irritate her.

"Who are you, and how do you know my name?" Oriana demands.

The man gazes at her for a moment. "Did you happen to see the sky?" he asks, ignoring her question. "It was stunning a few moments ago."

Oriana looks up, finding the sky has darkened. She mumbles something about not really noticing.

"Look at your coat! What a beautiful pattern is forming, like the fur of a harbor seal," he remarks.

"Oh that's funny," she chuckles, relaxing a bit and sliding her hands into her pockets. "It was designed for the changes to come at random intervals, so I don't always notice right away."

The familiar stranger moves too close for her comfort. Oriana begins to stiffen.

"Who are you?" she demands again.

"Come with me," he insists, grabbing her elbow and tugging her toward him. "We need to talk about your daughter."

"My daughter?" she gasps, snatching herself from his grasp. Oriana shoves him as hard as she can and kicks him in the shin. "Get away!" she screams, her mind suddenly frenzied with dread.

"Ahhh," he utters in a voice smooth and calm. "Relax, Oriana. Will you tell me, where are you going?"

Oriana's gums begin to ache, reminding her of the transgression she's committed. She turns to leave, but the man grabs Oriana's shoulders, squeezing hard to keep her from moving. Under pressure of his palms her fear gives way to anger and annoyance.

"Please let go of me," she says slowly and deliberately.

"You don't want to run from me," he suggests, turning her around to face him. "I am only asking you to tell me where you are going."

Oriana stiffens, wanting to run, yet powerless to move. The pressure inside her chest increases, and she pants with the effort of trying to escape the man's grasp. She tries to calm down. *How stupid to be out at night alone.* She reassures herself that alarm sensors have by now been triggered by his touch and help will soon arrive. She can almost hear the hovercraft whooshing up Main Street, and see in her mind's eye the security-bots grabbing the man's arms and lifting him away.

But VISHNEW isn't sensing the threat, because she is no longer connected, not even partially, after what she did to herself before leaving home. Her fantasy of being rescued vanishes. The cold stones under her feet transfer a chill into the marrow of her bones.

The stranger exhales through his scarf, and the warm moisture of his breath falls across Oriana's face. His breath smells of the sassafras tea her grandfather drinks every morning. She relaxes in spite of herself.

The strangely familiar man releases her, folds his arms across his chest, and waits for an answer.

Oriana has no intention of telling him anything about herself, and besides, as to where she is heading, she simply does not know.

The man turns his gaze toward the pink and blue glow fading on the horizon. "Don't be afraid, Oriana," he says softly. "I don't want to hurt you."

His compassion seems authentic, the words landing on her chest as a soothing hand. "Maybe I wouldn't be afraid of you if I could see your face," she whispers to the scarf-enshrouded man.

The stranger extends a hand toward Oriana's mouth. He places a thumb at her lips and gently wipes away the blood that has gathered in the corner. He knows what she has done. "Geez," he exclaims. Oriana ponders how strangely comfortable his touch is, even through thick gloves. The terror begins to dissipate from her limbs. Her shoulders ease and knees soften. The dim light of dusk fades into the darkness of silhouettes; tree limbs, widows' walks, and wrought iron lanterns outline the cobblestoned street.

"How are you feeling, Oriana?" he asks. "Are you uncomfortable or in any pain?" It's been so long since someone inquired of her being, without judgment or calculation.

"The truth is," she reveals, closing her eyes and covering her forehead with her palm, "I don't feel well at all."

"I'm sorry to hear that," he replies.

"You haven't told me who are you or why you have stopped me like this," she says firmly. She searches for the eyes she can barely see in the dim light. "What do you know about me?"

Saying nothing, he gazes sadly across Nantucket Harbor. Storm -damaged, sealed off from rest of the world, and protected by VISHNEW, the island no longer bustles with tourists, ferries and delivery boats. The man stares at the empty water. For a moment Oriana glimpses in him a deep sorrow, though tempered with strength and resolve. She smiles at him, then abruptly pulls back. No one is to be trusted.

"I have to go," Oriana announces. She steps off of the curb and heads up Main Street as quickly as she can.

"Oriana!" the man calls as he follows closely behind. "Please, for the sake of your child!"

Oriana stops and turns slowly towards him. Approaching her, he pulls off his gloves, holding his palms up to show her. Even in the dim light she can see that he lacks the implanted circuitry that connects most of the island's residents to VISHNEW. She steps back in awe and surprise.

The lights come on inside a nearby building. Oriana and the man grow suddenly still. Through the storefront window, they can make out the form of a woman setting up to take inventory of the island's techno-medical supplies. Stacks of bio-scanners and piles of nano-camera capsules line the long oak countertop. Once The Nantucket Pharmacy, The Repository had been a popular breakfast spot on the island where fisherman enjoyed scrambled eggs, corned beef hash, and onion-potatoes grilled up fresh, while summer residents favored the shop's gourmet coffee, fresh berries with yogurt, and warm, buttery croissants. Oriana's heart races over the thought of being spotted now that she has disconnected from VISHNEW. The strange man stands still as well, and grabs her tightly by the hand.

"Let go of me," she snaps as she tries to pull her hand free. This time there is no intrigue, no wonder or curiosity in her voice. Her eyes are ablaze. "Who are you, and why are you in disguise? Are you one of those Seekers?" she demands. "They'll soon catch you, you know. I'd get out of here quickly if I were you."

The man scoffs "huh" with a small, soft exhalation of breath through his mouth. He releases her hand, only to wrap his arm around her neck, clasping her tightly against his side. He covers her mouth, such that Oriana cannot speak. "Just stop for a moment," he says firmly as he pulls her away from the illumination of the street lamps. "We need to get out of view."

"That's impossible," Oriana replies into his palm in a muffled, garbled voice, wiggling to try to break away from his grasp.

The shutter of an abandoned building bangs repeatedly, lifted by the gusting wind. The lights go out in The Repository. The man and Oriana each become quiet again, in unspoken agreement about the danger they face. They watch as the woman leaves the building, swiping her hand over the door to lock up. And although she glances in their direction, she seems not to notice the pair in the middle of Main Street. The two remain still until they hear her footsteps turning the corner onto Centre Street.

The man backs away.

"Go on then, and do it your way," he says.

Oriana grabs the hem of her coat, lifting it to give her legs more freedom to run. The other hand she places under her heavy belly for support, her bare feet stinging on the cold stones as she takes off. Her stride is swift until a high-pitched screech startles her, and she stops to look in its direction. Oriana hesitates as she approaches a feral form crouched along the curb. The droopy ears and angry pinched face of the crabbit send a shudder up her spine. Jutting its head forward, the crabbit sniffs the air, then catches Oriana's gaze and stiffens. Scaly patches of pink skin and wisps of flaxen fur cover its crooked back. The chimera, an unfortunate product of the Molecular Foundry, lifts a scrawny paw and hisses. Feeling sorry for the loathsome animal despite its unpleasantness, Oriana jumps out of its way. But her pregnant state makes sudden movements nearly impossible, and the crabbit hops underfoot. Oriana stumbles, nearly losing her balance on the irregular stones of the road.

"Get the hell away from me," she curses.

The animal hisses, crawling toward her, low to the ground. Oriana prepares to kick it, as islanders are told to do when such a creature becomes vicious. Instead she picks up a handful of pebbles, lifts her arm over her head, and hurls them at its face. The crabbit scurries away through the tattered pickets of a fallen garden fence.

With nightfall, islanders begin to slip under their Hoods. It's been a few years since Oriana has gone under hers. All islanders are provided their own Hood for use from early childhood throughout life. The snug fitting head covering embedded with magnetic detection coils and tiny diodes connects with the user's brain. While under the Hood, remote viewing of the island is possible, including the inside of all public buildings as well as inhabitant's homes. It provides an entirely personalized education, and customized, user-prompted entertainment. The Hood is the only way to travel. Now disconnected, Oriana can no longer be observed.

She continues her trek up Main Street, passing by one darkened structure after another. She slows her gait at the intersection of Center Street, moving furtively past the elegant inns and the private homes that once belonged to Nantucket's whaling captains. One is of Southern design, its stately white columns supporting a tall front porch; another distinctively Federal, with horizontal clapboard painted blue, and a curved staircase to the side of the front door. Each represents a unique architectural design, reflecting the tastes of the wealthy sea captain who commissioned its construction.

Oriana reaches Pine Street. On impulse, she turns left, then left again onto Lucretia Mott Lane. "Oh no. It can't be," she whispers to herself. Half a block away, the shadowy figure of the man with the scarf leans against a fence post, waiting. She cuts through the side yard of an ivy-covered house, and then over to Judith Chase Lane, calculating how she might lose him. It's been many years since her childhood romps through the hidden alleys and gardens of this particular neighborhood, yet she has a sense of where she might go.

She crosses over the narrow street, passes through an unlocked garden gate, and makes her way through another yard. A dog barks at the sound of her movement, from inside a darkened house. She softens her step. The dim glow of two Hoods is the only light in the dwelling, yet offers her helpful luminescence. Oriana uses her hand to feel her way along a row of rose bushes. Firm grass cushions her bare feet as she creeps through the dark yard.

On reaching Ray's Court, she stops for a moment to recover her breath. Out of the corner of her eye she sees a woman standing alone under a wrought iron light post at the corner of Fair Street. The figure, thin and tall, wears a wide-brimmed hat. Across her shoulders lies a dark shawl. *She's got to be freezing out here without a coat,* Oriana thinks, feeling drawn to the woman and inclined ask her if she is okay.

As the difficulty of her own situation returns to Oriana's focus, she changes her mind and continues over Fair back toward Main Street. When Oriana stops again, it's to remove a pebble that's stuck to the bottom of her foot. She finds herself in front of a familiar building.

Perfect. There are no embedded cameras or sensors in here. This is a place I can be alone, and no one will ever know.

She heads through the gate of the picket fence, up the entry walk and onto the lower tread. The moon rises above the horizon, its whiteness highlighting the rooftops and trees. Oriana reads the faded text etched over the white clapboard siding:

#7 Fair Street: Erected by the Society of Friends, 1838.

Her mind returns to the first time she ever stood in this spot.

"This is where we Rotches came to be who we are." When Granddad stood by her side that day, at the threshold of this very door, the young Oriana peered inside the space of her family history.

"Come on, Granddad, let's go in," she had urged.

But he had refused. "There's no need for that. You can see all you need to see fine from out here," he grumbled, grabbing her hand to leave.

"Come on Granddad," the child had pleaded. "Can't we go in for a minute? I want to know what it feels like to be all the way inside."

Granddad was unmoved. He'd had more than his share of Quaker Nantucket, especially since his mate had expired. It was she who kept attending the Meeting, week after week, until the sickness made her too weak to go. So when Granddad looked into the Meeting House that day, with his young grandchild by his side, all he could see was the loss of his beloved mate. All he wanted was to go home.

"Go in there on your own damned time," he had replied to the child who was simply curious. "You can come back without me."

The years went by, and Oriana had neither the opportunity nor the inclination to return. Not, that is, until late last winter, and that was an occasion she had vowed to forget.

She glances back over her shoulder, checking to be certain she hasn't been seen. Reaching through the vines of an invading kudzu plant, Oriana feels for the front door. She spreads apart the entangled growth, the hairy, dried seedpods brushing against her face. She pats her hand along the peeling white paint of the old wooden plank, now warped, until the frigid metal doorknob is in her grasp.

She presses down on the iron latch, finding the lock completely rusted through. The door creaks as she leans her weight against its resistance. It opens just enough for her pregnant body to pass through. Oriana inadvertently pulls too hard, closing the door behind her. The rattle of windowpanes shatters the utter stillness inside.

The air, stagnant and dank, sends a chill across her chest. Its musty smell assaults her nose. One after the other, she places her feet onto the wide board flooring. Its surface, smooth against her heels and toes, provides relief from the rough ground outside. As her eyes adjust to the darkness, she takes in the room that was once the gathering place for the Quakers, those who called themselves Friends. Kudzu vines clinging to the eaves have spread their tendrils through window cracks and affixed themselves to the inside of the panes. The lunar brightness casts shadows of the objects in the room: whale oil lanterns mounted on white paneled walls; wooden benches assembled neatly in rows; the 'facing bench' at the front where esteemed elders would sit during Meeting for Worship.

It's a room long used for religious observation, yet without altar, icon, or ornamentation of any kind. All is utterly plain. Even the windows are bare of trim. Slipping further inside, Oriana is relieved to have found a place to hide.

Gong. Gong. Gong. Deep and metallic, the tone sounds from the nearby clock tower in the Second Congregational Church. Slowly, deliberately it rings. Gong, gong, gong. Hour after hour, day after day, decade after decade, century after century, clanging on as if to mark the endlessness of time.

Oriana's imagination takes hold. The year is 1840, and the house is filled with the silent faithful seeking the inner light. She walks down the center of the open room, heads lifting and turning to follow her, disapproving eyes squinting to see who is disturbing the worship underway. Arriving at the front, she takes a seat on a hard pine bench, her sense of present time and place restored.

The name Oriana, which is Latin for rising, like the sun, was chosen by her parents, Rebecca and Gardiner Rotch, on the same morning they selected her sex, her height, and the shape of her eyes. Her golden brown hair and green eye color were decided after heated discussion, but removing the Tay Sachs gene from the gamete that became Oriana was the easiest of their decisions. Her honey-toned skin was nature's choice.

Definitions of race are imprecise, arbitrary, and derived largely from custom, so it is no simple endeavor to categorize Oriana's genetic origins. Rebecca carried genotypic traits measured to be eighty-eight percent Semitic, though she maintained no specifically Jewish cultural or religious affiliation. She bore only a few Semitic physical characteristics, such as a beautifully prominent nose and wavy thick hair. Gardiner's family descended from the religious, cultural, linguistic, genetic, and social grouping of Nantucket Quakers, which made them largely white, European, New World immigrants.

So since Rebecca's ovum and Gardiner's semen were used to conceive her, Oriana is both Jewish and Quaker, so to speak, the Jewish part expressed in her genome, and, according to Granddad, the Quaker side evident in the strength of her determination and will. Because there are hardly any Quakers living on Nantucket Island anymore, and, more importantly, because she is not fully VISHNEW-connected, Oriana is an anomaly, infamous due to her obstetrical obstinacy.

Oriana slips her feet up under her thighs, crossing her legs under the warmth of her chameleon coat, which brings to her feet much appreciated relief. She pulls the coat tight around her midriff and does not resist when her eyes fall closed, until a loud bang against the wall startles her from her reverie. She rises from the bench, shuffling down the aisle as she makes her way back, pushing the door closed again. *It must have been the wind.*

Oriana returns to the bench where she sits peacefully for nearly an hour, cushioned by the thick fabric of her coat. She finds relief in the isolation she has finally found, until the reality of her act overcomes her. Disconnecting from VISHNEW is serious enough, so what must she have been thinking, she asks herself, to leave home on this, the night before the court-ordered retrieval of the baby in her womb?

As she rocks herself from side to side, she considers her predicament: the judge's decree that her baby be perfectly formed, and her mate's threat if not. "What have I done?" she murmurs into the darkness, her head in her hands as she moans. She lies down. Dread fades into sadness. Childhood memories fill her mind.

TRESPASSING

Old Wauwinet Road is rutted and nearly impassable. Yet Papa is determined to make his way out to what was once the Coskata-Coatue Wildlife Refuge, a place known for its pretty sliver of scalloped, sandy beaches. On this day the refuge is barely accessible, even on foot, which is why island ordinances decree the shore remain off limits to pedestrians and motor vehicles alike. Papa will not be deterred. He and Oriana and Granddad bump along in his new two-door ultra-light, until finally arriving in front of the abandoned Wauwinet Inn.

Oriana hops out first, followed closely by Papa, then Granddad. The old man shakes his head in disgust at the sight of the elegant old inn in shambles, its cedar shingles loose or fallen off, the bright white porches collapsed, the windowpanes missing or cracked. Papa takes a deep breath and smiles as he takes in the expansive view of Nantucket Sound on one side, and the Atlantic Ocean on the other.

Granddad grabs Oriana's hand, helping her to navigate the jagged rocks, debris, and stones strewn across the storm-damaged pavement. Getting to the water's edge is more difficult than they anticipated. Granddad's full belly, perched atop his skinny legs, throws off his center of balance. The old man stumbles once, then again. The third time he falls to the ground, nearly taking Oriana with him.

"Granddad!" she shouts.

"I'm fine," he replies, standing up, brushing himself off, and taking hold of Oriana's hand. They continue to trudge along. He pretends to feel no pain.

"I'm fine too. No need to worry about me," the child declares. It's unclear, however, whether either Papa or Granddad are listening.

It is Granddad's eighty-fifth birthday. Coming here to the old refuge is Papa's gift to him. Oriana plans to find a pretty seashell to give him. When they arrive at the water's edge, Granddad places both hands over his eyes.

"I can't bear to see it like this," he laments.

"Come on, Dad," Papa says. "It's not that bad."

"The hell it isn't," Granddad barks.

Oriana sits down next to Papa on a boulder. Granddad makes his way over the piles of rocks to a sandy clearing at the water's edge. "I wonder if the water's cold," he mumbles. Still standing, he grabs his left shoe to remove it, but loses his balance and steps into the water with his shoe still on.

"Holy crap," he scowls. The water is icier than he had expected and plus, he hates that he has accidently ruined a perfectly good shoe.

"It's been a long time since he was here," Papa explains to his only child, motioning with his chin toward the old man. "He was a kid then," Papa continues. "I thought it'd make him happy to come here, only I'm afraid it's making him sad instead." Papa runs two fingers through the hair that has fallen across his forehead. Oriana gazes at her grandfather, who is wandering in the surf at the water's edge, one shoe on and one shoe off.

"Papa, Granddad doesn't get sad! Remember? He's VISHNEW-connected." Papa ignores his daughter, looking out over the expanse of a seemingly endless sea.

"Back when Granddad was a boy, there were lots of plants here, like bayberry, beach plum, heather, and beach grasses. There were sand dunes, too. Not any more. It's all gone now," he says sadly.

Oriana shrugs. "That's a lot of stuff that's gone," she replies, taking in the rocky terrain, imagining all the sand and greenery that were once there and wondering where it all could be now.

Papa rubs his stubbly face. "This was once the largest red cedar savanna and woodland in New England." Oriana isn't sure what a savannah is, but starts to daydream about a book she once watched under her Hood where two children get lost in woodlands far from their home and become trapped in the house of a witch who plans to fatten them up and eat them.

"Gray and harbor seals lived in these waters when Granddad was a boy," Papa continues.

"Here, right where we are now?" Oriana asks.

"Uh huh," Papa utters with a nod.

Oriana looks back at Granddad, who has taken off his wet shoe and tossed it onto the rocks. She wonders what he is feeling, since VISHNEW keeps him from feeling sad.

"Hey Granddad. What are you doing over there?"

Her grandfather stands erect, hands on his hips. "Watching, that's what. I'm on the lookout. Come on over and help me, why don't ya?" Oriana teeters over the rocks, trying to keep her balance on the uneven surface. She reaches the spot where her grandfather stands and the two sit down together on a nearby boulder. She slides herself close to him. "Used to be that about this time of year dolphins would play out there in the surf," he explains, placing an elbow on her shoulder. Oriana squints to focus on the water.

"Really Granddad? Where?"

He points in the general direction of 'out there.'

"I was out swimming once when they came," he explains.

"Did they play with you, Granddad?" Oriana asks excitedly.

"Sure did, yup," he says proudly. "It was out past where that driftwood is floating right now." He points to an object Oriana cannot see.

"What driftwood, where?" she complains.

Granddad grabs hold of the child's waist and lifts her to a standing position, feet flat against the boulder. "Look to the left a little bit, Oriana. See it now?"

Oriana nods, not wanting to disappoint Granddad, or to remind him of her lack of visual enhancement. She truly wants to believe that she has spotted the object in question.

Granddad continues, "I was out beyond the sand bar, messing around, doing flips. All of a sudden a pair of fins broke the surface. Scared the bajeebers out of me, 'cause for a moment they looked like sharks."

"What were they?"

"What were they? I'll tell you what they were. A pod of dolphins, that's what," he says, stumbling a bit as he stands to set his only grandchild back down on the rocks. Oriana stares up at Granddad's face, hoping for some indication that he is having a happy birthday.

"You know," he continues, "dolphins will come right up to you if you dive under the water." His blue eyes bulge as he recalls the excitement of the experience.

"Wow," she whispers.

Granddad turns his gaze back to the water, one hand on his waist and the other outstretched toward the horizon.

"So I swam over closer to where I'd seen them come up and dropped under the surface of the water to wait. Seemed at first they'd gone back out to sea. I'll tell you one thing, I sure wasn't going to take any chances of losing sight of the direction they went, in case they came back again. So I stayed right where I was under the water, coming up for air only when I had to."

"Whoa," Oriana sighs softly.

"All of a sudden three of them came right toward me, I tell you. One was looking me right straight in the eyes."

"OOH!" Oriana coos, bouncing up and down gleefully.

"Now don't go and fall there, girl. These rocks are mighty loose," Granddad scolds.

Papa stands up from the boulder he's been perched on nearby, rubs his sore backside, and places his hands in his pockets. He gazes intently out over the sea, leading Oriana to believe a dolphin pod might actually appear.

"Then what happened, Granddad?" Oriana asks watching carefully. The excitement makes his loose hanging jowls quiver.

"Well now, would you believe that the pod started swimming circles around me?" Granddad says, taking his seat again on the boulder. "I was working so damned hard to stay under the water that I got sort of confused. Couldn't tell whether those dolphins were over and under me or swimming like this," he says gesturing to demonstrate a circle around his body.

"What did you do then, Dad?" Papa asks gleefully, knowing full well the answer. This is a story that Granddad has told for decades, one Papa delights in hearing.

"Well, as I said, I was struggling to stay down under the water, holding my breath long enough to get a good look at them. I reached out to touch the one that was hanging right in front of my face, the one that was looking at me, you know. But by golly, before I could get a touch, the whole lot of 'em was turning to swim away."

"So then what did you do?" Oriana asks, her mouth, eyes, and eyebrows scrunched with curiosity.

"Went up to the surface, that's what, and snatched a quick breath of air. Don't ya know that by the time I flipped back down under the water the dolphins were completely outta sight?"

"Oh no! Where did they go, Granddad?"

"Can't say exactly." Granddad rubs a hand over the bald spot on his head then pulls his hands through the remaining shock of soft white hair. "I sure was disappointed to lose 'em. I'll tell you one thing," he chuckles, "I was ready to swim with those dolphins to anywhere they were going."

"When can I see dolphins playing in the ocean?" Oriana questions as she pulls on Papa's shirttail.

"There's no day like today!" Papa replies. "You can watch dolphins under your Hood when we get home."

Granddad picks up his wet shoe and pulls it over his bare foot, the moist salt making it annoyingly sticky. "I'm leaving," he announces abruptly, starting back over the rocks. "No need to hurry yourselves," he says. "I'll be fine 'til you come." He heads towards the old road.

Father and daughter stand side-by-side, baffled by Granddad's leaving.

"Come on, Papa," Oriana says, pulling off her shoes.

"Let's go find Granddad a birthday present from the sea."

Papa slips his feet out of his sandals and follows her into the outgoing tide. "Be careful Ori," he warns. "The rocks in the water can be wobbly."

A small wave breaks at their ankles. Oriana catches a glimpse of an unfamiliar object floating in the shallow surf.

"What's that over there, Papa?" she asks, gesturing at the strange thing. Papa, who is preoccupied with navigating the jagged rocks, doesn't seem to hear her at all. "There it is again, Papa. What is that?" she asks.

"Kelp, Oriana. You know that," he replies after a quick glance.

"No, not that, Papa. That."

A sealed pouch entangled in a mass of puckered brown seaweed bobs on the surface of the water. Oriana squats to get a better look at the suspicious object, pulling it from out of the vegetation and taking it into her hands.

"Eeweee," she exclaims, finding it strange to the touch, spongy and pliable, light in weight. Seawater comes off the article in streams, running along its surface in rippling little waves. Holding it makes her feel queasy yet excited at the same time.

"Look at this, Papa," Oriana shouts, lifting her discovery up for him to see. Papa turns his head over his shoulder to see what she might be talking about.

"No!" he shouts, lunging in her direction. He snatches the package from her hand and hurls it out over the shallow, breaking waves.

"Papa, you said never to throw anything into the ocean!" she scolds. "Remember, Papa, 'anything we throw in the sea will come back to haunt us.' That's what you always say."

"It was already in the ocean, Oriana," he says, "along with other sorts of techno-medical waste." He grabs hold of her hand. "We are getting out of here," he commands. "Put your shoes back on and let's go."

"What about Granddad's present?" Oriana whines, kicking her foot against the rocks.

"Forget that," Papa insists.

Papa ushers Oriana back out onto the ruins of the road. Confused yet contrite, the child follows along.

"Slow down, Papa, okay?" she implores.

Papa ignores her request. "You'll have to clean your hands carefully when we get home," he admonishes her. And then he falls quiet, quieter than Oriana has ever known her Papa to be.

A sense of dread overcomes Oriana as she wonders what she has done and why Papa won't even respond to her request. Her six-year-old mind searches for a reason for her Papa's reserve; eventually grasping onto the possible significance of the object she had in her hand.

The October sun falls swiftly over the southwest horizon of Nantucket. The rutted, pot-holed road is even harder to walk in the dusk than when they first set out on their trek to the shore. Oriana tries hard to keep up, until finally she begins to cry.

"Papa, what was that I found back there in the water?"

Papa stops in his tracks. His eyes lock onto the child's with a forlorn expression.

"Well, Oriana." he replies, "A female body contains a very special organ called a womb. You have one," he explains, patting over her navel. "Some babies live in the womb inside a woman's body until they've grown enough to be born. Some do not. They live in a womb outside of the mother."

"When I was a baby, did I grow inside or outside of Mama?" Oriana wants to know, cocking her head to one side.

"You developed inside Mama's uterus, Ori."

"Where's is Mama's uterpus now that I'm out?"

"Uterus, Oriana. That's another word for womb, the place where the mother keeps her baby safe while it grows. It's a place with warm fluids to protect the baby, where it is fed and cared for until birth."

Oriana lifts her shirt, studying her belly. "It must be squishy in there," she deduces as she presses on her stomach.

"Yes, I suppose," Papa responds in a dour tone. "It's better than the alternative."

"Well, anyway Papa," she continues, "You don't have to tell me the rest because I know all about the atreeval."

"Re-trie-val, Oriana," Papa corrects. "Would you mind calling it a birth?"

"Okay, Papa."

Papa tucks Oriana's shirt back into her pants. "What you found in the water back there was a uterus sealed inside a specially designed pouch," he explains as they walk.

"A pouch? Oh, like a kangaroo!" Oriana says, hopping.

"Yes, inspired by the kangaroo, Ori. The pouch is designed to keep the uterus fresh for use by the growing baby."

The young girl stays silent as they navigate the furrowed road. She wonders how a womb can be a safe place for a baby to live, if it is sealed inside a pouch and floating in the ocean.

"Where is its mama, Papa? And where is the baby who belongs in it? How can the baby get a birth? I don't understand," she asks, searching for an explanation. Tears of confusion build at the corners of her wide, green eyes.

"Of course you don't understand; neither do I. It is a very difficult matter to sort out," Papa laments. "These wombs are grown in the Molecular Foundry, to be used for babies who grow outside of their mothers." Papa picks up a stone, and launches it against a rotting tree stump. Oriana recalls that Granddad's heart was grown in that place, and so were his new eyes.

"Well, where is the mama who had that womb in her, Papa?" she persists.

Papa crouches down to meet his daughter eye to eye. "That's what I am trying to explain to you. That was never in a mother's body."

Oriana considers this information carefully. "Well," she announces, "when I grow up and get a baby, I want it to live in the uterpus inside my body, not in a kangaroo pouch in the ocean." Oriana looks out at the horizon as she and Papa continue their trek back along Wauwinet Road.

"That would be best, Oriana," Papa chuckles. "And it would make me proud," he adds. He strokes the top of her head. Oriana likes how she feels when Papa does this. "I only wish you could conceive your babies on your own, Oriana. But it's simply not possible."

Oriana worries over her capacity to please Papa. "Conceive?" she asks. "What's that?"

Papa sighs in response. "Never mind, Oriana. I just wish it didn't have to happen in a lab, that's all."

When father and daughter arrive back at the place where they had parked, the vehicle is gone.

"Where in the hell . . .?" Papa blurts out. He catches a glimpse of the vehicle's shiny surface farther down the road and around a curve. "I guess I forgot to secure the brakes. The wind must have pushed it along," he confesses. "That's one thing I hate about these damned ultra-lights."

Oriana takes off running down the road.

"Granddad, guess what I found!" she calls toward the vehicle, figuring Granddad must be in it. Suddenly she stops, steps back, and places her hands on her waist. Granddad is nowhere in sight.

"Where is he, Papa?" she shouts to her approaching father.

"Oh no. Not again!" Papa exclaims. He peers into the windows of an empty car. "This is terrible. Poor Dad."

"Where is he, Papa?" Oriana asks again.

"Gone, obviously," Papa barks back.

"How come?"

"It must be VISHNEW, Ori. There's no other explanation."

"No! That can't be. We have to look for him, that's all," she exclaims. "Maybe he got lost. Maybe he fell into the water. Come on, Papa. Let's go find him," Oriana implores, her bottom lip quivering as she ponders the possible meanings of Papa's words. It scares her, that VISHNEW.

"Now Papa, before it's too late," she insists. "We have to go back to the water." Oriana pushes against her father's buttocks, grunting and panting in the attempt to move him along. Papa refuses to budge, rebuffing his daughter's pleas.

"Pull yourself together, Ori. We're going home now. There's nothing we can do," he declares firmly.

Oriana launches her foot squarely against Papa's calf.

"Damn it all, Oriana," he shouts. "That hurt!"

"We're going back right now to look for him," she insists, paying no attention to her father's howling.

Papa grabs Oriana by her shoulders, lifting her off the ground. The child kicks wildly and bites his upper arm.

"Stop this nonsense," Papa scolds as he limps to the passenger side of the ultra-light, carrying Oriana in his arms.

Oriana struggles to free herself from his clutches, tiring him, and making him even angrier.

The car doors unlock at their approach and open wide. Papa places his daughter squarely on the front passenger seat, locks the door, and slips into the driver's seat.

The lovely girl with soft green eyes looks straight ahead and takes a deep breath. With cheeks puffed out, eyes wide and bulging, she resists the impulse to breathe for a full forty-seven seconds. Oriana's tawny cheeks turn bright red. Finally, her pursed mouth gives way to a burst of warm air and soft spit.

"Too bad you didn't pass out this time," Papa says bleakly as he drives.

Oriana folds her arms against her chest and turns away, shifting her attention to the passing scene: abandoned beach houses cocked to their sides, their foundations tattered and exposed. She remembers what Granddad said about the Great Storms.

"It was seven days of relentless pounding against the shores that left our Gray Lady this way. She's a strong one, endured all kinds of storms over the centuries. This one was more than she could take. It's too bad you'll never know how pretty the island used to be."

She figures that the Nantucket she knows is fine now, so what does it matter what once was?

Oriana remains silent for the entire trip back home, at which point she heads straight upstairs to her bedroom. It is the next morning before she speaks another word.

"Hello?" she says, responding to the receivers embedded in the walls.

"That you, Oriana?" Granddad's voice replies, carried over the house-wide speakers.

"Yup," Oriana affirms, idly chatting away about what she'd found in the water the day before without bothering to ask, "What happened to you Granddad, and where exactly have you been?"

OSPREY

The rising moon reaches full height. The Meeting House interior comes more fully into view. Oriana sits up, eyes wide, and fixes her gaze on an illuminated fixture. *What am I doing in this place?* Oriana questions as she rubs the ache in the arm she's been lying on. The dank air cuts into her nostrils. She stands to stretch out her stiffened back, then placing her coat on the floor, she lies down on her back, feet flat and knees pointing toward the ceiling. Clasping her hands beneath her head, she studies the shadows on the ceiling above: a blotch of gray, a stitch of black, some sharp-edged angles, and a few less-defined curves cast against the white flaking paint. Ruminations of childhood carry on:

"Oriana, are you awake?" Papa asks, stroking the child's cheek.

No, she's not, though Papa's voice stirs her from sleep. His gentle touch invites her into her full senses.

"Hurry now, we want to get there before dawn," he prods.

Oriana groans. This is nothing new. Papa often awakens her early in the morning, and sometimes even in the middle of the night; he does this whenever he determines it is the optimal time to observe what he has in mind to see, such as the eye-shine of spiders, large insect activity, or sleeping birds. On this particular day, Papa is especially anxious to move quickly.

"Leave your pajamas on," he instructs as he pulls on her shoulder to turn the child from prone to supine.

She opens an eye and frowns.

"Don't worry," he reassures her. "No one will notice if you go out in your bed clothes. And anyway, who other than us would bother to be there?"

Oriana pulls the pillow over her head. She knows very well that anyone watching from under their Hood will be able to see her out in her bed clothes.

"Come on," he persists, pushing the fluffy mound off of her face. "Stop acting like such a child."

"I am a child, Papa," she quips. "I'm eight."

"This is important to me," Papa explains. "And it should be to you."

Yawning, she stretches out her arms for a hug from the man she considers the most important person in the entire world. Making him happy is her primary concern.

Papa reciprocates, his arms outstretched for a warm embrace.

"Okay, okay. I'm waking up," she says with another yawn. She buries her head in his chest and breathes in the yeasty bread and warm butter scent of his skin, which always reassures her.

Taking note of his daughter's smooth tan skin, wide green eyes, and wavy brown hair, Papa's brow creases involuntarily.

"Papa, what's wrong?" she asks, noticing his loosening hold on her. She senses that Papa sees in her the woman he lost eight years before.

The spell is broken. Maybe it is her innocent voice that does it, or the meekness of her inquiry, but the grief in Papa's eyes fades. It seems almost as if they are smiling. She closes her eyes as he cradles her close again. *At least you didn't lose me, too.*

What if he'd had a choice, his mate or the newborn child he didn't even know? What if, at the moment of Oriana's retrieval and Rebecca's horrendous death, the techno-medics had said, "We can only save one. Which one, is up to you." What if, right here and now, he could be with the woman he loved so passionately, waking her up early this morning, turning over in bed to get next to her warm body, holding her in his arms? "Get up now love," he'd say. "Why don't you come with me today?"

"Are you sure it's morning, Papa?" Oriana asks, peering around her father's arm and out her bedroom window. "It's awfully dark, you know." She may be young, but her father's resentment and pain are not lost on her, nor is the fact that at the moment he wishes it were Mama, rather than her, that he held in his arms.

"It's morning, alright," Papa affirms.

Oriana prefers to take her time to wake up. She likes to relish the dawn's light on her face, to take in the sun's shining at the start of a new day. The blackness of predawn offers her no such cheeriness. She is awake, yet feels serene.

"In fact," Papa continues, "for some creatures the day began hours ago." He slides his arms under Oriana's shoulders and lifts her to her feet.

Oriana bends back in a stretch and releases an exaggerated yawn.

"Be sure to rub warming cream on your legs and feet before you put on your socks," he instructs. "And you'd better wear sturdy shoes!"

"Why, Papa? Where are we going?"

"All the way out to Pimney's Point, that's where, to see what's going on up in that osprey nest."

"OOH!" Oriana squeals. She scurries to grab her favorite shoes, the bright yellow ones with the baby seal appliqués on top.

Ospreys had nearly disappeared from Nantucket due to shell thinning from organic chemical exposure. Their population was finally coming back when the Great Storms hit, bringing abnormal concentrations of salts and other minerals into the marshes. Native fish started dying en masse, and floated to the surface of the waters in thick, putrid groups. When the tides were low, the stiff smelly fish sank into the soft, mucky bottom, lifeless, and worthless to the osprey that depended on them for food.

Papa was thrilled when the species was sighted again on the island. As soon as he got wind of the exciting development, he went under his Hood to research what he might do to encourage Osprey repopulation. There he came across an image of a nesting platform built many years earlier out on the salt marsh.

"You and I are going to build one similar to that," he told Oriana.

A number of islanders happened to be tuned into the Rotch's home when Papa and Oriana were discussing his plans, and a flurry of commentary flowed through the community as a result. Papa's project was considered an abomination by most islanders who, being VISHNEW-connected, kept their distance from the dangerous, natural world.

"Why would a grown man endanger his daughter in that way?" they wanted to know when Papa and Oriana ventured out to put up the stand. Gossip spread that this, on top of the fact that he never had her connected, was further proof that Papa never should have been permitted to raise the girl alone. Islanders followed with intrigue every moment of the osprey stand rising, from under the safety of their Hoods.

A few weeks after putting up the stand, Papa and Oriana returned to the marsh to support the platform with a metal band, which also served to prevent raccoons from climbing up and preying on eggs or nestlings.

Islanders observed the stand from the safety of their Hoods for a few days. No bird activity was detected. Most got bored and switched to observing the activities of other neighbors around town.

Papa, on the other hand, went under his Hood every day for over a month, watching and waiting for some sign of osprey repopulation. Then, in the middle of March, something amazing happened. A white-breasted male landed on the platform and started to build a nest. An islander who happened to be scanning Hood activity at the time heard Papa's voice rise up in cheerful celebration and tuned in, too. Word then spread quickly among islanders.

About two weeks later, while watching from under her Hood, a curious islander spotted a female osprey land on the platform at dawn and reported it to the Audubon Remembrance Society. The Society members focused in on the discovery with great enthusiasm, and finally in late April, three remotely observing members simultaneously confirmed that four eggs were in the nest. None of the eggs had yet hatched.

Then, at 3:59 a.m. one morning, a man from the Society saw from under his Hood that three of the eggs were missing. One egg remained, and a tiny osprey leg stuck out from a crack in the shell. Papa learned of the occurrence at precisely 4:07 a.m. when the voice of the observing Society member came over his bedroom speakers.

"Mr. Rotch, Mr. Rotch, the remaining egg has now hatched!"

Papa grabs a flashlight in his left hand. With the other he grabs Oriana and heads out the side door.

"What about breakfast, Papa?" Oriana asks.

"You'll have to wait until we get back," he declares. "The sun will be up soon, and I want to get to the Point before it rises."

The air is still cool out by the marsh when Oriana and Papa arrive in the dark of early morning. The sensors in the child's pajamas trigger a flow of heat, but it is insufficient to keep her comfortable. She pulls herself closer to Papa.

"I'm cold," she complains.

"Here, put on my jacket," Papa instructs as they walk along the marsh's edge, searching for a clearing. "And try to whisper so we don't disturb any birds that may still be asleep." Papa squeezes the flexible tube in his hand.

"Can I carry the flashlight?" Oriana requests.

Papa quickly turns it off. Its light is brighter than he'd remembered. "We don't actually need this," he declares.

A full moon begins to set, casting a dim orange light across the grasses. Papa explains to Oriana that the outgoing tide provides them with a place to walk along the marsh's shore. The mud is mucky and sucks her shoes in as she walks. Squelch, squelch, squelch . . . this is a treacherous trek. Oriana reaches out and grabs for her father's elbow. His pace is too quick for her to reach him. "Carry me, Papa," she shouts.

"Try to be brave and walk on your own," Papa says, oblivious to her anxiety.

Oriana falls farther behind. Trying her hardest to keep pace with him, she slips off the path and disturbs a flock of nocturnal songbirds burrowed under some marsh reeds. The sudden sound of their pounding wings startles her. She jumps, and a panicked bird brushes against her face. "Whoa, Papa!" she screeches, flailing her arms wildly in all directions.

"Calm down, damn it," Papa scolds from about five yards up ahead.

Oriana's heart pounds hard. Strange, unfamiliar sounds keep her from feeling the calm Papa calls for. Finally she catches up to him, and Papa reminds her to be quiet. For a while, Oriana actually remains silent and still.

"What was that, Papa? I heard something over there," she whispers. Oriana grabs hold of Papa's arm.

"Nothing more than the windmills, I'm sure," he says. "You're not used to hearing their sound. We can't hear them in town."

"Oh," the child replies, unsatisfied with Papa's answer. "That's not what *I* heard," she mumbles.

"The herring, flounder, and other fish that were native to these waters haven't yet returned, so I am surprised the osprey are here," Papa says with a glint of excitement. "For years I've been watching and hoping. Eel and catfish are in the marsh now. Maybe they'll sustain the osprey."

"Catfish?" Oriana questions. She considers the oddity of combining a cat with a fish. "Yuck!" she exclaims, assuming it to be a novel creation of the Molecular Foundry. "That sounds pretty ugly."

"Some people think so," Papa agrees, taking a seat in a clearing in view of the platform and the osprey nest.

Oriana plops down by his side, the earth cold and moist against the thin fabric of her pajama bottoms.

"The return of the osprey is very important," Papa goes on. "The last time the ospreys came, Oriana, which was many years ago, they nested, then left without laying eggs."

Oriana notices something moving under the surface of the water. She pulls her legs in close to her chest in case whatever it is comes near.

"This time one stayed and laid four eggs," he says.

"I know that, Papa," she sighs. "I was with you under your Hood when we saw them. Remember?"

The surface of the water breaks. Something jumps up onto the ground. Oriana jumps too. She forces the squeal back into her throat. Papa darts her a stern glance. Oriana resists a giggle.

Dawn's brilliance spreads over the marsh, a glow that bathes the reeds and grasses in pastel hues of orange, red and gold. Papa squeezes Oriana's arm excitedly as the nest brightens under the daylight. He gazes up to the top of the platform through spectacles that adjust themselves according to the focus of his pupils; this is an item Papa had specially devised by Maker's Manufacturing to compensate for his unenhanced eyesight. A full-connect would have no need for such a gadget.

Papa peers through his oculars, able to get a great view of the hatchling. Oriana chatters away about dogfish, birdfish, lionfish, and other possible combinations. Papa focuses intently on his object of interest.

"I think the osprey will leave again because Nantucket is very stinky," Oriana remarks.

"Whisper, please," Papa scolds.

"It's too smelly for them here, if you ask me," his daughter continues. She has a valid point. "Why is that, Papa?" she wants to know. "Why does it stink so badly?"

"It's bad, Oriana."

"Yeah, that's why I have to cover my nose. The smell is pretty bad. How come?"

After what seems to Oriana an unnecessarily long pause, Papa offers answers. "One theory is that the odor comes from a combination of decaying protein and the presence of a type of algae that doesn't belong on Nantucket. In other words, it's non-native."

"Where does the algae belong, then?"

"Where *do* the algae belong, Oriana. The word is plural."

"But that sounds funny."

"We don't actually know where it comes from. No one around here has ever seen this species before. Even the marine biologists over in Woods Hole haven't been able to identify it. They suspect the algae may release toxins if eaten."

"Is that it, the purple and yellow stuff over there?" Oriana asks, pointing across the marsh with one hand and pinching her nose closed with the other.

"Yes, that's it," he confirms.

"Why not make it go away?" she inquires.

"We don't know how to get rid of it," he replies.

"Oh."

"The fact that it's here makes it difficult to keep the right kind of fish alive and abundant in the marsh. The algae smell is especially wretched at very low tides," Papa explains.

"Maybe the fish don't like the smell, either," Oriana mumbles.

"It's possible the algae will make the osprey sick," Papa goes on. Oriana touches her growling stomach.

"The next time you go for your tutoring," he directs, "I want you to search out the topics of survival, adaptation, and extinction in nature."

"I'm hungry," Oriana reminds him. Papa smiles tersely.

Oriana and Papa sit watching the platform until the sun has risen well up above the horizon. At around 8 o'clock, as Oriana is about to ask again for food, Papa's face lifts in excitement. He rises to his feet. Oriana stands, too. Papa puts on his special spectacles and focuses intently on the nest.

"Oh no!" he yells. "This can't be!"

He drops down into a kneeling position on the wetland mud. Oriana squats down next to him. "What's the matter, Papa?" she asks, patting his back. Papa's lenses fall out of his hands onto the ground. He buries his face in his palms and begins to moan.

Oriana reaches for the powerful oculars, picking them up and placing them over the bridge of her nose. They are too big for her face so she has to hold them up with her forefingers. She peers into them carefully, searching for the nest on the stand. Unable to find it, she stands and takes a step forward, trying to avoid getting her beautiful yellow shoes all wet in the putrid marsh.

"Oh! I see it now," she exclaims, spotting the legs first and then the feathery breast of the fully hatched osprey chick. She takes note of how it sits right by its mother's side "That's so sweet," she murmurs. And then she gasps, "Papa, I see the beak, but where are its eyes?"

"If you don't see them, Oriana, then it probably doesn't have them."

Oriana drops the lenses into the muck and grabs Papa's arm, sobbing. "I don't understand, Papa."

"Oh sure you do," he scolds. "If I have taught you nothing else, I've taught you about the mess we humans have made of this world." Papa stands, gathers his belongings, and begins to walk out to the road. "Let's get some food into your stomach," he proposes.

Oriana, following closely behind, turns her head to take one last look at Papa's osprey stand.

"Ooh my," she murmurs, as the shadow of a VISHNEW monitor drifts slowly above the nest, causing the mother osprey to take flight.

EMMANUEL

Oriana is twelve years old, and the only VISHNEW-independent child on the island. Generally she is used to the fact that she has so little in common with her peers. Yet this is a particularly lonely summer. Papa has suspended the lessons that Oriana usually receives from the Starbuck sisters, and encourages Oriana instead to explore the outdoors. She doesn't know how to do that all alone, so she finds herself mostly watching books under her Hood, observing stray animals, and waiting for Granddad to visit.

On one particular morning in July, Oriana gazes out the window, and catches a glimpse of her neighbor Emmanuel standing in the periwinkle patch in the side yard. "Well, I'll be a dolphin's fluke. They've let him out!" she imitating of one of her Granddad's expressions.

Emmanuel and his mother and father have just returned home from TEMPLE. Each carries a personal worship bowl in hand and wears the requisite expression of joy. Oriana pours a beverage into a tall glass and heads quickly out the kitchen door.

"You can come over here to my house if you want," she yells across the lawn to a Hood friend she has never met in person.

Emmanuel turns when he hears her voice. He looks as if he wants to reply to her invitation. Unfortunately, he probably can't.

The cause of Emmanuel's stifled communication remains unknown. 'Simple social incompetence' is the term the techno-medics use. When Emmanuel does talk, it is in cryptic sentences. He almost never uses direct eye contact when spoken to, observes rather than engages, and is non-communicative even when social-izing under his Hood. This is strange behavior, as connected chil-dren tend to be gregarious.

"Well, are you coming over or not?" Oriana shouts.

Emmanuel drops his gaze toward the ground.

"Oh come on," she chides, holding the glass out in front of her. "Papa made lemonade, and you can have some."

Emmanuel steps towards her with the soft deliberation of a cautious yet curious kitten.

"You're going to like it," she assures him. "This crop of Foundry lemons is especially sweet."

Emmanuel gently places one foot after another on the dew-soaked ground, causing a squishing squeaky sound with each step.

Oriana holds out the tall, ice-filled cup as he approaches, and the boy accepts it with a placid grin.

Emmanuel sips the drink, crossing his eyes as he studies the floating ice.

Oriana sees nothing wrong with him. She likes him, even though she finds him a bit aloof and disinterested. Being around him under her Hood makes her feel cheerful. Standing next to him in person makes her feel alive.

Emmanuel is the first young person to befriend Oriana. Once in awhile under her Hood she observes other island teens creat-ing fantasy worlds to play in. They limit her access to watch, and deny her the capacity to engage with because she and Papa are VISHNEW independent.

"Come on, let's sit down," Oriana invites.

Emmanuel and Oriana walk around to the front of the house, and take seats on the upper step of Oriana and Papa's home. Oriana looks at her friend with a wide grin, not quite sure what to make of him.

The boy stares out at the clearing across the road, toward what was once a grove of loblolly pines before the moths shredded them of their life force and the Great Storms brought their roots up out of the ground. He slurps down the remainder of his lemonade.

"What's so interesting over there?" Oriana asks him. She takes note of the rotting stumps, which bring to mind pale-faced witches with wild gray hair.

Emmanuel shrugs.

She watches him closely as he stares at nothing that Oriana can fathom. And then, quite unexpectedly, Emmanuel puts down his glass and places his hand on Oriana's knee. His gaze remains straight ahead. Oriana grows very still, not wanting to disturb the soft tapping of his three middle fingers on her patella.

"Emmanuel?" she says after a few moments. The boy's fingers fall flattened and his hand returns to the tumbler by his side. Emmanuel sips the melted ice.

"Emmanuel?" she continues, "Do you want to go inside the house and come under my Hood with me? We can make an amazing world together."

The boy doesn't answer. Oriana slides closer to him, an inch at a time, until her thigh touches his. The contact makes her feel tingly. He doesn't move away. He doesn't even flinch.

For nearly an hour they sit saying nothing at all. At times Emmanuel taps his knee. At other times he puts his hand on her shoulder or her thigh for a few moments. Then, for no apparent reason, Emmanuel gets up and heads back home.

"Hey, Emmanuel, can I go with you next time?" Oriana shouts as the boy rambles away. "You know, to TEMPLE. I haven't been there before." The boy looks over his shoulder, making brief eye contact with the only friend he has.

A few weeks later, Oriana spots Emmanuel coming toward the front door or her home, carrying a worship bowl in his hand. Gleeful over the chance to go to TEMPLE, she rushes up the stairs to her bedroom.

"Forget it, Oriana!" Papa shouts up the stairs.

"Why not?" she insists, demanding an explanation as she heads down the steps to confront him.

"You haven't got a worship bowl, and you've nothing appropriate to wear," Papa retorts.

She knows these are only excuses. "You don't want me to go, no matter what, even if only to the Worship Chamber."

"Enough Oriana."

"Didn't you keep Mama's bowl, the one she threw and kilned herself? Why can't I use that?"

"I said enough."

"I can wear my green and white striped dress."

"No, damn it!" Papa scolds.

Oriana storms back up to her room, pulling everything out from her closet and launching the items, one after another, down the stairs. "And what's so inappropriate about this?" she shouts with each article tossed.

Papa picks up the clothes and hangs each item on the banister at the bottom of the staircase.

Oriana, standing at the top landing, drops to her knees and bellows, "VISHNEW, VISHNEW, sustainer of life . . ."

"Stop that Oriana!" Papa shouts. "Where in the hell did you learn the TEMPLE chant?"

"VISHNEW, VISHNEW, sustainer of life…" she continues.

"If you ever say those words again in his house, I will put you out, and you'll go to live with Granddad!" Papa threatens, interrupting her incantation.

"Fine, then, why don't I go there right now?" she retorts, trying to sound tougher than she actually feels. Oriana stomps down the staircase and heads out the door to the front steps, trying to hide the tears that stream over her red cheeks.

Papa hears her quiet sobs as she passes him on the landing. "Don't be such a brat," he says. "You're overreacting, you know."

"What do you know?" she barks back. "You don't get it at all." Oriana plops down on the front steps and notices Emmanuel standing at the walkway's end. "Do you want to go for a walk with me?" she asks him.

"Can't," he replies, raising his arm to display the worship bowl, a shiny black vessel with a red and gold metallic rim. Emmanuel's mother approaches.

"Time to go, Emmanuel," she says.

"Can I hold that for a moment?" Oriana asks her friend.

Emmanuel carefully places the ceremonial bowl in her opened hands.

"What is this one made of?" she asks Emmanuel's mother.

"Wedgewood," she explains. "It was my mother's and her mother's before that. As you can imagine, it's very special to my family."

Oriana folds her arms against her chest, wondering what happened to her own mother's bowl. Although she's never seen it, Granddad has told her all about it.

"Do you want to go for a walk when you come back?" Oriana persists. The woman takes Emmanuel's hand, and he walks away without answering the question. Oriana settles onto the front steps and waits, knowing TEMPLE visits are short.

After a while, Papa comes out of the house and offers Oriana a batch of warm cookies and offers Oriana some. She raises her brow with appreciation and then sits quietly, eating one cookie after another. A pink rose petal, curled up at the edges and turning brown, blows along the street.

A skinny rodent with gray ears climbs the first two steps and grabs hold of a fallen cookie crumb. Oriana shudders, pulling her feet in close to her thighs. Its paws go up to its mouth. "Scat little rat. Get outta here," she commands. The varmint scurries back down the steps and into the loblolly graveyard across the street.

Oriana loses herself in thought over the possibility that TEMPLE has greater significance in Papa's life than he lets on. He's never admitted to going there but never said he has not. There must be more to his anger about TEMPLE than he has explained so far.

Her mind drifts to the time earlier this year when she'd asked Papa about a puppy that had been born blind. Oriana had wanted to take him home from the clinic as her pet, but Papa had explained patiently that the animal couldn't live that way and would have to be put down. All she wanted then was to hold the puppy while he administered the fatal solution into his veins. Papa slammed doors and yelled at her all day.

"I don't care what you want," he said, and tells her she is macabre and morbid. It was a reaction that made no sense to her at all.

"Walk to where?" Emmanuel asks, suddenly appearing in front of her.

"You're back from TEMPLE," she says. "I see you took your bowl back home and changed your clothes."

"Um hum."

"Where do you want to go on our walk?"

Emmanuel shrugs.

"You decide," he says.

"I don't care. Where do you want to go?" she asks as Emmanuel takes a seat by her side. She can hardly believe he's offering to spend time with her. There aren't many options available to them, other than to walk into the center of town and back, stroll down

Main Street to the old wharf, head out past the Whaling Museum near Granddad's house, or climb along the dike.

"Maybe to the tree," he says, drumming his fingers on her shoulder.

"Tree? What tree?" Oriana inquires. She assumes he is suggesting a game involving an imaginary tree.

"Oh," she says, gesturing across the street. She giggles, still unsure of herself in his physical presence. She hasn't yet learned how to interpret all the nuances of his expression. "You must be talking about that huge white pine over there, the one with the low branches we can climb," she says, pointing to a nearby meadow. Emmanuel removes his hand from her shoulder.

"No," he mumbles, dropping his eyes to the ground. Oriana sighs, placing her hand on his hand. She didn't mean to mock or disappoint him.

"Come on, Emmanuel, what tree are you talking about then?" she asks.

"From my dream," he replies in a whisper.

"Dream?" she asks. Oriana is puzzled because VISHNEW connects don't dream when they sleep. She wonders if he is suggesting they take a journey together under his Hood. "Sure," she responds. She rises and walks toward his house. "I'll go with you anywhere you'd like under there

Emmanuel heads across the street in the opposite direction from his home. Then he takes off running across the empty lot.

"Hey!" Oriana yells, following him, moving her adolescent legs as fast as she can. "Slow down, will you!" she pleads as he crosses the clearing and turns left onto the next street. When he finally stops, the two are standing in front of a bright blue hover-scooter parked on the side of the road.

"Whose is this?" she asks, panting, as she catches up to Emmanuel.

"Don't know," he answers, climbing onto the vehicle.

Oriana, still engrossed in what she surmises to be an imagination game, gets on behind Emmanuel and wraps her arms around his waist. She likes how it feels to have her stomach and chest pressed against his back, so she scoots in a little closer until her groin makes contact, too. That, she finds, is sublime.

"Let's go to a magical forest where the trees are huge and full of life," she suggests, closing her eyes to create the vision in her mind.

Emmanuel starts the engine.

"Hey, what are you doing?" Oriana exclaims. "I'm not allowed to ride on these. We'll get into huge trouble."

Emmanuel shifts into launch on a machine designed for both air and ground transportation. Shaped like an oblong dish with wheels, the vehicle has a windshield and a seat built for two, and its stealth motion makes barely a whisper as it glides upwards through the air. The control mechanism is a touch-sensitive panel on the windshield marked 'Forward, Lift, Lower, Slow, Stop.' It is simple to operate. The speed is regulated by the machine rather than by its driver, and is prompted by variable conditions such as traffic flow, wind, and the sunlight that provides it power.

Emmanuel and Oriana head out Orange Street onto Polpis Road, gliding over what the Great Storms have left of Quaise Pastures.

"This isn't a walk," Oriana exclaims over the cat-like purr of the engine.

"Yahoo!" Emmanuel shouts with glee as they soar further away from town and out over the desolate terrain. They land between two swaths of thick, brown scrub.

"A bog?" Oriana asks in amazement.

Emmanuel hops off the craft and takes off running for the edge of the thicket.

Oriana wishes he would take her by the hand, or say something, or at least look back to see if she is still there.

"Slow down, Emmanuel," she shouts breathlessly, jogging tentatively behind the boy.

Emmanuel raises his arms over his head, mimicking flight.

Back in the early part of the twenty-first century, Masquetuck Reservation was a fourteen-acre nature preserve, containing both native and non-native flora. Three-quarters of a century later it is unrecognizable. Scrub oaks and an entanglement of vines grow up and over the remaining stubs of once-robust deciduous trees and conifers. Kudzu, wisteria, a hearty variety of stinging nettle, and other aggressive non-native species have worked their way through the stumps and rot of what used to be a mature forest grove.

Emmanuel yanks at the encroaching vines, unveiling a rugged path through the overgrowth of late spring. Slowing his gait to accommodate the changing terrain, he pushes through briars, thistle, and robust shoots of poison oak as he moves to the commands of an untamed will.

Oriana trails hopelessly behind, unsure whether she is witness to a VISHNEW malfunction or a feral child.

"Take me home, Emmanuel. I want you to take me back home," she cries out to the boy who seems to have forgotten she is there.

When finally Oriana catches up, she finds her friend standing under a magnificent white oak. Huge by comparison to any tree Oriana has ever seen, its robust trunk and healthy broad branches astonish her. The tree is undamaged and full of young leaves.

"Wow, this one must be pretty old," she remarks. "I wonder how big it is." Trying to estimate its height, Oriana gazes up to its top, framing her fingers into a square and peering through them as she extends her arm outward. The change in perception fails to provide the information she needs to make more than a random guess at its size.

"Well, if size is what you're trying to figure out, I can give you an exact measurement of both its width and its height," Emmanuel blurts out, using more words than she's heard him speak all day.

Even when they meet under their respective Hoods, Emmanuel speaks very little. "I can gauge it to within a centimeter and even convert it into the English customary system," he continues.

The opal yellow of a VISHNEW-enhanced cornea washes over Emmanuel's eyes. He moves his gaze from treetop to roots. "It's forty-eight point seventy-five feet tall," he answers.

"Damn, you sure do think you're smart," Oriana mumbles under her breath. He may be trying to impress her, but it's humiliating.

"You can't do instant calibrations like that, can you?" he asks her.

"No, Emmanuel. I can't," she replies, putting her hands on her hips. "You know I'm different in that way." She hates this kind of insensitivity to her unconnected state. "And anyway, how is it you are suddenly talking so much? You usually hardly speak, and when you do it's no more than a few words at a time."

"I figured you couldn't do it," he retorts. "My dad told me you're handicapped on account of not being connected."

"Well what's its circumference, Emmanuel?" she asks, hoping he won't be able to come up with the answer and wishing the humiliation would end. Being with Emmanuel in person turns out to be a disappointment. Oriana feels stupid for the first time in her life.

"Can't you even make an intelligent estimate?" he retaliates.

Oriana wants to believe that Emmanuel's prodding is a desire to help her and not the harsh judging it seems to be.

"Well, I don't know how intelligent this estimate is, but I'll guess around twenty-five feet," she offers, hopeful that she is accurate.

"That's pretty close. Its actual width is twenty-one point five three," he returns. "Don't feel badly. I am a child of VISHNEW. Fully connected, that is." Emmanuel proudly displays his palms to confirm his claim.

"Bad," she returns. "The correct word is bad, not badly, Emmanuel. I guess VISHNEW doesn't know everything." Oriana pushes her friend's hands aside and walks around the tree. She is not entirely VISHNEW-independent, at least not in the way Emmanuel thinks. She has limited access from under her Hood, a hand-held device for basic communication, and, for security purposes, positioning implants embedded in the heels of her shoes.

The problem is that she doesn't have the direct brain interface of a full-connect, leaving her without enhanced information processing capabilities visual acuity, and global relays of data. So, for example, she has no idea of her exact geographic coordinates, as Emmanuel does.

Also, like Emmanuel and all the other VISNHEW- connected island kids, she is schooled under the Hood. But her lessons have to be supplemented by the Starbuck sisters, because she is limited in what she can learn from the virtual realities of the Nantucket educational program.

"How do you think this tree survived the Great Storms?" she inquires, hoping to impress him with her knowledge of historical events. Emmanuel doesn't acknowledge the question. Instead, he plops down on the ground and pulls off his shoes. Rubbing his bare soles on the loamy soil, he twists and turns them in the dirt with a purpose.

Oriana sits down next to him and pounds her shoe-covered feet against the trunk of the tree.

"Stop that," Emmanuel scolds her. "How would you like to be treated that way?"

Oriana notices his dirty feet, clumps of soil stuck disgustingly between his toes. "Yuck," she exclaims, pointing at them.

Emmanuel lifts a foot and rubs it against her bare leg.

"Hey, stop it!" she fusses as he laughs. He shoves his other foot against her calf.

The boy stands, and steps over an exposed root. Leaning his body against the trunk of the tree, he wraps his arms around it as much as he is able and slides his body up and down along the bark.

Oriana steps back in disgust. She may still be young, but Oriana knows enough about boys to suspect she is witnessing some kind of sexual perversion. And to make matters worse, Emmanuel begins to hum and moan, sliding his hands along the jagged bark and pressing his face against its surface. "Why are you doing that?" she asks.

"You should come try, so you can feel it too," Emmanuel invites her.

Oriana shakes her head 'no,' the soft ripples of her shoulder-length brown hair moving sideways with the motion. She is anxious and fears that actually touching the tree could cause her harm.

"Oh come on," he teases. She disregards his plea. Her own curiosity finally compels her.

"Feel what?" she asks, tentatively stepping closer to the trunk.

"I can't tell you what it is. You just have to feel it. Like me; do like I'm doing."

"Fine then," she replies, stretching her arms around the trunk. Before her face touches the bark, she scans the tree's surface for mites, lichen, or small vines that could lead to a contact dermatitis. Oriana has heard from other kids that it was a good thing that trees were nearly all gone from the Island, since they were so dangerous.

When she told Papa, he said such ideas were ludicrous and that she should check with him on anything she hears under her Hood regarding nature. "They should be so lucky as to be near a healthy, living tree," Papa had said.

Oriana leans in further to make full body contact with the tree's thick mass. No harm seems to be come to her as a result.

"Do you feel it?" Emmanuel asks, the pitch of his voice rising a bit.

She has no idea what he is talking about. "It's rigid and hard. Sort of rough," she huffs.

"No, I mean do you feel the tree?"

"I don't get what you're asking," she offers, longing to know what sort of sensations he might be experiencing.

"Well, maybe for you it would be better to turn around and try to feel it through your back."

Oriana follows his suggestion, pressing her spine along a vertical protrusion in the trunk.

"Why are you holding your head forward like that?" he asks her, tapping his foot in annoyance. "Go ahead and put your head against the tree. Make your whole body touch, or you won't feel it," Emmanuel instructs.

She leans closer to the tree, resting her head against the bark. When she imagines something crawling in her hair, Oriana begins to squirm.

"Calm down, or it won't work," Emmanuel instructs.

Oriana convinces herself that the crawling sensation is only her imagination, and continues to hold on to the tree.

Emmanuel begins to hum, no particular tune, just a droning on middle C. Oriana joins in with him. She ponders what might be causing his 'simple social incompetence' as she listens to the sound of his voice, which reminds her of the cooing of doves she once heard in a nature program under her Hood.

"Now let go," he instructs her.

"Let go?" she asks, as she begins to finally to relax. "If I let go, I might fall."

"No, not of the tree, of yourself. Let go of yourself and then maybe you'll be able to feel it all the way."

Once again she tries to imagine what Emmanuel feels. Pushing past the tears of frustration that are welling up inside her eyes, she attempts to let herself go. "You're not doing it. I can tell. You're not doing it at all," he accuses, with clear disappointment in his voice.

"Stop pressuring me, okay? I'm trying, really I am," she returns.

"Then stop thinking so much," he scolds, "so you can join with the tree." Emmanuel, no longer interested in coaching his friend, slips into a state of mind inaccessible to her. His humming drifts off into dead silence. His entire body is pressed flat against the tree.

"I'm alive," Emmanuel cries out suddenly, his voice carried upward along the branches in vocal vibrations aiming for the sky.

"Of course you are," she hollers in return.

"I am alive!" he cries out, louder than before.

"Me too!" she sings out.

Oriana hops up onto a low branch and hangs upside-down from the great tree. The blood rushes into her brain. She begins to sense something unusual in herself.

Releasing the tree trunk, Emmanuel lies down on the ground, wraps his arms around his knees, and curls into a ball. Oriana turns her attention to her friend who lies motionless on the ground, her perception askew from being upside down. She longs to know what he feels, and what it is like to be fully VISHNEW-connected like him.

"What are you doing down there?" she asks, slipping off the branch to curl up next to Emmanuel.

"I learned today that VISHNEW has determined me to be untreatable," he shares.

"What are you talking about?" she asks.

"I've been reclassified as a 'socially maladjusted youth,'" he explains.

Oriana places her hand on his back. Her friend's condition is more serious than she thought. Now he'll never be allowed to mate, and they definitely won't use his sperm for progeny. A feeling of sorrow overwhelms her.

Emmanuel shifts position, curling up around the base of the tree. The two lay silent for a while.

On rare occasions, the nano-wiring and tiny implants in a connected child can overwhelm the developing brain. Gradual yet adverse reactions, such as mental dissociation, physical fatigue, and, in Emmanuel's case, "simple social incompetence", can occur as a result. A shocking or horrifying incident or persistent emotional strain is usually implicated in the breakdown. Most islanders blame Emmanuel's mother.

Rolling onto his back, face turned upward toward the branches overhead, Emmanuel's expression softens.

"I guess you're feeling better now," Oriana surmises.

"The buzzing is gone. My head isn't hurting anymore," he exclaims, grinning, his teeth fully revealed, completely straight and nearly perfectly white. Oriana didn't know anything about this buzzing, or that he'd been experiencing physical pain.

"How come you feel better now?" she inquires.

"Dunno. The pain comes and goes. Maybe it's the tree," he suggests happily.

She reaches for Emmanuel's head, running her fingers through the soft blond strands that lay flat against his skull. She rubs her palm over his scalp with a gentle firmness, wishing she could make sure his suffering would never return.

"What time is it?" she asks, concerned that Papa must be really upset by now. She doubts her remote connection is working at all this far out, and surmises that Papa is bound to be growing anxious since he has no idea of her whereabouts.

Emmanuel sits up and lifts a hand to his forehead. "Hmm," he sounds. "Do you want Eastern Standard time, with the daylight saving factor, from the Nantucket Town clock? Or would you prefer the Coordinated Universal Time from the Cesium Fountain Atomic Clock in Boulder, Colorado?"

Oriana yanks hard on his left earlobe. "Could you stop being such a jerk and just tell me whatever time Papa has now?"

"Ouch," he complains.

"Well? What time is it?" she asks again.

"It sounds like you want to know if it's time for us to go home. To which the answer is probably 'yes.' It's been 138 minutes since we left your steps."

"We'd better go," she suggests.

"Not yet," Emmanuel replies with a smirk. "I'm not ready yet." Suddenly his body stiffens and his face tightens. He squints as a frown forms at the edges of his mouth.

"What's the matter?" she asks, touching his cheeks.

Emmanuel reaches for his shoes, slips them on, and stands slowly. He takes Oriana's hand and lifts her to a standing position. "It's my mother. Her voice, I mean. It's in my ears. She says I have to come home now."

"Oh yeah," Oriana comments. "She can talk to you whenever she wants to, right? That comes with being a VISHNEW-connect."

"Correct," he says, uttering the last word Oriana will hear him speak for weeks.

The two make their way back through the thicket, wordless, hand in hand. The ride home on the hover-scooter is peaceful, a barely perceptible breeze rocking the craft slightly from front to back as they glide. The vehicle lands itself exactly in the place where they found it.

"See you later, okay?" Oriana offers, climbing off the hover-craft. Although he says nothing, Oriana can read the desperation in his eyes.

Emmanuel catches a glimpse of his mother approaching. His eyes roll up into the back of his head. His eyelids flutter erratically, as VISHNEW senses his unease and attempts to make an adjustment to his brain chemistry.

"Are you okay, Emmanuel?" Oriana asks, wrapping her arms around his neck and pulling him close to her body.

"Let go of him," his mother demands as she reaches the pair. She takes hold of her son's arm, and steers him toward their home.

Oriana follows behind. She notes the stiffness of Emmanuel's gait, observes his dragging feet and his awkward stride. VISHNEW's adjustments are unsuccessful. Emmanuel's trauma persists.

As Oriana stops at the walkway of her home, she taps Emmanuel's back.

"See you later, okay?"

Emmanuel doesn't even turn around, continuing to stride arm in arm with his mother to the house next door to Oriana's.

A few weeks later, Emmanuel and his mother stand on Oriana's front steps. The two are locked arm in arm. A man, who Oriana assumes to be the boy's father, stands close behind the pair.

"Oriana, does your father know about your little adventure with Emmanuel?" the woman asks, raising her left eyebrow. She interrupts Oriana's attempt at a reply. "We do not approve of this friendship," the woman declares, lifting her index finger toward Oriana and scowling.

"We need to speak with Gardiner," the man tells Oriana as he pushes his way toward the open door. The man has blond hair like Emmanuel's, though much thinner and with flakes of dead skin caught in some of the front strands. He reaches for bangs that partially obscure his eyes, pulling his hair across his forehead and behind his ears to reveal the telling tiny scar at each of his temples. *Connected, of course*, Oriana verifies.

"Sure, I'll go in and get him," she replies, stepping inside her home. Papa appears at that moment and greets the unexpected guests, welcoming them inside.

"What a surprise," Papa remarks to his neighbors as they enter the foyer. He has never cared much for Emmanuel's parents. After all, they've never bothered to come by to say hello. In fact, they've made no effort whatsoever to communicate in a neighborly way in the years since Rebecca died, other than to leave a perfunctory note and a bouquet of virtual flowers in the greeting program for

Papa to find under his Hood. Papa had immediately dissolved the floral image and sent an auditory reply saying, 'How kind of you to think of me, and in a time of such deep grief.'

"My mate and I are here to assure that the boy and Oriana will not be socializing anymore," the woman explains.

"We'll be brief," Emmanuel's father promises.

"But why not?" Oriana protests from inside the foyer. "That's not fair!"

Papa gestures towards the living room couch. Emmanuel's mother seats Emmanuel between his father and herself. Papa's face folds into scornful glare as he wonders why they hadn't arranged for this meeting to happen under their Hoods. Politeness would dictate that such an austere declaration not be presented in person. The man continues to speak. Papa folds his arms across his chest and bites down on his lower lip.

"We have no choice, really," the boy's father exclaims. "The techno-medics believe VISHNEW has decreed this, and they are restricting Emmanuel's social exposure. The only interactions they will allow, other than with immediate family, are engagements under his Hood, as those can be closely monitored for his safety."

"Okay," Papa agrees. "Then Emmanuel and Oriana will continue to meet under their Hoods."

"Oh no, no. I am afraid that will not do," the boy's father continues. Emmanuel gazes through the panes of the triple-hung windows. "You see, even there his contacts must be only with pre-screened, full VISHNEW-connects."

The man pauses to study his surroundings, first taking notice of the object-filled shelves along the wall, and then contemplating the original glass of the windows. Although upgraded with ultra-thin film for protection from the elements, they still allow people to see outside from in, and vice versa. Very few private residences use two-way windows any more.

"How strange," the man whispers to his mate.

"Then how will we stay best friends?" Oriana implores, tears streaming from her eyes. "We only just met in person for the first time!"

"This reaction is a good example of exactly what concerns us," the boy's father states as he looks past Oriana to Papa. "Such emotional displays only serve to trigger adverse reactions in our son."

Emmanuel props his feet up on the couch, clutching his knees in his arms. A clump of hair falls across his eyes.

Papa takes notice of the boy's appearance: smooth dark skin the blue side of black, light yellow hair bordering on platinum, and pale, very pale blue eyes. He considers what an interesting set of design selections these parents have made for their only child.

The boy's father turns a stern eye toward Emmanuel. "Be polite and put your feet down," he scolds. Emmanuel's shoulders slump, and his head falls to his chest. His eyes fixate on nothing.

"He's not used to being in other people's houses," his mother explains, pushing down on Emmanuel's knees. "Neither are we, really."

The mother reaches for Emmanuel's face. She places one hand under his chin and lifts his head, and with the other she pulls the hair tightly across his brow and behind his ears like his father's.

Oriana's hands move unconsciously, drawing her hair forward over the exposed temples of her face, hiding the smooth skin, which has never been pierced for insertion of the standard hard wiring.

"It's okay for Emmanuel to sit any way he wants to on my couch," Papa interjects. Aggravation builds in his voice, and his deep blue eyes blaze. He runs his fingers through the black beard he's decided to let grow untamed.

"This furniture can't be hurt by mere feet," he adds. He slides his hands behind his neck, fingers clasped to support his head, elbows extended out to the side. "So he can keep his two feet right where they are. The couch can't be stained at all, not by anything. I think he's old enough to make his own choices about how he sits."

Papa stretches his legs out and slides forward in his chair, folding his arms across his chest. "Besides, other than for the sake of social tradition, there is no practical reason why Emmanuel's feet need to be on the floor," he sneers, not at all offended over placement of the boy's feet. "In fact, I insist," Papa goes on, standing up to pat Emmanuel's head in a gesture of approval.

Emmanuel releases his knees and puts his feet on the floor,.

"How about if I stay with them whenever Emmanuel comes to visit?" Papa suggests.

Oriana's face lights up, her eyes twinkling with adoration. He knows this is her only friend, and how much she cares for him.

"I don't think so," Emmanuel's father says as he stands to get a closer look at the items on the shelf. He reaches for a soft, rectangular object imprinted with the words 'The Last Child in the Woods.' "How odd," he comments, as he fondles it. "What is this?"

"It's a book," Papa replies.

"I've never actually held one of these in my hands."

"That one is a collector's item and one of my favorites," Papa says blithely. "The author makes a compelling argument about the end of a particular human era when children learned through playing out in nature, before such things as Hoods came into use."

"Sounds like nonsense," the father remarks.

Emmanuel looks at the relic in his father's hands and then at Oriana. Her soft round eyes meet his, and the two friends gaze at each other for a few seconds until the tap of Emmanuel's mother's hand on his shoulder breaks their connection.

"Would you like to borrow it?" Papa asks his neighbor.

"No, I would not," Emmanuel's father replies, anxiously putting it back in its place on the shelf between *A Field Guide to Nantucket Birds* and *Moby Dick*.

"We should go," he says to his mate.

In a little less than an hour, Emmanuel's mother returns. Papa spots her face pressed against the colorful windowpanes as he passes from the kitchen to the stairs. Apparently, the novelty of being able to see inside the house has made her forget her usual politeness. She anxiously motions for him to come to the door.

"Come in, please," he offers, opening the door. "And what brings you back so soon?"

Emmanuel's mother steps inside. Panting, she pauses to catch her breath.

"May I offer you a cup of tea?" Papa says. The woman clears her throat hesitantly and laughs nervously. Papa smiles, gesturing her toward the kitchen where she sits down at the table, her back rigid against the chair, her feet perched on its lowest rung. Emmanuel's mother pulls at the ponytail that lies across her chest, the flips it over her shoulder.

Oriana sits down beside her.

As Papa prepares tea, he chatters away in a genuine effort to ease her apparent discomfort. He talks about how his late mate Rebecca considered it important to have a cup each afternoon, and how she especially liked to use the silver serving set the women had kept in the family for many generations. The tea service was considered a treasure, and had been brought from Eastern Europe to the New World.

Papa tells his neighbor how he challenged his mate often over what he considered to be the frivolous use of a precious metal. He regularly suggested that it be donated to Maker's Materials and replaced with a plain polymer set from their stock, but Rebecca insisted that certain pleasures should not be sacrificed for material efficiency.

"An old-fashioned woman in many ways," he says, referring to her insistence that tea was made with the sassafras, chamomile, or mint that grew plentifully in her side yard.

Papa pours the warm beverage from the tarnished heirloom pot.

Emmanuel's mother sips the sweet drink with two hands. "Mmmh," she says. "You make a nice cup of tea."

Oriana leans over the teapot and gawks at the woman.

Papa smiles, as he remembers his mate sitting at that same table, relishing every sip of her ritual tea. His focus then shift back to the woman before him, who he finds unattractively pale, too frail, and annoyingly timid; quite the opposite of his Rebecca, whose full lips, wide hips, and unrelenting determination sealed the deal on their mating match.

Chin on hand, elbow propped firmly on the table, Oriana stares at her friend's mother. Emmanuel's mother strokes three fingers across her cleavage, peering coyly over her teacup at Gardiner.

"We need to ask you to leave, Oriana," Papa says.

"Aw, do I have to?" she whines.

"Yes, you do. And we expect privacy," Papa affirms, perplexed by his neighbor's behavior. He intends to get to the bottom of this, and Oriana's presence makes that difficult.

Oriana stands, sliding the chair aside as she heads out of the kitchen and down the hall to the room where her Hood is kept. She slips underneath it, resigning herself to remote viewing of the exchange between Papa and Emmanuel's mother. She is particularly interested in anything Emmanuel's mother has to say that might affect the time she'll get to spend with her only friend.

"I hate this," she sputters as she pulls the Hood down over her head and works her eye movements over the controls. She'd much rather be sitting with Papa and their guest in person. At least then she could get a clearer sense of the feeling in the room. Under the Hood, the best she'll get is to see facial expressions, and even though she'll hear every word, being right there would be so much more interesting. Oriana sets the view for 'one way observation', which generally counts as privacy.

"What exactly are you doing here? What is it that you want?" Papa asks of Emmanuel's mother.

"I feel I can confide in you," she replies, her head dropping a bit, her eyes focused on the cup of tea in her hands.

"What do you mean?" Papa asks. "Confide in me about what?"

"We had no idea he'd come out like this."

"Who? Like what?"

"All we wanted was to protect the child from ultraviolet exposure," she explains. "It's so dangerous for pale-complexioned children these days. We only wanted to keep him safe. It's just that, well . . . "

"Well, what?"

"Oh," she replies, lost in thought. "It frightened me terribly."

"What frightened you?"

"The boy, of course," she elaborates. "How can you not have noticed?'

Papa shrugs. "You mean his skin color?"

The woman nods.

"After the retrieval and connection were complete, they put it in my arms. I didn't know what to do. No one warned us. As you can imagine, I thought, 'How could this be mine? How could this have come from inside my womb?' At first I didn't want it."

"If you are talking about Emmanuel, I think you mean to say him. You didn't want *him*."

"Him, it, whatever. I was never so startled in my life."

Papa is not sure what to say. In a way, he understands the sentiment, because it is not very different from what he felt when they took Oriana from her dying mother's arms and placed her into his. He'd even tried to hand her back. He has since forgiven himself, realizing he was in shock during that horrific time.

"Do you mean to say you actually carried Emmanuel in utero?" he asks.

"Yes, it's a family tradition. My mother carried me," she explains. "And her mother carried her." Emmanuel's mother turns her focus to a dying spider plant hanging in the kitchen window. "We thought it best to keep him in our home," she continues, "out of the direct view of other Islanders. Somehow, sixteen years went by before we finally let him out."

"Are you saying that Emmanuel has been inside your house his entire life?" Papa asks in amazement. The woman keeps talking, paying no attention to Papa's interjections of, 'What?' and 'What did you say!?'

"After he and your daughter became friends under their Hoods, he became obsessed with wanting to go outside and see the island with his own eyes. I told him that would be a horrible idea, that he ought to try to understand; that his appearance would probably be as shocking to islanders as it was at first to me."

"I see," Papa replies.

"I didn't mean to hurt him. Really I didn't. I was trying to explain things to him the best I could."

"I can appreciate that," Papa reassures her.

"So we started taking him with us to TEMPLE. Ever since then, he's not been so well." The woman's eyes begin to tear. VISHNEW senses her depressive emotion and treats the condition immediately. A sweet smile comes across the lips of the mother who has yet to accept her genetic progeny as her own. "Ooh," she coos as the pleasure center of her brain is stimulated. "Recently we let him out like he wanted. Now something has gone terribly wrong," she announces.

"Apparently," Papa says. "What is his prognosis?"

"Not good if he continues to venture outside into the public domain," she responds.

"They have a special friendship, you know," Papa offers.

Emmanuel's mother clears her throat and places the nail of an index finger between her teeth. She gnaws nervously until the skin beneath it bleeds. A wordless moment passes is shared between the two.

"You ought to consider his emotional needs," Papa scolds.

Abruptly, Emmanuel's mother heads out the kitchen door.

Oriana watches from under her Hood as the woman marches down the steps, across the side yard, through her front door, and up the stairs to Emmanuel's bedroom. Oriana resets the viewing control to observe the inside of Emmanuel's home. To her surprise, Emmanuel's mother takes Emmanuel by the arm and escorts him out again. Oriana slips out from under her Hood and returns to the kitchen table.

"They're on their way back," she informs Papa.

At that moment, mother and son walk up to the side door. Oriana sits in her chair. Papa opens the door.

"So you're back!" he says to the pair.

The panther-skinned teenager with blond hair and clear blue eyes pulls his hand out of his mother's clutch and sits at the table beside his friend.

"Only one more chance. That's it," his mother scolds. "If anything at all goes wrong, that's it for Emmanuel and Oriana's so-called friendship. Back into the house he will go."

"One more chance," Oriana mumbles as her friend's mother gets up to leave.

The woman shuts the door with a bang.

STUNG

The clattering of the Meeting House windowpanes awakens Oriana from a deep sleep. She sits up, aware of an urgent pressure in her groin. The baby has shifted its position, making Oriana's need for relief rather pressing. She walks across the room to a side door, hoping to discover a toilet on the other side, but finds the knob locked.

"Damn it all," she cries out, her voice echoing across the worship benches of the empty room. She grabs her hair, pulling on the wavy strands. Moaning, she shifts her weight from side to side, resisting the urge to urinate. Oriana considers her options, including going back home. *I can't go back there, I can't.*

Oriana returns to her place on the floor. Lying down again on the chameleon coat, she convinces herself that the sensation will go away. She takes in a deep breath and relaxes with the exhalation. The cramping muscles soften. The burning sensation subsides. Oriana drifts back into deep slumber.

Within a few moments her bladder begins to leak, soaking her undergarments, the urine running onto the floor. Her dreams become fitful and disturbed. Images deluge her mind, ushering her back to her twelfth year since retrieval.

Papa is in the kitchen preparing a cake in celebration. Oriana is perched under her Hood, exploring a greeting card Emmanuel has sent. She misses him terribly, since his relegation to a life indoors, forbidden from direct contact with outsiders.

The techno-medics had told his parents that isolation was the only possible cure, and they accepted this diagnosis. They determined that the mental overstimulation from his relationship with Oriana, compounded by an emotional entanglement between the two, was a significant source of disturbance to his capacity to participate in the outside world.

Oriana browses through the images Emmanuel has created for her birthday greeting. She smiles over the sentiment he sends, enjoying the song he sings in celebration of her retrieval day. She misses the sound of his voice and the penetrating expression in his eyes. She remembers how it felt to be with him in the flesh, to touch his hands, and to feel his skin. But holographic displays are better than no contact at all.

"I hope you like the card," he says, tuning in to her from under his Hood.

Emmanuel's hands reach for her hands. He slides his arms around her waist, pulling her into a tight embrace. His lips touch tenderly to her lips and her virtual body swoons. Her actual body tingles, pulsating from her heart to her skin. She sighs as she experiences the display.

"I like that," she says. Emmanuel kisses her forehead, then her cheeks, nose, and lips. "Do that to my mouth again," she requests.

"I'm so sorry," she hears him say as his hands, arms, and finally his shoulders fade from view.

"Sorry about what?" she asks, "What's happening?" Their carnal expression is unauthorized. Emmanuel has been disconnected.

Papa spreads pink icing across the first layer of the cake. He then carefully places the second layer on top. Once he has centered it perfectly, he prepares to frost it in blue. Out of the corner of his eye, he catches sight of something moving outside. He looks up, distracted from the design of the cake, a techno-medic craft landing in the side yard of their home. A female and a fertili-bot step out.

"Oh no!" he yells suddenly. He drops the frosting knife, and runs to the household control room. By the time he gets to the panel and runs his palm across it to self-identify, it is too late to shield the house. The front door opens. The pair steps inside. They find Oriana still underneath her Hood.

She knows why they've come. She's been expecting them ever since she saw the blood on her panties and went under her Hood to find some other girls to ask about it. One of them must have reported it at TEMPLE. In a way she's happy that the techno-medics have come, because now she will be more like the other island girls. But she can't let on to Papa that she feels that way. He would never understand.

After only a few private minutes with her, the two emerge and declare Oriana to be extremely fertile, with a whopping 80,000 eggs available for extraction. Island girls, on average, have only 30,000 worthy eggs by the time they reach the height of puberty.

"We estimate that nearly 148 are healthy, viable eggs of a superior enough quality for fertilization," the female techno-medic says gaily. "That makes her special."

"The girl will be celebrated. Envied too," adds the fertili-bot.

Word of her fertility spread swiftly among islanders watching under their Hoods. Granddad shows up half an hour later with a special gift. He presents it to Oriana, who is sitting at the kitchen table having a cup of tea when he arrives,

"I guess I know why you are here," she says without looking up at him. Granddad hands her a brightly wrapped package. She ignores it, embarrassed and humiliated by the entire affair. She pretends not to care.

When he leaves, she carries the package up to her room and peeks inside. The contents overwhelm her with confusion, fear, and an unexpected sadness. She places the carefully boxed bowl under a blanket on the floor at the back of her closet.

"Let's go out and celebrate!" Papa suggests later in the day.

"Celebrate what?" she replies.

"Your twelfth birthday, of course!"

Oriana smiles broadly, relieved the focus is not her fertility, the revelation of which makes her feel exposed and invaded. She would rather forget the entire episode.

"That sounds great, Papa."

"Oh good. Let's go then," he returns. The pair climbs into Papa's vehicle.

"Where do you want to go?" she asks.

"How about to Mama's and my favorite place?" Papa offers.

"And where was that, Papa?"

"Oh, try to guess."

"Hmm. Maybe the place that used to be the town of S'conset . . . "

"You got it!"

Granddad's voice comes over the car speakers as they head out of town.

"Damn it all!" Papa says.

"Hey, I happened to catch sight of you two turning onto Milestone Road! Where the heck are you going?" Granddad asks, his voice breaking from agitation.

"None of your business," Papa replies.

"Hey, Ori, did you happen to open the package I gave you?" Granddad asks.

"No, Dad, I don't think she's opened it yet," Papa responds before Oriana has a chance to answer.

"And why the hell not?" Granddad barks. Oriana rolls her eyes

"I don't know. Ask her yourself, why don't ya?" Papa suggests. He glances at Oriana with a grin. She stares straight ahead. She'll open the gift Granddad has given her when she is ready. Meanwhile, it's not a subject she's willing to discuss.

"By the way, happy retrieval day there ole' girl," Granddad says, breaking into his rendition of the retrieval song.

"Happy retrieval-day to you, happy retrieval-day to you, happy retrieval-day ornery Oriana, happy retrieval-day to yoooooo!"

"He has some nerve," she says, tapping her fingers on the roof through an open window. "The geezer."

"Don't be so hard on the old guy," Papa returns.

Granddad persists in questioning them about their plans.

"Well, actually, we are taking a ride out to the shore," Papa responds, avoiding mentioning the specifics of the trip. Granddad gets jealous when the two go on private jaunts, and resents being left behind.

"Come back for me. I want to go," Granddad insists.

Papa declines, citing the danger to an old man in going out to the shore.

"Now don't you go trying to parent me, you son of a gun," Granddad yells. "I can decide for myself where I will go and when. And I'll have you know that I am quite capable of judging for myself when the risk is too great. So you bring your fat ass right back to town and get me."

His remarks start Oriana giggling. Papa is trim and fit, so the description doesn't fit at all, but still, she delights in the way Granddad says the words. Papa jerks the wheel to avoid a pile of debris and continues driving in the same direction.

Granddad starts chattering about how well protected he is as a full-connect, and how Oriana and Papa would be the vulnerable ones in a dangerous situation.

"You'd better be careful of the Seekers way out there," he warns.

Papa howls sarcastically.

"Oh come on now, Dad. You don't actually believe in that island intruder hogwash. Who do you think would want to intrude on us? There's not much left here on Nantucket for anyone to want."

Oriana's expression shifts from snide to concerned. She focuses her gaze on the vehicle indicators. The ride is rough and rather unpleasant. If the vehicle warning sirens go off, she'll insist that they go back immediately.

"I know what we've been told, Dad," Papa goes on, "about connected communities being vulnerable to attack. About the desperation of the Seekers to gain access. What I don't understand is why you insist on falling for it."

The vehicle sounds its first warning. Papa shuts it off with the punctuated voice command.

"Override," he commands the car. Oriana grabs the safety on the dashboard in front of her.

"It's nothing," Papa reassures Oriana, who is positioned to begin her plea to return to the safety of home.

"Alright already, never mind. The answer is still 'no,'" Papa says. Granddad grunts.

"We are heading for off-limits territory. I can't be responsible for you out here," he tells him.

"I'll have you know that I am still the parent here," Granddad tells him. "Turn that vehicle around and come back to get me, you hear me boy?" Papa puts his hand over the sensor panel, preparing to end the conversation.

"Absolutely not," Papa affirms. "I have no intention of coming back to get you, Dad. This is a father-daughter outing."

He swipes a hand over the communication control and the signal is immediately broken.

Papa clenches his teeth, frustrated and angry over the limitations Nantucket's Selectmen have imposed. Who are they to tell him what risks to take? The so-called dangers are not real but just another example of authority exceeding the boundaries of its legitimate domain.

"Are we going to be put in the Facility for coming out here, Papa?" Oriana asks, glaring at her father. Papa brings the vehicle to a stop, and the passenger door swings open.

"Don't worry, we will be fine," he answers. "Hop on out, and I'll show you where your Mama and I first began our mating rituals."

Oriana steps out onto the sandy surface.

"This used to be Broadway," Papa grimaces, as he explains about the destruction of the rose-covered, gray-shingled cottages that once lined the quaint hillside of S'conset. He glances over the felled roof of a whaler's cottage, once perched perfectly for viewing the open sea, now a pile of broken fence pickets, splintered heart pine flooring, and shattered glass. "This one stood for over three hundred years," he remarks, pointing to the dilapidated structure. A tangled mass of vines spreads out from under a seam of the roof. A single bloom catches Oriana's eye.

"Wow, it's so pretty here!" she exclaims, looking down the battered hillside over the expanse of water.

"It saddens me that you will have to rely on your Hood to know what it once looked like here," Papa says, remembering the rolling dunes that swept down over the wide beach and the flower-covered cottages that once perched on the edge of the hill.

"Let's go," Papa says suddenly, and the two head over the pebbles and scrub. Oriana follows behind, distracted by the thicket of deep red beach plums. She finds it intriguing to be in the same place Papa and Mama had been when they courted. "Don't talk to anyone about our little celebration today" he tells Oriana, with a taut smile on his lips to secure their outing as a secret.

"Not even Emmanuel?" she retorts.

"Not even Granddad."

"Why not? He already guessed we're coming here."

"Let's try not to make things more complicated than they are. I'm asking you not to talk about it."

Papa knows that he could get a fine, or suffer an even worse punishment, for ignoring the town ordinance that prohibits trespassing on storm-damaged areas.

Although the ban ostensibly protects public safety, Papa suspects its real purpose is to keep residents under tighter control. With or without the restrictions, fear of nature keeps most islanders from venturing into the open wilderness of Nantucket waters. Given the building debris, pot-holed roads, beach erosion and unpredictable undertows that have resulted from the Great Storms, connected folk would never expose themselves to the danger of venturing outside of the domain of VISHNEW's awareness.

Papa trusts himself, has measured his strength, and believes he has a pretty good feel for the ocean. Furthermore, he'll do as he damn well pleases.

"Hurry up, Oriana," he calls, running through the wild grasses and across the storm-ravaged dunes.

The nearly round moon of a late summer evening rises over the horizon, soft and round, and throws a pale pink light across the undulating water. Although Oriana never knew her mother, Rebecca's presence pervades the longing spaces of her mind, and Papa's frequent adulations feed her imagination. The words 'courageous' and 'fearless' come up often in his reminiscences about his mate.

Papa slips out of his pants, drops the towel, and plunges into the water. Oriana watches as he disappears for several long moments. Finally his back breaks the surface about twenty-five feet out. Oriana puts her hands on her hips and begins tapping her foot on the coarsely pebbled ground.

"Damn it, Papa! You promised to take me with you!" she accuses as Papa's eyes waterlogged eyes focus on hers.

"What happened?" Papa demands to know as he moves towards her. "I thought you were right behind me."

The young woman pouts, sensing that once again she has failed somehow to live up to the indelible image of her mother engraved upon her father's heart. Rebecca's love of adventure earned Papa's undying devotion. She would have dived into the water with him without a moment's hesitation.

A wave rises up behind Papa. "Watch out!" Oriana shouts, pointing to the quickly rising mound. In an instant Papa disappears. A moment later his head pops up, right in front of where Oriana is standing on the shore. "Wow, that's incredible!" she giggles.

"Come on in, Oriana!" he calls, walking in her direction. "I'll be a leatherback sea turtle, and you can climb on my back for the ride out."

Papa often talks about animals, especially extinct ones. His long-standing passion for them led him to embark on a career as one of the only animal techno-medics on the island. Oriana is proud of him but doubts she has the capacity to follow in his footsteps, even if she had the desire to.

Papa's purpose in life is to restore nature and to help animals, but Oriana's ideas are quite different. She views life and the world much more broadly. Papa believes the Earth is dying by human hands, while Oriana figures the Earth will survive well beyond the age of humans.

Papa reaches toward Oriana as she wades tentatively into the water. A wave breaks at her thighs. She is determined to keep going. As she moves in deeper, a second wave crashes around her waist and throws her off balance.

"When we get out deeper and a wave approaches, you'll have to slide underneath before it breaks," Papa warns her. Although increasingly ambivalent, even a bit afraid, Oriana convinces herself that she can handle the water.

The next wave catches even Papa by surprise. It breaks hard and fast before they can prepare for the dive. The thundering collapse knocks them both under its rolling mass. Oriana tumbles head over heels, her chin shoved into the sand. Papa topples all the way back to the shoreline. Dazed, he stands, pressing his hands against his knees, spewing salty water from his mouth.

"Ori!" Papa calls, searching for his daughter. Oriana, coming to her feet about forty feet away from him, rubs her sand-matted head. "Are you all right?" he shouts. She wipes the running mucous from her upper lip. She looks startled but intact.

"Let's try again!" she says giggling.

Papa's brow furrows, lips turning downward into a frown.

"I don't think so," he responds.

Oriana cocks her head to the side in curiosity over his odd expression. It reminds her of a strange night, a few weeks before, when Papa had brought her with him to the clinic for an emergency veterinary case. A puppy had been found lying limp and bleeding under a forsythia bush on Cabot Lane.

Papa worked on the dog for over an hour, cleaning the wound, reinserting the displaced intestines and sealing the gash with an application of suture gel. Oriana sat quietly, watching as Papa repaired the laceration.

"This animal was probably attacked by a feral chimera, possibly a crabbit; more likely a ferret-clawed canine," Papa had explained. Oriana shuddered at the thought of such a vicious attack.

"Look here, Oriana," he said to the girl whose reaction to the operation was a mixture of fascination and queasiness. "Look at the distinctive teeth and claw marks in the skin. It's a horror."

Papa often despairs over the popularity of designer animals: dogs, cats, ferrets, and rabbits altered with the genes of fish, reptiles and birds to provide unique colorings and patterns on their coats; odd combinations of feather, scales, and fur; and unusual characteristics in personality. He considers this kind of tampering to be unethical.

Oriana slid her chair closer and leaned her head over the dog's tail. Papa stared intently at the puppy. Oriana, trying to please him, became as inconspicuous as possible, hardly breathing or moving. "All right now sweet little puppy," Papa said as he ran his hands over the puppy's back. "What a beautiful boy you are. Don't be scared. Everything will be all right; I promise."

"Animals are not as disconnected from humans as you might think," Papa explained that day. "Look at how aware this one is, such gratitude in his eyes." At that Oriana stood, leaving the animal treatment clinic for home. She sat alone at the kitchen table for nearly two hours, sipping on cups of sassafras tea. *Maybe*, she considered, *Papa feels I don't appreciate him enough for taking care of me all these years.*

Later that evening Papa walked into their home, slamming the door behind him. "What's wrong, Papa?" Oriana asked.

"Leave me the hell alone, Oriana," he answered, walking past her to go under his Hood.

"Papa," she asked, "are you alright?"

Most of the time Oriana feels secure about her Papa's love for her, although she wants to know that she means as much to Papa as he does to her. "What am I supposed to do?" he shouted that night, slamming his hand down hard onto the surface of his Hood. "I have had enough."

"Enough of what, Papa?" Oriana asked, approaching cautiously. Oriana had seen Papa distressed before over such matters as wildlife habitat loss, species disappearance, and rude islanders who refused to return his 'hello.' She was not accustomed to seeing him this angry.

"Animal work," he answered, lifting the Hood. "The hell with it, I'm done." He lowered the Hood down until the apparatus completely covered his head.

"Don't say that," Oriana warned, even though Papa was no longer able to hear her. She worried that he might be on the verge of giving up the thing that most motivated him.

For hours, Papa sat under his Hood. Oriana, perched quietly on the darkened foyer staircase, watched him in anguish. At one point she thought she heard him crying. Clearly he was heartbroken.

The next morning, when Papa came out from under his Hood, Oriana asked again what had upset him so. Papa's voice cracked as he explained to her how a stray cat-gerbil had died of heart failure in his hands.

"I don't know if the animal died because of being abandoned or as a result of trying to live as two things at once," he said.

"Hey, head's up!" Papa warns, noticing the big wave forming in the distance. He makes his way through the surf and over to his daughter's side.

Oriana's excitement rises as the growing swell moves in their direction. "I can do it this time!" she exclaims, lifting her arms in anticipation. The wave breaks at Papa's hips and across Oriana's stomach.

Papa's worried expression changes to glee.

"Then let's go!" he says, lifting his daughter onto his back.

Oriana stretches across his back and wraps her arms around his shoulders. She likes the feel of his bare skin. The pair rides up and over the swelling green waves. The warm water of mid-September runs over the top of her head, down her back, and along her legs. A wave rises up in front of them and Oriana lifts her head, grabbing a quick breath of air.

"We're almost there!" Papa shouts.

He leans forward to take a breaststroke. Oriana closes her eyes and buries her head in Papa's neck. He has to swim much longer than she expected in order to reach the sand bar, but eventually they arrive.

"Woo-hoo!" Papa shouts, his feet touching the soft sand as he stands. The water pours from his saturated hair, dripping over his shoulders and onto hers. "The sand bar is still here, and even bigger than I remembered it! Get down now," he instructs. "You're a bit too old for a piggyback ride."

The shore is awfully distant. Oriana grabs his neck tightly. "Come on now, let go," Papa scolds, prying her hand away. She slides slowly off his back. Realizing the water is shallow; she sits her bottom down on the soft sand.

"It feels good out here," she remarks. The clear, warm water courses under her neck. Through it she can see the rippled sand underneath. She runs her hand along the fine grains, searching for a shell. Suddenly, her face goes white.

"Papa?"

"What is it, Oriana?"

"Ow," she whimpers.

"What's wrong?"

"I don't know," she replies. Oriana stands, extending her arm for him to look at. Blotchy discolorations have formed on her knuckles, palm, and wrist, and it feels as though a thousand tiny needles are poking into her skin. The fiery itching on the top and bottom of her hand turns into a searing pain.

"Papa! It really, really hurts!" she shouts, beginning to cry.

Papa splashes ocean water over the splotches on her skin. "I think I see the problem, Oriana. Is this where the pain is coming from?" he asks, pointing to her wrist.

"I don't know," the twelve-year-old cries. She rubs her itching eyes.

"Don't look," Papa warns as he takes hold of his penis.

Oriana covers her face. The warm urine flows over her hand.

"Better now?" he inquires.

Her eyes widen as she watches the splotchy redness spread across her skin. Blisters begin to form.

"Papa, what's happening to my arm?" she sobs.

"I'm not certain," Papa admits. His eyebrows draw in toward and his upper lip begins to quiver. "I do know that I need for you to calm down."

The sea begins to heave, salt water sloshing at their waists as the tide rises and rolls toward the shore. Oriana's breathing becomes shallow and erratic. "Everything hurts now, Papa, not just my hand and arm. My back and my stomach hurt too."

"Get control of yourself!" Papa shouts, grabbing his daughter's shoulders and shaking her.

"Stop it! Stop yelling at me!" she returns, pushing on his stomach. "I'm not one of your animals, you know, that can be in pain and manage to stare gratefully into your eyes."

"Give me your arm," Papa commands, his grip firm on her wrist.

He studies her arm carefully, from the tips of her fingers, up her forearm, and past the knobby joint of her elbow, over her shoulder, and across her neck, turning her arm over and back again. The puffy patches throb and pulsate beneath her reddening skin.

"Papa?" she asks quietly.

"I think this is a reaction to a bite or sting," he replies. "But I can't figure out what could have caused it."

Turning her around slowly, Papa studies Oriana's back and chest, trying to identify the source of the sting. "Ouch!" she yells, doubling over. Yellow and green globs of undigested supper spout from her mouth as she clings to her father's hairy chest.

Papa lifts her onto his hip, side-stroking until they reach the water's edge. Carrying her, he treads across the pebbles and scattered mounds of sand until they finally reach the vehicle. He places her carefully inside.

"Try to sit quietly, and stay very still," he advises.

"I can't breathe, Papa," Oriana gasps.

"You have to get hold of yourself," he replies, mumbling curses under his breath as he pushes beyond speeds that are reasonable on such a rutted road. Oriana senses the weight of his own emerging panic.

She slumps to one side, her breathing shallow, her pulse is erratic and rapid. Papa curses the day Rebecca died, and curses himself for his daughter's predicament. He knows that if Oriana were fully connected, a techno-medicraft would be approaching.

By the time they reach the infirmary Oriana is barely conscious. Granddad, who's been under his Hood watching for their return to town, catches their dramatic entry. Minutes later he arrives in a fury, marching up the infirmary corridor to find them.

"Now listen here, son," he spits out in front of the entire techno-medical staff. "You can do as you please for yourself. As for your daughter, you are to keep her remotely connected to VISHNEW at all times!"

Granddad tells Papa that he was irresponsible in taking Oriana into a forbidden area, but reminds him that if she were fully connected the stinging culprit would have been sensed before it stung, averting the attack altogether. And even it that had failed, VISHNEW would have alerted the techno-medics to bring her immediate treatment.

"Instead," Granddad charges, "you knowingly put the girl in danger."

"Where am I, Papa?" Oriana asks as she opens her eyes the next day under the covers of a strange bed. The room is decorated with cheerful curtains in an ocean motif. Colorful sea life murals drift across the walls, and picture windows offer unobstructed views of the harbor and sky. Oriana takes in the familiar gray of the overcast Nantucket morning.

Granddad, arms across his chest, stands by her bedside with Papa. They talk in hushed tones while two techno-medics busy themselves at the far side of the room. Oriana glances up at the glass door to her room, reading: "ERAC EVISNETNI CIRTAIDEP."

A security-bot glides inside. "Would someone tell me what's going on?" Oriana asks. A woman in a wide-brimmed hat leans against the end of the bed, her fingers curled around the footboard. Her quiet presence and warm smile comfort Oriana, and she wonders why Papa hasn't acknowledged her presence. She squints to get a better look at the woman, but the image fades.

The security-bot grabs hold of Papa's forehead from behind. Papa's lips close, and his eyes begin to twitch.

"Papa?" Oriana asks weakly. She reaches over the bed's edge, catching hold of his shirt, which slips through her hands as the bot lifts Papa away.

"I have to go, Ori," he sputters. His voice is strained and he forms his words with difficulty.

"What are you talking about, Papa?" Oriana tries to sit up, but falls back onto her elbow from weakness.

"Where are you going? Don't leave me here!"

Again Papa tries to move his mouth, but the security stun has by now taken its full effect. Papa is arrested on the charge of being a threat to the interests of the island and its adolescent girls. Granddad looks toward the woman in the yellow hat, mumbling something about his only son being a hopeless and irresponsible renegade.

"She's lucky to be alive," Granddad grunts.

Oriana looks up and meets the gaze of the smiling woman who is still standing at the foot of her bed.

"Who is that, Granddad?"

"What?" he replies.

"Who is that you're talking to?"

"Myself, I suppose," he returns, seeming to walk right through the mystery woman.

"Oh? Granddad! That's weird."

"You're lucky to be alive, Oriana. And your father is a fool," Granddad says.

"No, he's not, Granddad," she retorts, forgetting for the moment about the apparition. Oriana wants to return the insult with something like 'Crusty ole' Yankee,' 'Pink Lipped Possum,' or 'Horney Fat Bastard,' all of which she heard once while watching an island couple fight in their bedroom when she was under her Hood. Except that she doesn't want to hurt Granddad's feelings.

"That's exactly what he is, a fool!" Granddad insists. Patting Oriana on the head, he sits down on the mattress beside her.

"I'm scared, Granddad," she admits. Looking out the window, Oriana notices that a ray of sunlight, struggling through the clouds, has cast an odd yellow light over the rooftops.

"Well then, you ought to get your wits about you," Granddad states petulantly.

With furrowed brow and pursed lips, Granddad studies the grid embedded under the taut skin of his palm, searching for any indications of irregularities in the beating of his laboratory-grown heart. When he had the one he was born with, he knew if it was broken or sick by the way it beat under his ribs. But he cannot feel the new one at all.

"I feel flu-ish," Granddad says, dropping his hand to his stomach.

This makes Oriana even more anxious. 'Fluish' describes the early symptoms of global C60 poisoning, an affliction that caused the deaths of her maternal grandparents along with a third of the world's human population and nearly a quarter of all aquatic mammals. The epidemic began when a research study linking fullerene C-60 to longevity led to mass production and high dose ingestion of the closed-cage carbon molecule. Oriana's mother was the only member of her maternal family who survived the poisoning's rapid spread. Papa's mother didn't survive, and Granddad barely did.

Papa, young and frightened, waited the poisoning out in quarantine along with other healthy islanders, until island techno-medics concurred on the cause of the illness. Once lab tests showed his tissues were free of C-60, Papa turned his attention to helping others who were not well. Apparently, he hadn't eaten any seafood that month and had therefore not been exposed to the carbon nano-balls that had saturated the food chain. Granddad had eaten plenty.

Oriana tugs at her grandfather's sleeve.

"Take me to see Papa," she pleads.

"Wish I could there ole' girl, but it's not gonna happen."

"Granddad, when will we see him again?" she persists, pulling hard at his plaid flannel shirt, the elbows worn and the fabric threadbare.

"Now what makes you think I'm the person to ask?" he barks.

Oriana pauses. A panic begins to rise in her chest and yelps burst from her throat. Two of the techno-medics approach her bedside.

"I tried to warn you to get control of yourself," Granddad scolds, standing up.

"Where's Papa?" the girl shouts, kicking off the sheets and climbing out of the bed. One techno-medic grabs her head and the other places a small black box over her face.

"Papa?" she whimpers as the quieting pulses begin to seep into her brain. She collapses onto the bed, her long brown curls damp with perspiration.

Granddad harrumphs, watching in dismay as a techno-medic lays his granddaughter on her back, tightly tucks the white sheets across her, and places a quilt with a lighthouse design on it over her limp body. His despair turns to resolve. He marches out of the infirmary room, ranting.

"A VISHNEW connection will solve this problem once and for all."

"This should have been taken care of by her fool father long ago," he continues.

Oriana rolls onto her side, curling into a ball. "Yesterday was my birthday," she remembers. Despair engulfs her, eyes open wide but unfocused, as Oriana fades away.

TEMPLE

The Meeting House grows colder. Without waking, Oriana rolls over onto her side and cushions her head with a bended arm. Two hours pass, and the sound of her own moaning stirs her to the awareness of her wet clothing.

She sits up, slips off the drenched undergarment, and shifts to a dry spot on her coat. The new life in her uterus turns three times and a heel protrudes at her left side. The baby's head descends further into birthing position. Clearly it's nearly time now.

Oriana drifts into a place between sleeping and waking. Momentarily she dozes again, and drifts between sleeping and waking. Her mind returns to the day when she removed Grandpa's present to her from her closet, where she'd hidden it away.

Oriana slips off the wide white bow, then carefully removes the colorful wrapping. "Mama made this," she whispers. The bowl is lovely, with deep blue and brown baked onto the clay in a pattern that reminds her of Nantucket. *This must be the same bowl Mama used for her extraction,* she surmises, *which means this is where my life began.*

As Oriana prepares for her appointment at the TEMPLE, she talks out loud to a father who is not there, one who is paying his debt to society for nearly taking her life. "Don't be upset with me, Papa. Really, I had no choice. Now that I am just like the other island girls, it's important that I go to TEMPLE. We're all supposed to go at thirteen.

"Anyway, it would be selfish for me not to. Granddad says this way is best for all concerned, and anyway, it's my duty to our island. I'm not afraid at all you know, Papa. From under my Hood I can see everyone talking about how lucky a girl I am, with so many eggs to offer. Come home soon, okay?"

She washes her face and neck, puts on the blue dress that Granddad had placed on her bed for this occasion, and parts her hair carefully along the center of her scalp. Making four braids, she leaves two hanging in the back, and then pulls the other two along the crown of her head. These last two she secures with a hairpin.

"See you later, Granddad," Oriana calls as she pulls shut the front door. She strides across the front porch, down the old wooden front steps, and up the cobblestones of Broad Street, head up and shoulders taut.

As she rounds the corner and proceeds up the hill Oriana slides a hand down along the sides of her dress, smoothing the bunched fabric that has gathered at her knees. Carefully she holds on to the bowl that had once belonged to her mother, as she takes the short walk to Cliff Road.

Oriana knows from watching under her Hood how other girls are presented with a special gift from their mothers on the day they go to TEMPLE. She's seen how the mothers speak to their daughters about the gift of VISHNEW that assures successful progeny. She knows how uplifting the words can be, how they encourage and empower the daughters with a sublime sense of womanhood.

Under ideal circumstances, the mother accompanies her daughter to the TEMPLE. But Oriana is used to doing things alone. She strides along, neither excited, nor afraid, but brave in the acceptance of her obligation.

From the outside, the building where TEMPLE is held looks much like it used to many years ago, when it was the home of a Louisiana whaler. The majestic clapboard structure is still painted white, and its original columns stand upright and stately along the raised front porch. Oriana climbs up to the beveled glass French doors.

"Welcome, Oriana. Please come inside," a voice says through the speakers embedded in the trim. Inside the foyer float holographic images of Nantucket children from the last three hundred years. Oriana shields her eyes from the display as she passes by what was once a formal parlor but is now the Sanctuary where incubating wombs are displayed.

Across the hall is the Worship Chamber. Islanders know that today is her extraction day, so Oriana anticipates that at least a few live worshipers will be inside, and that the room will fill with the sounds of swooning chants, of "ooh-ing" women, and "ah-ing" men, waving symbolic bowls. Today's extraction, like all extractions, will be done with reverence and adulation.

Oriana passes through a narrow corridor to the closed door of the Inner Chamber. She knocks twice, and the door opens.

"Welcome, young friend, how'd do?" says the matron who greets her there. The woman's voice is inviting, and ebullient, yet warm. Her body is draped in a flowing purple gown. Her eyes, deep, dark, and piercing, beckon Oriana to follow her inside.

"Come now, child, and take my hand," the matron offers. "My name is Mrs. Wyatt, and you must be Oriana Rotch."

Oriana steps inside of the room where the procedure will take place. The set-up is much like a techno-medical clinic, but it feels more like a home. Oriana notices an examination table draped in white cloth, and bright lights suspended above it. Colorful murals of yellow, green, and blue adorn the walls, and handmade ceramic tiles cover the floor. The sweet aroma of dozens of roses placed in vases around the room fills the air. A deep soaking tub occupies the center of the room. Mrs. Wyatt reaches for the bowl in Oriana's hand.

"I'll take that, dear," she says, smiling as she leads Oriana across the dimly lit room to the ceremonial cleansing tub.

"Go ahead now, child, remove your garments and climb in."

A fertili-bot enters the room. It is human-shaped, but smaller in stature than Oriana. It has a female simulacrum, with soft eyes, a mouth and nose, and no hair or ears to speak of. Its form is covered in a pale, tan, skin-like substance. It has palms for hands, with no digits to serve as fingers. Instead it has octopus-like tentacles. Oriana is startled by its presence as it moves towards her.

"Relax now, dear heart," Mrs. Wyatt remarks as she prepares the extraction equipment. "Let the robot do its good work."

The fertili-bot coats Oriana's skin in course sea salt, which seeps from its eight rubbery tentacles. Its palms, functioning like sponges, rub her from forehead to feet. Warm water is then released over Oriana's entire body from inside the round top of the bot's head. Oriana steps from the tub and is dripped with rose oil before being patted dry with a towel. Finally, she is dusted with a layer of soft minerals.

"Feeling nice?" the matron asks with a broad smile.

"I feel lovely," Oriana replies.

"You are the epitome of beauty, my dear," Mrs. Wyatt remarks. She strokes Oriana's hair, pulling her fingers along the hanging braids. The woman seems almost proud of her. "I promised to take good care of you," she says.

"Promised whom?" Oriana questions.

"Time for silence, dear," Mrs. Wyatt remarks as she continues with her work.

The fertili-bot places the egg-rich girl on the procedure table, flat on her back, and lifts her legs into cushiony stirrups. Oriana's heart begins to beat faster.

She has actually never seen the procedure performed. She tried to learn about it by watching other girls in TEMPLE from under her Hood, but since there are no surveillance cameras in the walls of the Inner Chamber, all she has ever seen of the ceremonial procedure are the adoring, chanting worshipers.

"What happened to my bowl?" Oriana asks faintly. She surmised long ago that the bowl was important, but still has no idea why.

"It's being disinfected," Mrs. Wyatt explains as she turns off all but one powerful examination beam. "Time for silence, remember?" she reminds Oriana.

Mrs. Wyatt proceeds to light a special arrangement of Maker's candles. A warm glow basks the room in shimmering light. Lying on her back, Oriana looks at a live image of the Worship Chamber projected across the ceiling overhead. One person has arrived. He holds a ceremonial bowl in his hands. Oriana recognizes immediately the dark skin, contrasting blond hair, and awkward movements.

"Emmanuel!" she cries. "They let you out!"

Mrs. Wyatt puts a finger to her lips.

"SHHH," she asks most patiently. "That's only a hologram, dear. He's participating from under his Hood."

Three women enter the Worship Chamber. Two are quite mature, as determined by VISHNEW-measured bodily state, the third one aged 'early fertility.' One wears a dark red ruffled dress, and the other two have on skirts topped with brightly colored shirts. Each holds a distinctive bowl.

Emmanuel's image begins the chant.

"VISHNEW, VISHNEW, sustainer of life!" Strong and clear, his words carry above the others. Oriana finds it soothing. She closes her eyes. His voice, melodic and deep, helps her to relax.

The matron douses Oriana's groin with nano-silver antiseptic, then inserts the micro-tubal pump into Oriana's vagina. The worshippers lift their voices in celebration.

"VISHNEW, VISHNEW, sustainer of life!" The chanting fills the room.

"What a good girl you are. Your Mama would be very proud," Mrs. Wyatt says as the procedure comes to an end. The bowl is filled to one third. "Take a look, if you want," the matron offers.

Oriana sits up, eyes wide, and gazes at the sterile blue liquid holding all the eggs her body had contained. Soon they will be stored for screening and selections. A pang of joy interrupts the sorrow Oriana feels over being reminded about her mother by the fertility procedure.

"Did you know my Mama?"

"I knew her very well."

Clothed and cleared for discharge, Oriana receives a parting gift of three freshly cut sunflower stems from Mrs. Wyatt. With gratitude she takes the bouquet in one hand and holds onto her bowl in the other.

"Thank you from the entire community," Mrs. Wyatt remarks, following protocol.

Oriana knows that one day VISHNEW will assign her a mate whom it determines is an ideal match for her, and this mate will claim her along with the best of her eggs. Eventually, fertilization of one of her best ova will result in a genetically perfect child. Young women in need of genetic material may bid for what is left of her abundance.

Oriana sniffs the sunflowers, whose clusters of bright yellow petals surround dense orange interiors. There is no sweet scent to them, and yet they are quite beautiful to her eyes. Left in the soil, they would have one day developed a swirling pattern of tightly packed seeds, hundreds of them, each one encased in a rigid black and gray shell to protect the soft, small, fertile material inside.

PART TWO.
FERTILITY

GONE

When Oriana moves into the house on Broad Street, Granddad is already in his early nineties and living there alone. Though energetic and as healthy as any VISHNEW full-connect, he is happy to have his granddaughter's company. Oriana knows, however, that he is furious with Papa for leaving him no choice but to take her in.

Soon they are spending much of their time together. During warm weather they take morning strolls to the bayside, and in the afternoon they walk together down to the harbor dike. In the evening they sit on the front porch, and Oriana listens as Granddad tells stories.

When winter comes, Granddad settles in his upholstered chair in the parlor and props his feet up on the footstool. Staring into the empty hearth, he muses with Oriana over what she is learning from the tutors under her Hood. Sometimes they travel together under their Hoods to wonderful and exotic places.

Once in a while Granddad tells Oriana that he appreciates her help in taking over many of the chores he once did for himself,

such as programming the vacuum system, dispensing the disin-
fecting mists, running the laundry through the silver ion machine,
and preparing most of their meals, but that most of all he simply
enjoys her company.

"Hmm. Maybe the place that used to beOne evening, in particular, Oriana and Granddad eat supper on the front porch.

"It's the lobster chowder I miss," Granddad announces, finish-
ing the last of his tomato soup. No fresh, local seafood has been
available on Nantucket since the Great Storms.

"What was so special about lobster chowder?"

Granddad tells her he can't quite describe its taste, that it is
similar to corn chowder, only with thick chunks of sweet lobster
meat. According to Granddad, the lobster substitutes grown in the
food laboratories don't compare.

"Only nature's own can fill a mouth with the sweetness of the
sea," he says.

Eating an animal that scavenges the bottom of the ocean
sounds unappetizing to Oriana.

"That's nasty, Granddad."

"It's wicked depressing," he declares as he sniffs the enticing
aroma that wafts from his cup of sassafras tea.

Granddad gulps it with a slurp, then puts his cup down and
starts in on the topic of Nantucket in its tourist heyday. He tells
Oriana that when he and Grandma sat on their porch at night,
hundreds of people would walk past.

"The streets were crowded back then," he says. "And loud, I'll
tell you. What with the ferry coming and going, blowing its horn
from early morning until late at night . . ."

"I thought you liked the sound of the ferry coming in," Oriana
interrupts.

"I did, and I miss it. All I'm trying to say is that the place was
mayhem in the high season, and with the traffic-jammed roads
and all, it was more than your Grandmother could take sometimes.

There were lines and crowds of tourists everywhere, comin' and goin' with their shopping bags and beach bags and groceries."

"Not a Nantucket I would recognize, huh Granddad?"

"Believe you me," he says a bit too loudly, "huge car-carrying ferries and fancy high-speed boats would run in and out of the docks all day long!" He takes a deep breath.

"Folks would crowd onto the island for the beaches, whaling history, walking-talking tours, and shopping on Commercial and Main Streets for a bunch of worthless, pricey crap they'd proudly carry home."

Oriana recalls that Granddad made good money selling some of that 'crap.' He brought to Nantucket a treasure worth more than all the whales, clams, lobsters, bluefish and cod ever brought out of these waters: nano-titanium powder.

'Magic coat,' he called it. Granddad had a few hundred pounds shipped to the island, then convinced the Preservation Commission to hire him to mix it with varnish and paint it over the surface of every historic structure in town. And they did. As a result, most of the structures behind the new dyke in town stand as they did before the Great Storms, clapboard, brick, slate, wrought iron, cobblestones and all.

"Wow! I guess there were a lot of people passing by here who you could talk to back then," Oriana surmises.

Granddad shakes his head in disagreement.

"Nope," he corrects her. "Visitors tended not to speak unless they knew each other. And the local people rarely said hello to total strangers unless, of course, they were customers. Your Grandma and I liked to watch it all."

Granddad points up the street to where a popular bookstore had been, and to the tavern next door where lines of customers waiting to eat dinner would wind all the way around the block.

A fog rolls in. Oriana snuggles up close to Granddad, putting her head on his shoulder, and tries to imagine the past he just described. A woman walks past, but the thick fog and fading light make it difficult for Oriana to make out who she is.

"Good evening," Oriana says to the stranger.

The woman slows, turns, and looks up onto the porch. She tips her broad brim hat and waves a hand.

"Who was that?" Oriana asks Granddad as the woman disappears into the fog.

"Beats me," he replies, running his hand through his beard as if trying to figure that out for himself. Oriana doubts he has any idea who the woman is. He didn't seem to notice her. "Maybe you see things that I can't, ole' girl, and I'm not talking about your eyes having better enhancement than mine. I am beginning to think you may have the other kind of sight."

"What kind is that?"

"Well, if you're seeing someone I'm not, then it's another kind of vision for the un-seeable, I guess. Your grandmother had something like that. She used to say there were folks walking up and down the street wearing black cloaks and top hats from hundreds of years ago. Didn't mean a thing to me. I just let her go on about it, figuring she was just seeing different is all. "

"I've never wanted to be different, Granddad. It's lonely."

"Yes. I suppose it is. You sure have had more than your share of that."

Granddad says goodnight and heads inside to bed. Oriana remains alone on the porch for a while, staring at the empty street and listening to the deafening quiet of her island home.

When morning comes, Oriana opens her bedroom window for some fresh air and hears the sound of clacking feet hitting the cobblestones from the far end of Broad. She stretches her neck out of the window, looking over the porch roof to see who might be approaching. The thick shock of black hair can belong to no one else.

"Papa!" she cries out. "You're home!" Oriana runs down the staircase, across the foyer, and out through the front door. She wraps her arms around Papa's neck as he steps up onto the porch.

"Too bad he's out," one islander exclaims, watching from under his Hood. Numerous others, tuned in to Oriana's house, voice similar sentiments.

"She was doing so well without him," someone replies with a snarl.

"What happened to you, Papa? I missed you."

"I missed you too, Ori."

Papa takes a seat on the porch couch, patting his hand on the blue paisley cushion. Oriana accepts the invitation and sits down next to him. His broad smile exposes discolored teeth and dark gray gums, which surprise Oriana. So much has changed over the four years he's been gone. Papa's voice is tight and hoarse, his eyes dull and hollow.

Some of the island kids had told Oriana that people in the facility get put into catatonic states. Maybe it's true. Papa seems so different. She slides in as close as is possible, pulls up her feet under her thighs, and snuggles under his armpit.

"Are you all right?" Oriana asks him. Papa strokes his daughter's cheeks and hair.

"I'm fine as a dandy."

He doesn't look so dandy to her.

"How about you, are you all right?" he asks, searching her eyes.

"Oh yes," she replies, chipper and reassuring. "Everything is better than ever." Papa's brow furrows into tightly rippled lines. "Didn't Granddad tell you?" she queries in response to his obvious puzzlement.

"There was no way for Granddad to tell me much of anything, Oriana. I was in the Facility. Remember? They had me under almost the whole time I was there."

"Under where?"

"I guess Granddad didn't explain that to you," he says. "What do you mean better than ever?" Papa twists his unruly eyebrow hairs between his fingertips.

Oriana notices the moisture forming on his forehead and the suspicion in his eyes. She brushes her hair away from her face and tucks it behind her ear, revealing the tiny graft of skin over her temple.

Papa leans toward her, squinting.

"Oriana, are you . . . ?"

"Isn't it wonderful!" she exclaims, proudly displaying her palms. "I'm fully connected now, and I even have friends under my Hood!" A pained expression replaces Papa's smile. He bites down on his lower lip.

"What's wrong, Papa?" she asks.

Her father grabs her arm, squeezing it too tightly. His eyes are ablaze.

"How could you, Oriana? How could you deceive me?"

"Stop it," she whimpers. "You know the security-bots will come if you keep hurting me."

"I'm sorry," he says, releasing her arm from his grip. Tears fall over Papa's gaunt cheeks.

Oriana remembers when she used to cry. Seeing her father's face, she wishes she still could. Sadness now feels like a balloon slowly filling inside of her chest. Suddenly the balloon pops, slamming against her ribs, and the feeling changes to joy. Oriana giggles.

"Don't be sad, Papa. It's ok now."

She notices that her skin is red and irritated from the pressure of Papa's hand. She rubs it gently and considers Papa's sentiments and the torment he seems to be suffering. She observes that his hand shakes as he rubs it across his forehead. The Papa she remembers was not nearly so fretful. She worries that he will never again be the man she once knew.

"Are you all right?" he asks again.

"I told you already Papa, I'm great. Even better than before." Oriana takes Papa's cheeks between her palms, as she did when she was a little girl. The feel of his beard is rough and prickly, and she remembers the smooth, soft skin of his clean-shaven days.

"You know what, Papa?" she whispers softly, "I can hear Granddad speaking to me inside my ear, even when he is all the way down Broad Street. I can hear him even if I'm upstairs and he's out here on the porch, or if he's in the kitchen and I am taking a walk by the dikes. And if I want to, I can listen to any kind of music at all, any time, by pressing on this part of my hand. If I want to call you at the clinic or in your car, all I need to do it to press over here, and we can talk to each other. And you know what else? My eyes can see really tiny stuff now, far away. And when I …"

"That's enough, Oriana. I don't want to hear another word." Papa removes her hands from his face.

"Oh, Papa," she laments, her head falling onto his chest, her nose burrowing in to be sure he still smells the same. " Granddad said this would happen, that you wouldn't understand."

Papa stands abruptly and storms through the front door. Oriana jumps up behind him, the swinging seat slipping forward and banging against her thighs.

"Ow!" she yelps as she chases after him. "Wait a minute! I was talking to you. There is something else you should know, Papa."

He ignores his daughter, stomping down the center hall to the parlor where Granddad sits perfectly still under his Hood.

"Don't bother him right now, Papa," she pleads. "He's watching the Daily Global Report."

"Damn you, Dad!" Papa screams.

"Leave him alone," Oriana implores.

Papa pounds his hand down hard against the Hood. Granddad jumps, slamming his head up against its hard underside.

"Gardiner, what 'n the hell do you think you're doing?" Granddad demands, lifting the bulky mechanism from over his head. He rises to his feet, his face flushed with rage. "Are you out of your mind? You could hurt somebody doing that!" Granddad hollers, shaking his over his head.

"What in the hell have you done, Dad?" Papa retorts, taking hold of Granddad's shoulders. Granddad scowls, and Papa backs away. "How dare you go over my head and do this to my daughter!" Papa cries, placing his hands on his hips. He begins to hyperventilate.

"Oh, so that's what ya think, do ya, son?" Granddad replies. "Well, I'll have you know that even if I had instructed them not to, they'd have gone and done it anyway, because after that little stunt that nearly killed your daughter, you lost your parental rights, my boy! It's your own fault this time, buddy, so don't go looking for someone else to blame!"

"The hell it is," Papa snarls.

While VISHNEW's gift has advanced to the point that all island children can be, and are, connected immediately upon retrieval, this hasn't always been the case. Not so long ago, islander parents would have to elect to have their babies fully connected, usually within the first year of life, after it had been determined that the nano-wiring, blood-bots, and brain enhancements could be implanted successfully. Parents could also refuse to have their children connected, as Oriana's parents had done. If parents wanted to have their children fully connected, but this was not possible because of physical issues, limited access to VISHNEW could be provided through subcutaneous implants and access to a Hood.

Papa had febrile seizures as an infant, so the techno-medics advised against the full procedure for him. Therefore, he was a partial–connect when he met Mama. Mama was never connected, having spent her entire life as a VISHNEW-independent. Once Mama and Papa were mated, Papa disconnected altogether in order to make Mama happy. Eventually he came to enjoy the fact that he was independent.

Oriana puts a hand on Papa's back.

"Papa, this is what I want," she explains.

At first, Papa's expression goes blank. His nostrils flare. He grabs Oriana's shoulders, his eyes searching her face. "Ori, have you been to TEMPLE?" he demands to know.

"Three years ago," she admits, head down, avoiding his gaze.

"As a worshipper, or for the extraction procedure?"

Oriana simply nods her head, indicating 'yes.'

"No!" Papa wails. "No, this can't be! I tried my best to protect you, Ori!" Papa shouts. He begins to shake her. "You can't trust VISHNEW, Ori. It killed your mother. Now it's taken away your fertility. Oriana, what have you done!"

Granddad intercedes. "Ten, nine, eight, seven . . . soon they'll be back to get you, ya know. She's fully connected now. Six, five, four, three . . . the security-bots are on their way!"

Papa lets go of Oriana and steps back. Oriana moves to the corner of the room, taking a seat on the needlepoint stool next to Granddad's chair. Placing a palm over each ear she squeezes tightly, rocking and humming quietly to herself.

"Now look at what you've gone and done," Granddad exclaims. "Why can't you leave her alone?"

Oriana presses harder, unable to muffle their voices entirely.

"Easy out for you, Dad," Papa barks.

" Get control of yourself, son. Do you hear me?"

"Let's go, Ori," Papa says, ignoring Granddad. He leads Oriana into the sitting room at the front of the house.

"Aren't you taking me home now?" Oriana asks. Papa drops onto the velvet couch that's been in the same spot for nearly 80 years.

"Why were you gone for so long?" she continues. "I went under my Hood every day to look for you, Papa. You were never there."

97

Oriana sits down next to him, running her fingers across the soft surface of the upholstery.

"I had no access to my Hood, Oriana. They put me under. I already told you that."

"Why, Papa?"

"Okay. Let's both calm down," he says, with his head in his hands, his fingers rubbing his scalp. "I am going to try to explain everything to you." Papa sighs deeply. "Do you remember, Oriana, what happened that day we went for a swim in the ocean?"

"Yes, I remember, sort of. Something hurt me. Granddad says it was a sea animal that never used to live around here before."

"You had Irukandji syndrome, brought on by the sting of a species of jellyfish that comes from Australia. It moved into Nantucket waters with the Great Storms."

"Yes, I understand. They are too small to see, although I might be able to see them now that I'm connected," she suggests.

Papa slides his hands up behind his head and leans back against the couch. Oriana takes note of the deep crow's feet extending from the corners of his eyes, and the white hairs at his temples. It saddens her to see that he is choosing to age.

"I don't know anything about what this connection to VISHNEW can or cannot do for your abilities," Papa says. "What I do know is that by nature's design, plants and animals strive to survive."

"Does that include the plants and animals from the IPC?" Oriana inquires. "From the Institute of Playful Creativity? No, not those, I'm talking about nature's creatures," he answers.

"According to Granddad, the IPC creations and nature's are molecularly identical, In fact, they are indistinguishable," Oriana informs him.

"Forget what Granddad says," Papa snaps. "I am trying to explain something important to you."

Oriana settles back onto the couch.

"Okeydokey. I'm all ears."

"When an entity comes along that threatens the survival of one of nature's creatures, that creature protects itself just like you or I would do. We do what we can to keep from being hurt. Jellyfish don't have the capacity to sort out whether or not you mean to hurt them. They're simply not that intelligent. All they know is that something has come along that's not for consumption or for breeding and might be intending to eat them. So what do they do?"

"They protect themselves, obviously," she answers, looking down at her palms. Oriana notices that on the left hand the grid has turned pale blue, while the right is still the color of her flesh.

"It wasn't one jellyfish. It was many. You were hurt because you frightened them. They perceived a possible threat to their survival," Papa says.

Oriana shrugs, continuing to study the VISHNEW grids.

"As with each and every one of nature's creatures, the Irukandji wanted to stay alive," Papa continues. "Everything in nature wants to live, Oriana, jellyfish, seaweed, humans."

"Even Mama?" she asks. "She was from nature too, right? Did Mama try to stay alive?"

Papa's face sags.

"Did she or not?" Oriana persists. Her lips purse as she waits for his reply. No one has ever explained to her why a mother would choose to die at the moment of her own child's retrieval.

Papa searches for words and isn't quite able to find them. He takes another deep breath.

"Papa, why didn't Mama protect herself?" Oriana insists.

"I already told you that. VISHNEW was the cause of your mother's death." He pulls Oriana close to him and she breathes in his comforting scent. *This is Papa alright,* she concludes, *and he still smells of yeasty bread and warm butter, just as he always did.*

"Obviously it's true, Oriana, that Mama was also one of nature's creatures. If she could have fought something, stung something, bitten something, or run away, I am sure she would have done it to stay alive with you. It's what we all do, we creatures of the Earth."

"As a VISHNEW-independent, Mama had planned to birth you at home. Her best friend, Grace Wyatt, was the only person on the island who had the experience to do that. The moment she arrived, she took one look at your Mama and called for the techno-medics to come for her," he explained. "It nearly broke Grace's heart. For one, they'd made their plans, and Mama was opposed to the standard retrieval, and for two, they both knew that a conventional retrieval would require that Mama be fully connected, which meant that her independence would have to be sacrificed. She was willing to do it for you, to be sure you were protected and safe."

"She loved me before I was even retrieved," Oriana says softly.

"Absolutely she did. The actual connection went surprisingly fast and the implants were successfully inserted. Then the techno-medics assured her that you were healthy and ready for retrieval. Mama's feet went into the stirrups, but all of a sudden the system went down."

"How can that be, Papa? It makes no sense for it to just stop like that. VISHNEW needs no power source. It's a self-generating system."

"No one knows why, Ori. It looked to me as if there were a short circuit, or power interruption, or maybe a surge. It was a chaotic hell. There were red and yellow lights flashing all over the place, materna-bots jammed and twitching, and techno-medics running around, throwing up their hands, yelling about multiple malfunctions registering from inside your Mama's brain."

Oriana grimaces over these horrid details.

"They had your Mama up on the retrieval table, her legs suspended high in the air. I was so proud of her. She was so brave." Papa wipes his brow. "It was obvious that you were cresting. I briefly saw the top of your head, your golden brown locks matted with her blood."

At this Oriana doesn't even gasp. She just sits staring, her eyes blank, her face without expression.

"Fighting for her life and for yours too, Mama reached down between her legs and grabbed hold of your exposed chin, essentially birthing you herself. The techno-medics watched in awe. Once you were out they cut the cord, and Mama put you up to her breast. That was not part of the protocol. They tried to take you away. 'Critical assessments have to be made right away,' they insisted. But your Mama refused to let you out of her arms, and she held onto you until she expired."

Oriana begins rapidly twisting strands of her hair onto her index finger. "You mean she was holding me, actually nursing me, when she died?"

Papa's voice drops low and firm. "I told you, Oriana. VISHNEW killed her."

"Why, Papa. Why?"

"They couldn't explain it. They said nothing like this had ever happened before."

Father and daughter sit motionless, neither saying a word. Oriana glances down at the grid on her palms. She closes her hands into fists.

After a few long minutes, Papa sighs. "Listen to me carefully," he scolds. "I should have known better than to take you out to old S'conset that day. The jellyfish aren't intelligent. I am. And I can use my mind to calculate how dangerous the ocean might be, to determine whether or not to go in. It's not the way it was when Mama and I would go there. Everything has changed since then."

Papa takes hold of Oriana's cheeks, stroking the soft olive surfaces. "You had a very serious reaction to the stings. By the time we reached the infirmary your throat had nearly closed, and you were getting very little air. Anaphylaxis, it's called. We are very lucky you're alive and that your brain survived without damage."

"That's what Granddad told the woman," Oriana says.

"What woman, Ori?"

"That pretty woman who was wearing the white hat. You know, the one who was standing at the end of my bed in the Infirmary. I'm surprised you don't remember her, Papa. She was smiling at you."

"Hmm, I don't seem to recall anyone being in there with us, other than Granddad and the two techno-medics," Papa ruminates. He places the palm of his hand on Oriana's forehead to see whether a fever has made her delusional. She promptly removes it.

"Nothing is wrong with me, Papa," she insists, recalling Granddad's suggestion that she may have inherited the gift of second sight.

Papa slips off his worn brown loafers and props his feet up on the pine seaman's chest that serves as a coffee table. Oriana knows Granddad would not approve, as this particular item has been in the family for centuries. "Oh well, whoever she was, it's not important right now," he concludes. Oriana runs a finger across the leather handle attached to the side of the chest.

"What you need to understand is that I was put into the Facility as punishment for this entire catastrophe. What happened to you was entirely my fault. I am sorry Oriana, I am so, so sorry," Papa says.

Since coming to stay with Granddad, Oriana's evening ritual has been to sit on the cushioned ledge of the bay window and watch nightfall approach. Nearly every night for four years she's waited right there, hopeful to hear Papa's footsteps approach and to see him climb the steps.

"You don't have to apologize," she says, moving from the couch to windowsill. She presses her nose against the pane. She spots what she first believes to be a June beetle banging against the windowpane. Upon closer inspection, she realizes that the odd green object is actually a mechanical device. She sits quietly as nightfall casts shadows of the trees, their stark outlines pressed against the pavement. Her breath condenses as she exhales, forming a wet fog over the glass.

"Getting connected didn't hurt at all, you know," she offers, as she returns to the couch and sits down next to Papa. "Neither did the removal of my eggs." Papa's eyes narrow to a squint, as sweat beads begin to form across his upper lip and brow. She places her head in his lap. "Don't worry, Papa," she whispers. "Everything is going to be okay."

Granddad pokes his head through the living room door. "I'm heading up for bed," he announces.

"Goodnight, Dad," Papa returns, his eyes fixed on Oriana's scarred temple.

"Goodnight, Granddad," Oriana chimes in, rising and giving him a hug and a kiss.

"Papa, I'm happy this way, you know," she says, returning her head to his lap.

"I know, Ori. It's just that I never wanted this for you," Papa complains.

"What about Mama? What did Mama want for me?"

"We'd agreed, even before you were conceived. She was passionate about wanting your independence, Ori, and so was I."

"I suppose she couldn't know what it would actually be like for me, even though she was one too. Maybe it was different back then. All I know is I didn't like being an independent. I had no friends. Did Mama?" Oriana's gaze falls on her father's worn, cracked hands.

Papa puts a hand over the girl's mouth. "Stop it. No more of this kind of talk," he instructs.

Oriana jerks her head aside, breaking the unwelcome touch. "It's true, though. I used to feel like an imbecile. Now I am smart, as smart as anyone. And I can say whatever I feel, thank you very much," she protests.

Papa chuckles over his daughter's independent spirit and folds his arms across his chest. "Can't you understand that we wanted to keep you free, aware, and insightful, in ways that VISHNEW-connected children can never be?" he retorts.

"I like all the things that I can do now, Papa, like math problems really fast in my head. I can spell or define any word and recite all kinds of facts. Do you want to know the total number of tons of whale blubber that were brought onto shore by Nantucket ships between 1700 and 1853? I can find out almost instantly. And the Starbuck sisters don't have to school me anymore. I can go under my Hood and learn from VISHNEW every day, like the other kids. And when . . ."

"No! This is not what I want for you! Trust me, Oriana. It's no way to live!" Papa shouts, standing.

"Then why is everybody else on Nantucket fully VISHNEW-connected?" she returns, sneering.

"Maybe because their imbecile parents decided that having instant access to unlimited information, continual communication with other people, and safety from physical harm, along with being happy all the time, make for a better life."

"Well, doesn't it?"

"Not necessarily, Oriana. Mama and I believe that something of our humanity is actually lost in the process."

"Mama's dead, remember?"

Papa ignores her.

His conviction leaves Oriana unconvinced. Her mind fills with thoughts. *I like being connected. I don't get sad or afraid, as I did before. I feel content with life. Why wouldn't that make him happy for me? He probably doesn't remember what it was like to even be a partial-connect. How could he understand?*

"Don't you get it?" Oriana persists. "Now I'm better than I was before in every single way. I even have friends under the Hood, Papa, real friends. And I'm smart, too, super smart. If you loved me, you would have done this a long time ago. Good thing Granddad got to be in charge for a while. He says you were too irresponsible to father a VISHNEW-independent child. And I agree with him."

Oriana begins to shake. Her eyes roll up under the bone that encases them, to leave mostly the whites exposed.

"What are you doing?" Papa scolds, appalled at the grotesqueness of it. "Don't play around that way!"

Oriana's gaze locks upward.

"Stop it, I said. Quit it right this minute!"

Papa stands to search the pockets of his jacket and pants, and looks around at the floor behind him.

"Damn it all, where in the hell is my . . .?" he mumbles, groping for the small ophthalmoscope he keeps on hand.

"I don't need any of your stupid, outdated devices. I am all right now," Oriana spits as she regains ocular control. Papa turns around to see that her fern green irises are wide and bright, her pupils clear and warm.

She explains to her father what the techno-medics had told her; that sometimes the eyes of a VISHNEW-connected child will roll back in the head because of routine adjustments being made by electrical impulses that are sent into the cerebellum.

"It keeps me synchronized with other full-connects," she says proudly, "and in mental equilibrium."

Papa cups his head in his hands and groans.

"Please don't cry again, Papa," Oriana pleads.

"I will not accept this situation, nor tolerate being disrespected," he snaps. "I have every intention of raising you my way." He lifts his index finger and shakes it at Oriana's face. "And I expect reparation from the VISHNEW authorities who took advantage of my incarceration at the Facility."

Oriana shrugs. "Authorities? What authorities?" she challenges him. "Where are you getting such nonsense? Those of us who are connected are grateful for it. Why would we ever complain? You have no appreciation for how fortunate we are."

Papa well knows that VISHNEW is autonomous. There is no central authority, not even an operating facility. VISHNEW is disembodied. Generous though it may be in provision of information and support of human life, VISHNEW is an immaterial and obscure force of being. This is all widely understood. So why does Papa badger me in this way?

"You'd be much more pleasant as a full-connect," Oriana mumbles.

Gently, Papa pulls her head against his chest, holding it there. With utmost affection he caresses her scalp and smooths her hair.

"Oriana, come now," he says. "You're smarter than this. All you are doing is receiving feedback from a highly sophisticated computer program. Can you understand that? There is no VISHNEW other than that. Those techno-medics did what they wanted to, not what some disembodied, omniscient entity led them to do. As for you, all I can say is you were vulnerable and had a lapse in judgment."

"Don't worry though," he adds. It will all turn out okay." He strokes her head softly. Oriana relaxes in his embrace.

"Papa, do you remember that tomorrow is my sixteenth retrieval day?"

"Your birthday? Of course, yes. No reminder needed. You and I are going to spend it on a picnic out where Surfside Beach used to be."

"I'd rather we celebrate at home on Copper Lane," she replies. "Granddad can come and we can get birthday cake fresh from the Foundry. Would that be okay with you?" she asks, her wide eyes gazing up at him. Papa continues to stroke Oriana's head, noticing how much longer and darker her hair has gotten in four years, and how much looser her curls have become.

"Sure, that's a great idea. We can celebrate your birthday and my homecoming at the same time."

Exhausted by the emotional reunion, Oriana dozes off in his arms with the thought, the hope that they can be happy again, and soon everything will be all right, just as Papa has promised.

When her breathing becomes deep and regular Papa lays his daughter on the couch, carefully releasing her from his arms, and then tiptoes up the stairs to the second floor.

The sound of his bare feet padding across the hard pine boards above causes Oriana to stir. She can make out Papa walking out of Granddad's bedroom, down the hall and into the bathroom. With enhanced hearing, she picks up every sound. When she hears him opening the bathroom cabinet, Oriana heads up the staircase to find him.

"What are you doing up there?" she calls out quietly as she approaches the second floor landing. Papa's lanky shadow dances against the wall, fluidly and with purpose. "Papa, what's going on?" she whispers hoarsely.

"Hush Oriana!" he scolds. "Granddad is trying to sleep." He pokes his head out of the bathroom door and dismisses her with a wave of his hand.

Refusing to be deterred, Oriana steps onto the landing as Papa emerges from the bathroom, his hands filled with objects she cannot quite make out in the dim light. Her eyes, turning the opal yellow indicative of VISHNEW-supported vision, refocus for a closer look. She sees that Papa is carrying a tube of analgesic.

"We've got to hurry," Papa says, as he treads back down the stairs and into the kitchen. Oriana follows him. "Sit here." He points to the ladder-back chair with the peeling red paint.

Oriana plops down on the Nantucket blue cushion tied to its seat. "What's going on, Papa?"

"Oriana, I love you," he says softly. These words are pleasing to her ears after so many years of silence.

"I love you too, Papa." He kisses her forehead, and then quickly swipes an impregnated cotton ball under her nose. "I am going to fix this little problem of ours," he says as the sedative begins to take effect. "And you, my dear, are going to promise me that you won't ever let those techno-medics try to rearrange your perfect body again."

"What do you mean, Papa? What problem?" Oriana asks, slurring her words.

Papa waves the cotton ball under her nose again.

Oriana notices that it has a strange smell. Its pungency makes her nostrils flare and sting.

"Don't be afraid. I am doing this for you, Ori," he reassures her. "I am certain it's what Mama would have wanted."

"OOOH," she utters, her arms and chest falling limp across the kitchen table, her tongue and lips flopping like sliced bologna.

Still conscious, Oriana feels Papa's hands on the back of her neck, pulling against the skin of her foramen magnum where the medulla and spinal cord exit the skull.

"Got it!" Papa announces. He slides a sharp, cold object into her right ear, probing as he pushes and prods. "Damn it all!" he curses as he works. Oriana feels a warm substance flowing across her cheek and down her neck.

Lifting and turning her head with his hands, Papa opens her mouth and inserts the scalpel.

Oriana feels Papa pull up on a tooth and squeeze her gums. The pain in her mouth is dull, but in her ear it is excruciating. *If only there were some way to let him know,* she tells herself, *then certainly he would stop.* Oriana moves her lips and tongue. Her efforts to speak produce only incomprehensible sounds.

"Shh, try to relax," Papa commands of the semi-conscious young woman. He yanks off the skin graft from her temples, grimacing in empathy with her pain. He applies more analgesic.

Papa, please, you're hurting me! Oriana's mind cries out to a father who is too preoccupied to sense her pleas.

Papa feels for the small knot at her sphenoid. Finding what he is searching for, he grabs hold of the end of the tiny tube inside the bone and swiftly snatches it out.

As Oriana drifts further from consciousness, she smiles to herself, comforted by the awareness that she'll soon be sixteen years old. Then everything will be okay. She begins to dream of freefalling through a cumulous cloud. The mechanical beetle, now inside the house, flies frantically around her head.

Less than two minutes later, at exactly 9:12 p.m., a security hover, followed closely by a techno-medical craft, approaches Granddad's house on Broad Street. The low drone of the landing vehicles sends vibrations through the house. Oriana is stirred briefly into consciousness. Papa takes his daughter into his arms and hugs her tightly enough to assure she knows he cares.

The front door opens. Three bots make their way down the center hall, one grabbing the girl, the other two apprehending Papa. Granddad, barely awake and rubbing his sleep-encrusted eyes, descends to witness the removal of the child. At the sight of the blood that soaks her shirt and skirt, the old man stumbles and falls.

It is the sound of Granddad's bellowing cries that sends Oriana deep inside the shelter of her mind.

LESSONS

A band of women scuttles across a forest floor in search of edible roots. Oriana, from under her Hood, climbs into the program on her knees to join them.

"Think of it this way, Oriana," suggests the program's instructor. "Early in its evolution, the hominid species related to Earth as Mother, the source of life." The voice attuned to Oriana's sensitivities chooses words that will help her feel comfortable on her first day of advanced studies.

"What about Father?" she inquires. "Was he seen as a source of something, too?"

Adjusting its semantic algorithm to Oriana's current state of mind, the instructor continues.

"What a marvelous question, and the answer is definitely 'Yes,' Hold on, though. We're coming to that momentarily."

"Okay," Oriana agrees, reaching for a berry growing on a small bush. She turns the soft red fruit in her fingers and pops it into her mouth. "Yuck, that's nasty!" she exclaims.

"Eating that berry with the seed still in it will kill you very quickly," the instructor scolds.

"Well, it's a good thing this one is not real then, wouldn't you agree?" Oriana replies, scurrying to catch up with the root-gathering band, which has moved on to a watering hole.

"For centuries, the maternal metaphor persisted across cultures," the instructor continues, "with Homo sapiens enacting sundry mother-worship rituals. That changed when humans gained control over matter. With the ability to manipulate substances precisely, people had little left to worship. The body itself became less essential to procreation, and both parental metaphors dropped out of use," the instructor states. The scene fades, only to be replaced by the blackness of deep space.

"Take a look," the instructor suggests, "at Earth coming into distant view. This is not the only place in the universe that can sustain life, although it's the only one yet found that is as compatible with hominid existence," the voice relays.

"Wow," says Oriana. "It really is blue, like Papa told me."

She finds it reassuring that at least some of her father's teachings are corroborated by the same instruction other islanders receive. Oriana watches closely as the Earth comes into view, circled by the moon, orbiting the sun with the other planets of the solar system.

"It's stunning."

The program's perspective pulls back, and within seconds the solar system is engulfed in the Milky Way. Soon the entire galaxy is insignificant in the vastness of space.

"Ok. Now watch," the program tells her. "The universe folds in on itself."

"Holy crap, this is unbelievable," Oriana utters, in awe of its sheer vastness.

"The same feeling arose in your ancestors when they first saw the Earth from this vantage point. Clearly, humanity's sense of itself had to change drastically," the tutor surmises, "just as it did when the world was discovered to be round, rather than flat."

"Who could have believed otherwise?" Oriana asks with a giggle.

The image fades, replaced by a diagram showing the evolution of human technological progress with each stage correlated to the myths that informed its era.

The tutor continues. "Before gaining technological prowess, humans worshiped natural energies and elements as gods. Earth, fire, water, wind, and basic elements such as gold were sources of power, so they became objects of devotion. Perhaps you might understand it metaphorically as the infancy of humanity, when worship and adoration of Mother occurs in recognition of the care, sustenance, and nourishment Earth provides."

"What's that?" Oriana inquires as a new image appears.

"Step inside and see for yourself," the instructor suggests.

Oriana walks through the massive wooden doors of a gothic building. "Oh wow, where am I now?" she asks.

"This is St. Patrick's Cathedral at 5th Avenue and 51st Street, New York City."

"It's amazing," she says. "The columns and arches are huge. And the room is so long. Oh geez. Over there are shorter rooms extending out to the sides," she says, perplexed by the odd-shaped architecture. "Is that significant?"

"Yes. The lines of a Latin cross inspired its design. Go ahead, walk all the way up to the front," it instructs, responding to her interests as they become apparent. Oriana approaches the altar slowly.

"What's this building used for?" she asks. "There is certainly nothing resembling such a structure on Nantucket."

"The cathedral was designed to be a tower of gifts from men."

"Gifts? To whom?" Oriana wants to know.

"To their god. The aim was to reach his domain, far above Earth, physically, mentally, emotionally, and spiritually."

"Why?"

"To appease and appeal to that which was perceived to have ultimate power. You see, as Earth came more and more under the control of your species, some turned their eyes to a greater power, a superior creator, Father."

"So that's where he comes in," Oriana recognizes.

"The cathedral was meant to be an outward sign of the inner potential that human beings were given by that father god."

"It's sort of overwhelming."

"Don't feel intimidated, Oriana. No need to anymore. That only worked in the past, when people believed in an all-powerful entity, separate from humans, and therefore frightening. VISHNEW would never require that kind of sublimation," it assures her. "Anyway, at least for the connected, VISHNEW and human beings are as one."

"It's cold in here," Oriana complains.

"Of course it is. Look around you. Notice the materials that were used for the construction."

"Stone?"

"Correct. Can you imagine the challenge of heating all this?"

"Aren't there solar cells built into the roof? Or radiant hydrogen in the floors?"

The instructor chuckles, and Oriana laughs in return, realizing that it is probably a silly question.

"Tell me more," Oriana requests of the program, which speaks in a patient, human-sounding voice.

"As monotheism took hold, paternalism rose to prominence. Earth, still seen by some as a mother figure, lost its awe-inspiring thrust. In fact, once they became empowered with tools and sophisticated techniques, many humans began to oppose the Earth, seeking to dominate and control it, using it for their own purposes.

"Think of this as the adolescent phase of evolution," the tutor continues, "when humans sought independence from the mother. And even though the Earth–Mother paradigm continued in some mythology, it lost the early reverence it had earlier enjoyed. People continued to need their Mother, but they began to reject being dependent on her."

The cathedral fades. Oriana wiggles to ease the stiffness of sitting for so long in her chair, stretching her legs and arms.

"Furthermore," the instructor continues, "efforts were made to control the female and contain her, too. Mother-worship was sublimated to that of Heavenly Father, Allah, and other male deities. Woman became subjugated to the will of Man, who saw himself as the emissary of God."

"This is getting confusing," Oriana confesses. "Not to mention depressing."

The instructor takes note of Oriana's hand wringing. EEG frequencies picked up by her Hood suggest fatigue. "Would you like to take a break?" it offers.

"No, it's okay. I don't want a break now. I'd rather we finish sooner than later. Maybe then I can take a longer lunch."

"You seem uncomfortable," the instructor persists.

"Well, my head is a bit sore, actually."

"Perhaps you should loosen the diodes a little," the voice suggests. "They may be attached too tightly to your scalp."

Oriana adjusts the controls in the armrests of her chair. The lining of the Hood retracts half a millimeter.

"You were right. That's much better now. Thank you," she says.

New images form on the screen. First, a grazing herd of elephants becomes a mass of bones strewn across a wide savannah. Then a lush, old growth forest defoliates into stumps, branches, and dust. Deep, flowing lakes fade into silt-filled puddles. Fertile land across southern Europe becomes desert before Oriana's eyes. Huge expanses of ice begin to melt at both poles.

"This is what Papa told me about," Oriana whispers.

"What you are watching is the ecological shift that resulted from alterations in human consciousness. As humans expanded their capacity to penetrate and manipulate matter, their ego drives and desires increased, too, leading them to create with great hubris and disdain. Something had to change. Now watch."

Oriana's Hood fills with a totally silent darkness. She feels herself floating face down, surrounded by nothing. A deep humming sound begins to emerge. Then a vast, seemingly endless body of water appears below her, its contours enshrouded in a dark mist.

"Ah," Oriana remarks in awe.

Over the water a thin layer of light appears, shimmering in yellows and blues, transforming itself into an intricate flower with many petals. Then a voice, quiet yet clear, whispers, "It's time to begin. Now create." Oriana feels a sense of excitement that quickly gives way to confusion and fear.

"I don't understand at all," she complains.

"Your species has always had the freedom to create. Now, for those of you who have embraced VISHNEW, the Earth, your bodies, and the whole universe are entirely in your hands."

"I'm sorry. This is confusing. Control of what?"

"Of life, Oriana. Your species stands at the threshold of controlling life and death."

"Really?"

"VISHNEW functions without biological constraints. Through VISHNEW, you now have the ability to slow the degradation of living cells; to identify and arrest most diseases; to collect and share information without limits, via cognitive exchange; to keep yourselves safe from the threats of the natural world; and to overcome the limitations of anatomy and the vagaries of genetic determinacy."

The tutor continues. "When the Virtual Information System for Human Noetic Evolution and Welfare emerged, it was detected in very few localities on Earth. No one knows exactly how VISHNEW came to be. Exquisitely intelligent, it appears to have formed independent of human design."

"How is that possible?" Oriana returns. "What keeps it alive?"

"Discretely linked in time and space to the global circuitry of ubiquitous nano-systems, it by all accounts appears to garner its power and knowledge from the hundreds of thousands of satellites that orbit close to the Earth's atmosphere. One theory suggests that its emergence constitutes the first phase of the long-predicted singularity."

"Oh that," Oriana grumbles. "Papa told me about the convergence of human and machine intelligences."

"Another view suspects it to be a cleverly-orchestrated system of social manipulation, contrived by an unknown entity. Then, of course, there are those who believe VISHNEW to be a technological incarnation of God."

"Papa says VISHNEW can never replace the Inner Light," Oriana declares.

The program hesitates briefly as it taps into her father's files.

"Your father descended from Quakers," the instructor replies. "He meant well, Oriana, but he failed to reconcile the teachings of his Quaker heritage with rational trust in the emergence of supreme human intelligence. "

"Papa taught me that one of the most serious problems with humans is our unbridled desire for control."

"I know," remarks the tutor. "As I said, he meant well, even though he sought to manipulate you. Just look at what you have become as a result of your father's teachings."

"Manipulate me? How dare you criticize him that way!" she exclaims. "He raised me and taught me most of what I know about the world and life. He devoted himself entirely to me, because he cares about me. You are suggesting he was wrong?"

"Exactly."

"I'll tell you who's wrong. You; whatever the hell you are. You are the one who is wrong. All this so-called history you're feeding me, and these images you're showing me, how is it not manipulation? Isn't this lesson just your effort to alter what I think and believe?" Oriana chides.

The disembodied voice chuckles.

"And what do you mean by 'what I have become?'" Oriana interjects.

The program falls silent.

"Who do you think you are?"

There's still no response.

"Papa never trusted VISHNEW, and now I understand why," Oriana shouts.

"Your belief in him, Oriana, is that of an ignorant, adoring, emotionally-dependent little girl."

"You will never be able to fathom the belief I have in my father. It has to do with a kind of connection you have no knowledge of!"

With that she swipes 'off' on the controls, lifts her Hood and slumps down in the chair. "How much longer can I go on lamenting the loss of Papa?" she wonders aloud.

AFRICAN MEETING HOUSE

"Good morning, Albert Rotch!" booms a pleasant female voice. "How will you be spending this fine day? Why not enjoy extended, uninterrupted entertainment under the Hood in the comfort of your own home? Remember, there's no charge on Saturdays. Missed a weekday program? Watch it today. Ready to catch up on that sporting event? No problem to claim your preferred seat in the stadium. Never got the chance to see those foreign lands, fly over the surface of Neptune, or explore the deep sea? What are you waiting for? Today's the day.

"Take in a vintage anime or cartoon. Watch a book from any library in the world. Laugh at an old black and white comedy. It's a new day! Want to start a new course of study? Pick your subject! Feeling a little bit lonely? Tune into the homes of other islanders or invite someone into a simulation. Whatever you wish for, your Hood can provide. Settle in underneath and get that gray matter working . . ."

Oriana rolls onto her back, eyes still closed even though she's all the way awake now, and pulls the covers over her head. Her urgent need to empty her bladder would have woken her even if the Hood advertisement hadn't. She tosses the sheets and blanket to one side, climbs out of bed, and picks up the blue plaid bathrobe lying on the floor at her feet.

"Granddad," she yells, "why the hell have you got your alarm set so early?" She crosses the hallway to the bathroom.

"I've got big plans for the day," he hollers back as he exits the bathroom door to face her.

"I figured I better wake up extra early," he added, rubbing the top of his granddaughter's head enough to worsen the tangles of the messy mop left by her restless night's sleep.

"Well, would you mind turning the volume down on those damn house speakers, so a girl can get her rest?" she asked, firmly removing his hand from her hair.

"I'll have you know," he says as he begins his descent down the staircase, "those speakers are set exactly where I need them to be, so don't you go telling me what to do." Granddad disappears into the kitchen, and Oriana gets dressed.

Most of the island's adult inhabitants are employed in only a handful of places. The Institute for Expansive Realities is where Hoods are designed and maintained. The Molecular Foundry provides the organic and macromolecular synthesis of food and beverages. The Facility detains islanders who are unable to abide by Nantucket's laws and ordinances, or who are otherwise socially maladapted. Island Security protects the community from outsiders. Island Maintenance services the utilities, waste management, and public buildings. The Biomaterial Labs grow replacement limbs, wombs, and other organs, and repair DNA. And the island's largest employer, Maker's Materials, transforms non-food refuse into consumer products such as vehicles, appliances, instruments, and toys.

After Granddad's hardware store went out of business, he took up employment at Maker's Materials, where he was able to put his knowledge to use as a molecular re-assembler. Retired now, Granddad spends most of his time under his Hood. Recently he has developed a keen desire to go out to sea.

About a month ago, Granddad joined the crew of *Relief Light Vessel # 58*, which dropped anchor on Nantucket New South Shoal in 1894. She was a flush deck steam vessel, schooner-rigged with a steam whistle between two masts. Granddad happened aboard her on a day when the sea rose up with unexpected fury. Sudden gales caused enough rolling and pitching to knock the glass out of the lanterns, heave the candles off their holders, and toss the beds out of their berths. It was an exciting but harrowing excursion for Granddad.

The next time he went onboard was on a calm evening. All the crew had to do besides maintaining the lights was to weave rattan baskets to sell back on shore. Granddad didn't mind at all. He enjoyed being with the sailors, listening to their stories, and sharing with them meals of salt beef, potato, and onion stew.

Granddad got the idea that it would be exciting to captain a slave ship. So he did, and he found it to be exhilarating. That was exactly the problem. The obscene sense of personal power he derived from the experience revolted his Quaker conscience. Shamed, he decided his penance would be to go under the Hood the next time as a slave.

This time, Granddad climbed aboard a ship called the *Feloz* commanded by Captain Jose Barbosa and bound for Bahia. In accordance with the settings he selected, the moment Granddad stepped onto the deck his skin turned black, his lips filled out, and his hair coarsened. The second in command caught a glimpse of Granddad and accosted him. Granddad was at a loss for words when asked why he was wandering above deck. But it would hardly have mattered what he said to the man in reply.

With a red-hot brand, the officer impressed the owner's mark on Granddad's arm, the branding burnt in with a red-hot iron.

Then he took him under the grated hatchway of the bottom deck and stowed him in a space so low he had to crouch down between the legs of another slave. Granddad could not move or even change positions at all, and the stench overwhelmed him.

Oriana was in the kitchen at the time, making their lunch. In the adjacent parlor, Granddad sweltered in the putrid underbelly of the ship. Suddenly, the old man lifts his Hood and runs towards the bathroom located just outside the kitchen door.

"What in heaven's name is going on with you?" Oriana demands as he runs past her.

"None of ya' damned business," he answers. Oriana hears the toilet flush, and Granddad returns to the kitchen. He takes a seat at the table where Oriana has placed a bowl of chili and warm bread. The food remains untouched while Granddad sits brooding in front of it for nearly an hour. Then he heads back to his Hood.

"So where are you going now?" Oriana asks as Granddad reaches up to pull the rigid covering down over his head.

"Get back, girl. It's no place for the likes of you out there."

"Out where?" she asks.

"Get back, I'm tellin' ya."

"Let me guess. It's another slave ship."

"Nope, it's a whaling ship, and a famous one at that! I'm going out on the Essex to lend a hand in harpooning whales with some African seamen. So leave me alone for a few hours, would ya?"

Granddad is fascinated by the whaling boats of the 1700's that sailed out of the harbors of Nantucket, Martha's Vineyard, and New Bedford. Once, while under his Hood, a Wampanoag whaler tried to teach him a traditional hunting technique. As Granddad explains it, the man leapt off the ship and onto the back of a passing whale, driving a wooden plug into its blowhole, suffocating the animal. On seeing this operation up close, Granddad lost his breath and became dizzy, forcing an early end to the Hood session. The next time under he used a harpoon with detach-able barbs, another invention whalers had adopted from Native Americans

"That's enough, Granddad."

"Humph."

Oriana places a hand on his shoulder. Granddad pushes it off as he slips under his Hood for another adventure.

"Granddad, how many times do I have to remind you? You get headaches when you stay under too long."

"Back off now, girl."

"Come out for lunch, already! You don't even know when you're hungry anymore."

Oriana notices a brightly colored bag on the parlor mantle. On peering inside the mysterious bag, she finds a pair of thin metal rods and a ball of colorful, stringy material. She puzzles over what she sees. Reaching inside, she takes out a note from Granddad say-ing, 'Happy 18th Retrieval Day, Oriana. These are knitting needles and a skein of yarn. A long, long time ago, islanders made their clothing by hand.'

Oriana removes the knitting supplies and the other contents of the bag, taking the rods into one hand and squeezing the soft mound of yarn with the other. "Wow, Granddad. This is an in-teresting gift," she says, tapping on his Hood. Granddad lifts his Hood enough to hear her.

"I really don't know what to do with it," she says.

"It's simple, Ori. You go under your Hood, load up the courses on historic handworks, and select 'How to knit.'"

"The color is really pretty," she says quietly.

"It's supposed to look and feel identical to hand-dyed, hand-spun, historically-authentic indigo Nantucket sheep's wool," he says proudly. "That skein in your hand is entirely fabricated of na-no-fibers, not grown on a stinking, dirty sheep, but in a clean lab! Now whad'ya think about that?" he asks.

"I think you ought to get going before the ship sets sail without you," she suggests.

Granddad returns to his adventures, and Oriana goes under her own Hood in the parlor across from his.

"Welcome to the world of craft," a voice says gaily. "So you want to learn how to knit?" Oriana reaches for the virtual needles floating in front of her.

"These are size 12 needles for your first try at casting on. Which do you want to learn first? The Loop, Backward Loop, Knitted, Cable, or Long-Tail cast on?"

"What?" Oriana asks.

"Point your thumb toward yourself, under the yarn," the tutorial instructs, a diagram materializing before her.

"Human depiction please," Oriana requests. Human hands replace the diagram.

"Turn your thumb away from you." Human hands replace the schema. Oriana struggles to watch both her own hands and the virtual ones working in front of her eyes. "Slip the needle up into the loop on your thumb." She bites down on her lower lip, her hand muscles tight as she attempts to hold the virtual needles and maneuver the yarn at the same time.

"There was a time, not too long ago, when sheep grazed on Nantucket meadows, and their wool was shorn for spinning, dying, and knitting," the voice explains. "Hats, scarfs, gloves, blankets, booties, and sweaters were knitted by hand, as you are now learning to do.

Oriana sighs. What am I supposed to be making?

"Now slip your thumb out, then repeat steps 1 through 3 until there are enough stitches on the needle," it continues.

"Enough what?" Oriana replies, increasingly frustrated by the process.

"Stitches: loops around the needle."

It seems as though it should be simple, even fun. But Oriana feels dumb, awkward, and anxious. Still, she persists with the tutorial for well over two hours until finally she has the confidence to try it on her own. She shuts off the program, comes out from under her Hood, and heads for the front porch rocker, knitting bag in hand.

She puts the skein up against her cheek and inhales the naked, raw scent of synthetic lanolin. The best part of knitting, she finds as she settles in, is the texture of the wool, so springy and fluffy to the touch. *I wonder if there's enough here to make a small blanket? That seems simple enough.*

"Good morning, Sunflower!" says a voice coming from the sidewalk in front of Granddad's house. Oriana looks up from her craft to find a visitor. An embroidered black hat perches low on the visitor's head, obscuring her face. Two long gray braids hang over her shoulders, and a floral skirt falls just short of her ankles. Her outdated appearance is almost surreal. "Happy 18th Retrieval Day to you!" she offers.

"Oh, thank you," Oriana returns, thinking the woman looks familiar.

"Blustery day, isn't it?" the woman suggests, shifting the balance of her weight to hold the bike in place. Her plain black shoes are tattered and scuffed, her skin wrinkled, deep brown, and creviced. She reaches down deep into the pocket of her sweater and pulls out a handful of loose raisins. "Have some?" she offers with a wide, warm grin.

"I'll pass."

The woman pops one into her mouth. "Ooh, that's good," she remarks. "The produce coming out of the Foundry tastes more and more authentic all the time."

Oriana nods. "Their lemons are my favorite," she returns. "They're great for making really good fresh lemonade, if you add enough of the basic sweetener."

"What's that you're doing?" the woman asks, slipping the remaining raisins into her mouth. Oriana notices her missing teeth, and guesses that it might take the woman a while to finish chewing.

"I'm knitting," Oriana responds proudly.

"Oh, I see. And who taught you how to do that, my dear?" the woman asks, her words garbled by the mush in her mouth.

"No one. I was tutored under my Hood by the handworks instructional program." *This should be obvious. How else would I learn?*

"That's tricky work. Must come natural to you," the woman compliments. "Like your Mama. She made beautiful things with wool."

Oriana freezes, a strand of yarn wrapped around her index finger hard enough to cause a palpable pulsation in its tip. She looks up from the needles at the woman, who is now bent over and pulling up a long black sock.

"Her specialty was haberdashery," the woman goes on as she untwists the fabric gathered tightly around her ankle and heel. "Why do socks always have to do this?" she mumbles to herself.

"Haber-what?" Oriana asks.

"Hats. Your Mama was especially talented at making women's hats. Like this one," she says, taking her hat off and handing it to Oriana. Oriana's jaw drops.

"It's you, Mrs. Wyatt," she utters, recognizing the old woman as the matron who cared for her at TEMPLE exactly five years ago.

"You didn't recognize me at first?" she asks.

"No, I really did not," Oriana chuckles as she studies the old woman and the hat that her Mama made. Detailed in lovely embroidery, felted to fold on one side, and rounded with perfection across the top, the hat is impressive, yet at the same time disconcerting. Nobody ever told her that her mother had been a hat maker. *Why didn't Papa or Granddad say anything?* Oriana's hands begin to quiver. "What else do you know about my Mama?" she asks, craving any information she can get about her dead mother.

"Your Mama was a very sweet lady," Mrs. Wyatt offers as Oriana hands back the hat. "What a wonderful presence she was in TEMPLE. We spent a lot of time holding the hands of anxious young girls while they waited for the fertili-bot to come in and retrieve their eggs. This was back when volunteers like your mama were allowed to help during the procedure. Same with the likes of me now."

"How well did you know her, Mrs. Wyatt?"

"Quite well," she replied.

As the woman talks, Oriana feels hers consciousness fading, the awareness of her own body weakening. It is as if she were drifting out of her own head.

"Rebecca and I were best friends," she explains. Oriana thinks she understands the concept, because back when she was connected she had a few buddies for a while under her Hood. *She must be an independent, just like Mama. That would explain their friendship. And it would also explain why she couldn't hold a job anymore.*

"What was my Mama like?" Oriana asks, putting her knitting aside. She leans forward, elbows on her thighs.

Mrs. Wyatt moves onto the porch steps, waving her hand in an expression of delight. "Your Mama was a lot like you, Sunshine. Beautiful and very smart."

"Would you like some lemonade, Mrs. Wyatt? I made some fresh this morning."

"No thank you, dear." She opens her arms in invitation. "How'd you like to come with me for a bike ride?"

"I don't have a bike," Oriana returns.

"Well, that's not a problem at all, dear heart. Mine has a place for a passenger, see?" The old lady points to the small platform mounted behind her seat, obviously designed for carrying a basket or hauling small packages.

The thought of riding behind someone who barely seems able to keep herself upright on a bike amuses Oriana.

"Come on now, you've no reason to worry over being with me," Mrs. Wyatt offers, rolling her index finger inward in a coaxing gesture. "I'll have you back here before you know it. There's something I want to show you."

Oriana decides to trust the oddly warm feeling she's beginning to have for Mrs. Wyatt.

"Okay, I need a moment," she replies, "to let Granddad know that I'll be gone for a while."

Oriana finds Granddad still under his Hood, foot pounding and hands clasped together as if he's holding onto something for dear life. She decides not to interrupt him. She places her knitting on the kitchen table and makes her way back out to Mrs. Wyatt.

Oriana climbs on the bicycle, noting the firm muscles of Mrs. Wyatt's arms as she leans her weight against the handlebars. Apparently she is not the feeble old lady she appears to be, despite her obvious decision to age.

"Take ahold now!" Mrs. Wyatt instructs, as Oriana settles onto the rear of the bicycle.

Sliding her arms around Mrs. Wyatt's waist and across the front of her stomach, Oriana props her chin along the top of Mrs. Wyatt's broad shoulder. Down the narrow cobblestoned streets of Nantucket Town they roll, across Center Street to India, over Liberty Street to Main, out Pleasant and finally to York at the Five Corners.

"What is this place?" Oriana asks as they stop in front of the old African Meeting House.

"Way, way back, they called this community 'New Guinea,'" Mrs. Wyatt explains. "It was once a racially-segregated place. Hop off, and I'll show you where I first met your Mama," she says blithely, taking Oriana's hand into hers.

The two walk along the broken stone path up to the clapboard post-and-beam building.

"Mama was here?" Oriana asks as she peers inside the windows of the seventeenth century structure. Inside are simple wooden benches laid out in straight rows.

"Let's sit down under this old tree," Mrs. Wyatt suggests.

Oriana notices the dusty ground below her feet and hesitates.

Mrs. Wyatt lifts the lid on the basket attached to the front of her bike and pulls out a blanket and a small cloth bag. She covers the ground and invites Oriana to sit down. Sunlight dances between the branches above their heads, casting a golden beam of light across Mrs. Wyatt's face. Illuminated, her brown skin is rich and deep, her old eyes bright and wide.

"This was once a magnificent tree," she declares. "It was a real beauty in its day, framing the African Meeting House. That was way back even before your Mama was born. Interesting, isn't it, that we happen to be here on the eighteenth anniversary of the day she died?"

Oriana would rather not acknowledge that her retrieval day is the same as the date of her mother's expiration.

"Isn't this something!?" Mrs. Wyatt exclaims. "How this old tree still stands." The woman stares in wonder at the life form in front of her. Oriana muses over Mrs. Wyatt letting herself age. "I'm surprised it survived the Great Storms," Mrs. Wyatt goes on.

"Also known as 'the week of ten tornadoes,' right, Mrs. Wyatt?" Oriana asks. Granddad often refers to the devastation with this old expression.

"That's right, Sunflower," Mrs. Wyatt confirms.

Oriana likes how Mrs. Wyatt uses terms of endearment with her, especially since this particular moniker happens to represent her favorite blossom.

"I've never understood about all that, Mrs. Wyatt. Granddad says no one can explain what caused the storms."

"Well, if you really want to know what I have to say about it, I'll tell you. What happened is what will always happen when the People of the World go messing around acting as if they have all the knowledge and the power."

"'People of the World'," Oriana repeats, surprised to hear the not-so-neutral expression used by someone other than Granddad. "Are you a Quaker, Mrs. Wyatt?"

"I do my share of shaking and quaking, Sunflower, but I have never bowed my head in the company of any formal group, and never will."

"Well, then, do you mean to attribute the storms to some kind of omniscient, all-powerful presence in the universe?"

"It's the Tower of Babel, and it will happen again, and again, and again, until the end. We Children of the Light don't seem to learn what we need to, despite our fancy techno-toys."

"Children of who?"

Mrs. Wyatt raises her brow but doesn't answer.

"I guess you must have known my Papa, too."

"What I know is that your Mama loved your Papa very much, and they had many wonderful times together. I think your father must have told you so. And I am certain you must have seen holographs of their happy times together."

It is true that Oriana had seen many such images: of their mating day and honeymoon at the Seven Seas Inn, of picnics together at Long Pond, of the two of them planting trees, and of them riding bikes along what was left of the Nantucket trails.

"Behold true love, Oriana!" Papa would exclaim, referring to the fact that he and Mama had come together without the use of any mating compatibility program or any assurance from VISHNEW that they would produce perfect progeny.

Mrs. Wyatt stretches out on her back, hands beneath her head, and closes her eyes.

After what seems like a long time, Oriana speaks.

"I miss my Papa so much," she sighs."

Mrs. Wyatt reaches for her hands and squeezes them tightly. "Precious Sunflower, I can only imagine how much it hurts you that he's away in the Facility like he is. When was the last time you were with him?"

Oriana pulls her hands away and covers her face with them. "Maybe we shouldn't talk about this. My grandfather says it's time

I get over it, that I'll never see him again. He's been gone for six years, except for the few hours he was home the day before my sixteenth birthday."

"Oh dear me," Mrs. Wyatt remarks, "Your birthday isn't a very happy day for you, is it? It's the day that your Mama died, and also the day they put your Papa away. What an amazing girl you are."

"Not really," Oriana responds. "I don't feel amazing at all. I'm pretty uninteresting, actually. I haven't got any talents or abilities like most people around here have. Boring is a better word for what I am. Something akin to a slug, I'd say."

Mrs. Wyatt's eyes narrow to slivers as she looks up.

"You need to stay strong," she says, looking from Oriana to the decrepit old tree and back again as if, by the sheer force of her will, she could support both in their endeavors. She turns her head to gaze at some passing clouds, and then closes her eyes.

"What are you doing?" Oriana inquires. "Are you tired?"

"Not at all. What I am doing is relishing memories of your Mama."

"Such as?"

"Oh, like the time we first met."

"Will you tell me about that?

"Well now, let's see. I guess I'll begin by explaining it this way. We independent women folk used to sometimes gather here at the African Meeting House and share our personal stories. You might have called ours an affinity group, so to speak. One night your lovely mother walked into our gathering. So gorgeous she was in her wide white hat and yellow dress. Very politely, she asked if she could join in. Ours was a small group, but we welcomed her."

"That's very interesting to me," Oriana says, lying down next to Mrs. Wyatt.

"Well, Rebecca kept on coming to our gatherings, but she would usually just listen. Then one night she surprised us by telling us about her genetic connection to the infamous Sadie Lee." Mrs. Wyatt grins, taking pleasure in revealing to Oriana this previously unknown tidbit about her heritage.

"So you know that makes you related to *her*," Mrs. Wyatt exclaims.

"What do you mean?" Oriana asks, sitting up again.

"Sadie Lee was your great-great-grandmother's great-great-grandmother. Don't you know about her, Sunflower?" Oriana stands, putting her back against the trunk, trying to feel the tree. This is the first she has heard about this ancestor.

"She was one of the most cherished, beautiful women on the island, a black woman who was born a slave and brought to the island by a whaler from the Carolinas," Mrs. Wyatt continues. "One of the families of the Nantucket Friends Meeting bought her and then freed her. She became the pride of the Meeting."

"That's wonderful," Oriana exclaims.

"Well, maybe not," Mrs. Wyatt continues.

"She ran off with a Wampanoag tribe man and got herself pregnant, but he died before their baby was born. Poor Sadie Lee. She was expelled from Meeting not so much because of the pregnancy, but on account of her association with one of The World's People."

"And that's supposed to be a happy story?" Oriana comments. "I wonder how Mama felt about it."

"She's coming back you know, little girl," Mrs. Wyatt adds.

"I'm not a *little* girl."

"You'll see. She's coming back through you."

"Who's coming back, Mrs. Wyatt? What do you mean 'through me?'"

"Both of them are, really, as one, Sadie and Rebecca. They've always been one and the same soul. I've been seeing her around you. She'll be coming along when the time is right."

"No wonder the islanders think you're nutty," Oriana mumbles. "You have some very strange ideas, that's for sure."

"Oh, now don't go getting yourself confused by the chitchat of folks around here. You'll come to realize it soon enough."

"Granddad's probably wondering where I am right now," Oriana worries. "I'd better get going."

"You're not scared of me now, are you, Sunflower? It's who you are, that's all."

"Mrs. Wyatt, could you please take me home?"

"Not so fast. First I have something to give you," Mrs. Wyatt says, putting the bag she's been holding into Oriana's hands.

"What is this?" she asks.

"A Happy Retrieval Day gift," Mrs. Wyatt replies, as Oriana peeks inside. But of course, you and I are going to refer to today as your birthday."

"I don't understand. What is this?" she asks, taking the object in her hand.

"This is the bowl that your mother brought with her to TEMPLE on her appointed day of extraction."

"Are you saying that . . .?"

"Yes. This is where your life began. This is where you started out." Oriana studies the bowl despondently.

"No, it's not. This one is plain white. Mama's bowl was blue and brown. Granddad gave it to me years ago, on the day they counted my eggs. I used it when I went to TEMPLE for the extraction."

"Oriana, that bowl probably belonged to your father's mother. I can assure you, this one was your mother's."

"But I can't use Mama's bowl now. It's too late. My eggs are all gone," she laments. "I don't want this, Mrs. Wyatt. Take it back." Oriana shoves the bowl into the woman's gut. Mrs. Wyatt pushes it away.

"You calm down now, girl, and take it. I am giving it to you not to use, only to cherish." Oriana begins to sob, and Mrs. Wyatt pulls her into a tight embrace. "Your Mama loved you," she affirms. "She gave over her eggs with complete devotion to your conception. All she wanted was a daughter, you know. That's what she told me on many an occasion. This bowl represents her best efforts to bring you into this world as healthy and as well-formed as you could be."

"I wish you'd given it to me before, so I could have used it on the day I came to TEMPLE," Oriana says, her head on Mrs. Wyatt's shoulder.

Stepping back, she takes the bowl, returns it to the bag, and puts it in the carrying pouch hanging over her shoulder.

"Thank you," is all she says, her sobbing diminished. And she can tell from the expression in the old woman's eyes that for Mrs. Wyatt, those two words are quite enough expression of appreciation.

"You are most welcome. Now come on, Sunshine," Mrs. Wyatt says as she folds the blanket and places it back into the basket. "Let's get you back to your Granddad."

Oriana glances over her shoulder at the bolted door of the three hundred year old African Meeting House. She wonders how it would feel to walk in and sit where her mother sat. She considers what it might have been like to be among those who used this building regularly: an African American or Wampanoag school child perhaps, or a runaway slave seeking refuge, or perhaps a white minister to the island's brown, red, and black peoples. Loneliness envelops her as she thinks about the mother she never knew.

Mrs. Wyatt climbs onto the bike.

"Why do you use the title 'Mrs.'?" Oriana asks as she gets on behind, wrapping her arms around the old woman's waist. "It's so archaic. Mates don't use that term."

Mrs. Wyatt chuckles. "Oriana, I was never 'mated,' as you say. But long ago, I was married. Not here, though. I wasn't married on Nantucket."

"What do you mean? Where did you come from? How did you end up here?"

"I came from Martha's Vineyard, dear one. As to how I got to Nantucket, well, that's a conversation for another time and place."

MAMMAL

S ince Papa rendered her VISHNEW connection impossible to re-store, except for minimal communication options with other con-nected islanders and security implants in her gums and inner ear, Oriana's days consist mostly of spending time with Granddad, visiting his friends the Starbuck sisters in their home, and going under her Hood in search of Emmanuel and Papa. Even though she doubts that either Papa or Emmanuel has access to VISHNEW's network right now, she hopes that one day they will become connected to it. When they do, she wants them to find her waiting there for them.

She thinks of Emmanuel everyday, and wonders how he is, where he is, and whether he ever thinks about her. She can imag-ine no one else she'd rather have as her mate. Her father, too, is never far from her thoughts. She wonders how it is, after so many years, that she still feels anything for him at all and even cries her-self to sleep some nights.

Granddad is no substitute for Papa's company, yet she gen-erally enjoys being with him. Oriana finds, however, that at just over one hundred years old, he is aging in noticeable ways despite the enhancements and life extension treatments he receives. He is much crankier than he was even a few years ago, and at times rather mean-spirited, even belligerent.

The breaking point occurs on a day when Granddad and Oriana sit talking together at the kitchen table, eating pea soup and warm corn bread.

Granddad complains that she is spending too much time with him, and should instead be under her Hood having fun.

Oriana tells him that she is waiting to find companions who like her and want to be around her.

Granddad, putting a spoonful of soup into his mouth, calls her a stupid old cow and tells her she is being altogether ridiculous.

Oriana's feelings are hurt. Still, she never intends to tell him to go screw himself. When those words come out of her mouth, Granddad slams his spoon down into the bowl, spraying the hot, green liquid all over the table and his shirt.

"Granddad," Oriana pleads, wiping up the mess. "I'm so sorry. Forgive me."

He gets up from the table and walks away.

"What in the world are you doing, walking away from your supper like that?" she asks. "Come back here right now and finish your soup." Sometimes she can't help speaking to him as if he is a child, although she doesn't usually see him that way.

Her remarks agitate him even more.

"Don't go using that patronizing tone of voice with me," he shouts, bursting into a diatribe about lonely women who squander life, the many disguises of sexual frustration, and baby birds that are afraid to venture out of the nest.

The last part angers her, not because she is still living at home, but because it brings back the memory of the day she and Papa went to observe the newly hatched osprey, only to discover that it had no eyes. Even though that event happened years ago, the image of the mother bird leaving her baby behind is etched vividly in her mind.

"Granddad, I don't know what to say," she replies, following him into the hallway. "What is it that you expect of me?" Granddad turns his head in her direction and grumbles.

"You, my darling granddaughter, are becoming an old hag. Just look at you, already lonely at an age when women should be mated."

"Granddad," she whispers, "please don't."

"You gave up too soon, Ori. You should have been more social, and kept trying until you met someone under your Hood," he accuses. "Now all you do is watch people when you go under there."

How do you know what I do under there?

"You're too damn old to have never even been touched," Granddad continues.

I don't believe that's any of your business.

"It's time we did something about your frigidity!"

"What did you just say?" Oriana screams.

Granddad marches into his bedroom. "I'll fix this," he announces, slamming his bedroom door.

The old man is strangely quiet all day, barely saying a word to her. Until, that is, the household sensors alert that two people are climbing the steps to the front porch. Granddad yells to Oriana that she should answer the door. As she heads down the steps to the center hallway, he slips out the back door.

Oriana looks out the parlor window and discovers a delivery team from the specialty department of Makers Materials standing on the porch. "What is this?" she inquires as she opens the door.

The pair is holding a large rectangular carton.

"Excuse us," one says, passing her as the two head into the foyer and up the stairs. "The order instructs us to deliver this directly to your bedroom."

Oriana follows behind, intrigued. Once the delivery team has left, she shuts her bedroom door and hurries to unpack its contents.

"As I suspected," she says, grimacing as the carton's final fold falls down onto the floor. "Damn that insensitive old man." She knows exactly what it is.

Well, why not? It's not as if I haven't tried. What harm would it do? The men I've met under the Hood just aren't interested in me.

In fact, the few men she's identified as even the least bit interesting had cut off contact with her when they found out who she was.

"Are you the girl whose father trashed her VISHNEW connection?" one had asked.

"Aren't you the one with all those great eggs stored at TEMPLE?" said another.

One had actually said he wanted to 'get next to her' in person so he could 'run his hands over the body of a woman without a VISHNEW connection, just to see what would happen.'

She stares curiously at the face of the creature standing before her. "Oh my," she remarks, when its eyes open wide. She removes the bright red bow from its neck and tosses it onto the floor. Then she instructs, 'engage conversation,' and watches as the array embedded in its forehead lights up brightly in response. The object before her, humanoid in form, is the size of an average adult female. Its essence is rather primate. Smooth hair-like follicles cover its chest, arms, legs, and also its upper lip, cheeks and chin. Its eyes are deep and wide, larger than a human's, and strangely alluring. The robot cocks its head to one side. She's heard about these creatures, but has never seen one, and certainly never fantasized owning one.

"You must be Oriana, the offspring of Albert Rotch," it states matter-of-factly, using olfactory sensors to determine her identity. The machine seems to Oriana like an obnoxious kid showing off its VISHNEW-provided knowledge.

Oriana issues the command 'personalize.' The creature's voice changes from adolescent boy to adult male, the accent morphs from Rahway, New Jersey to Savannah, Georgia, and its speaking shifts from inarticulately rapid to moderate and well-enunciated. Its forehead flashes in colors of green and blue.

"That's me," Oriana affirms. "And who are you? Do you have a name?"

"I am whatever you want me to be. Why don't you name me yourself?" the life-like machine throws back. Its palms, she notices, are thick, very thick in fact, smooth, taut, and covered with something resembling skin. Wide-knuckled fingers accompany a long, opposable thumb. The being's fingernails, smooth, and oval, resemble acorns.

"Then I'll call you Mammal," she determines.

"And you're a virgin," it concludes, bluntly.

"That's a personal matter, don't you think?" she retorts.

"It's my responsibility to know my client," Mammal responds, offended. "Tell me, do you prefer women or men?"

"Well, I suppose that depends on the company," she returns with a smirk.

Oriana changes the mode to 'fine tune.' Curious, she adjusts the personality setting from 'Mischievously Social' to 'Dominant and Directive.'

"Take off your clothing. I want to see you naked," it barks, as if shouting directions to a disobedient dog. To Oriana's surprise, the prospect of submitting to the creature appeals to her.

"You want me to take off my clothing?"

"All of it. Every item, until all I see is your glistening skin. But do it slowly."

She turns her back on the gloating creature, her mind racing to justify continuing with this experience. *What would Papa say? Mama would be horrified. Damn that Granddad. He has some nerve sending this to me.*

"First your shirt. Unbutton it slowly and then take it off." Although her back is turned to it, Oriana obeys. "Now your bra. Unhook it and let it fall across your shoulders . . . now your skirt. Slide your fingers over your waist and under the edge, and pull it down over your hips . . ." The apparatus behind her moans, groans, and then grunts.

"Hold still for a moment," it continues. "Slip your fingers under the lace on your panties . . . hold there for a moment, sliding your fingers along your skin . . . now, pull your panties down and let them fall to the floor . . ."

I like the way Mammal looks at me. I like the way its nostrils flare when it speaks. Something about his scent appeals to me.

Oriana becomes aware of its pleasure, and of her own. A mounting desire disinhibits her and she feels surprisingly daring. But when she turns to face it, she suddenly feels embarrassed and ashamed.

"I think I want to stop right here," she asserts, continuing to remove her undergarments.

Mammal's eyes widen and its eyebrows lift. He gazes at her intently, processing the ambivalence of her request.

She opens her mouth to repeat her refusal, but hears herself say something else instead.

"Never mind. Let's go on." She can't seem to break the captivation, enraptured by the sensations in her pelvis.

I've gone this far already. What's the harm in seeing what happens next?

Oriana wonders whether she should continue playing the submissive or change to something new. She considers the full range of its mechanical possibilities and picks up the accompanying instructions.

"Put that down," it scolds.

"What?" Oriana questions. She looks directly into its eyes.

"You are to keep your head bowed and your eyes on the ground. Only after I give you permission to address me may you open your mouth to speak. And you are to refer to me only as 'Sir.'"

Oriana giggles nervously as she scrolls through the digital pages of the manual.

"Put it down now. I can answer any question you may have about how to use me."

Oriana stops, head down, her eyes focused on the wide pine boards of her bedroom floor. The hair-covered toes hold her attention. She stands still in obedience to the creature.

"You make speak now."

"If I may," she says softly, deciding to maintain its current setting, at least long enough to know if the domination will please her.

The creature nods in approval.

"What can you actually do? I mean, physically," Oriana inquires, lifting her gaze to its.

"You were not given permission to look at me," it scolds firmly. She has disobeyed it. She has forgotten the rules that quickly. The creature clears its throat.

"Forgive me, sir," she whispers, beginning to enjoy obeying his orders. Her gaze returns to the ground as she listens to his response.

"I am a personal attendant, and you are my sexual property. I know exactly what it is that you desire." The creature speaks with confidence and authority. "You will be bound and collared."

Oriana's fantasy is broken. "The hell I will," she scoffs, and adjusts the controls to modify the relationship. Mammal's voice becomes polite and unassuming.

"My dear Oriana, may I presume to suggest some ways in which I might provide you service?"

"Never mind, wrong direction," she retreats, not knowing what she wants from it, or for herself, for that matter, mostly frustrated over the pitiful state of her lonely life. Oriana has never had a sexual or even a social life, and somehow she doubts she ever will. She turns the knob to the setting 'Mysteriously Jungian.' She has no idea what that means.

Look at me, she laments as she faces the mirror above her dresser. *How did my life come to this?*

"Tell me what you see," Mammal says, moving close behind her. She stares at its image reflected in the mirror, a dark figure barely taller than her. The upturned mouth and wide eyes suggest a desire to please and to be helpful, but the soothing intensity of its voice is baffling and a bit disturbing.

"What do you mean, 'What I see?'" she inquires.

It places an unexpectedly warm hand on her shoulder.

"Hmm," it says, looking along with her at their reflection in the mirror, "I see a beautiful feminine body, Eve-like, a shapely full curvature, powerful and alluring. Perhaps you see something different? Or imagine something other than what you see, like perhaps a phallus at your pelvis, erect, powerful, and potent?"

"That's repulsive," Oriana replies, feeling excessively exposed. She steps aside.

"You're weird," she declares, turning to face it directly. She pokes an index finger at its chest saying, "Back away from me."

The creature looks at her intently, its pupils constricting to small black dots against the widening whites. She feels helpless, and yet oddly comforted by its presence. Intrigued, she wants to know more.

Oriana glances nonchalantly at its crotch, not wanting it to catch her looking. "Let's turn down the lights," Mammal suggests as it adjusts the ambience controls of her room. Her study of Mammal interrupted by the dimming of the lights, she is unable to make out further features of its anatomy.

The personal attendant moves across the room, sitting down on the cushioned window seat. Bathed in the moonlight that dances over its form, its shadowy semblance seems almost human. Its wide, round eyes gaze back at her longingly, and it extends its hand to her.

She takes a few tentative steps forward.

Mammal takes hold of her wrist and pulls Oriana close, gently and without hesitation. It guides her down onto its lap. Her bare bottom sinks into its soft, warm hair.

She grows more uncomfortable with each caress. A yet-to-be-deflowered woman, she wonders over the full meaning of 'personal attendant.'

"I have a story to tell you," the creature speaks softly into her ear. "It is a mythic adventure of lust, heroics, and deceit which features you, lovely woman, as a damsel in distress."

Oriana relaxes into Mammal's embrace, enthralled with her vulnerable role in the tale. She settles into the comfort of its lap, enraptured by the detail in its storytelling, soothed by the calm of its deep, melodic voice.

When it gets to the part where a grimy witch ties Oriana naked to a stake, builds a fire around her feet, and begins to prod her genitals with the head of a snake. Oriana squirms. "No way. That's enough for me." Only then does she realize that a rigid probe is gradually penetrating her. Its movements are steady and searching as it slips through the opening of her vagina. She writhes in delight and disgust.

Mammal tightens its hold around her waist. "What would you like? I can make myself wider, or go deeper into you," it offers.

Oriana is horrified, yet gripped with a pleasure from which she does not wish to be released. Held firm in Mammal's embrace, she closes her eyes tightly. Hiding herself inside of herself, she hears her own voice request that Mammal use its own judgment in determining what would most please her.

"What I can do," it replies, "is help you to figure that out for yourself." The probe continues its rhythmic pulse. Mammal's head leans back, its eyes drifting lazily along the curves of her body, as it gauges what else she may desire. When it senses she has released and is subdued, the robot deflates the probe.

Oriana shudders as a warm liquid oozes down from between her thighs, and she revels in the strange bliss of having given herself over for the very first time, her virginity claimed by a bizarre and hideously enticing creature. For a few moments Oriana sleeps deeply, relaxed in Mammal's tender embrace. And then she awakens into a quiet rage.

She stands, walking calmly to the pharmaceutical cabinet on her wall. From it she takes a cloth and dries herself, and then pumps mists of silver nitrate spray over her crotch and thighs.

"No need for that, darling," Mammal says softly. "I'm totally clean."

Ignoring it, she quietly dresses herself, and then remotely disconnects the personal attendant from its power source. It slumps forward, head over chest, back hunched into a curve. Its arms dangle at its sides. Oriana stands motionless in the dim stillness of her bedroom until the fury explodes in her skull, racking her entire body.

With both hands, she shoves mammal off of the window seat, and the limp creature falls to the floor with a hard thump. She shrieks and curses, waving her arms wildly above her head until she collapses with exhaustion, sobbing. She presses her forehead and nose against the beveled glass and looks out onto the quiet emptiness of Broad Street below. Islanders observing under their Hoods shudder over the emotional display.

"Why did *it* have to be my first?" she cries in despair, speaking out loud without realizing it.

"And why are you so upset?" a female voice sounds over her bedroom speakers.

"Oh crap, who are you?" Oriana ask of the disembodied voice.

"I've been watching you all afternoon. How beautiful and what fun!" A holograph of a woman of considerable age forms in the center of the room. Her white hair hangs long and straight over her shoulders. Her face beams with a frisky expression, her bold brown eyes alight and glistening.

"Did you not enjoy that?"

"Damn it," Oriana curses as she checks the panel set into her wall. Her room is registering 'multi-viewing visibility and sound.' She holds her head in her hands and shakes it back and forth in disbelief.

"How many others are watching?!"

"Don't be embarrassed," the woman returns. "Lots of women on the island have personal attendants. I wish I did myself. In fact, the woman who lives right next door to you has one, too. Only, she prefers to program hers to have a female form."

Oriana is speechless. She had no idea robots were so popular, and it never occurred to her that her sex life would be a source of such entertainment for others.

"So this is how you get off, going under your Hood to watch me in my bedroom?"

"You know, Oriana," the woman explains, "even the women of 18th century Nantucket got lonely sometimes, very lonely. Their men were gone to sea for many months, even years, at a time. Maybe you don't know about this. They, too, had ways of mechanically pleasing themselves. It's a natural thing to do."

"That's not the point," Oriana retorts. "The point is that nothing can replace the genuine companionship that the human heart longs for, wouldn't you agree?"

"No, I would not agree, because that is not what we are talking about here, Oriana. What we are talking about is a fundamental physical need. We are humans with hearts, yes, but we also have bodies that long to be stimulated and caressed. For human beings, sexual release is a physical need. That is a simple matter of fact.

"Why would you want to deny this essential part of yourself? Maybe you think you are a bit better than everyone else, or just different because you were raised as an independent? The fact is that all of us, connects and also independents alike, have bodily needs."

Oriana takes a moment to consider this assertion, trying to believe enough of it to absolve herself of the guilt she feels. Her mind turns to a memory of Emmanuel and the last time she saw him. His eyes were a bottomless blue bliss of delight, and his adolescent body aroused hers. She remembers the way he teased and played with her, the comforting sound of his voice reciting the TEMPLE chant, and the cheerful radiance of his face when he looked at her from under his Hood.

Emmanuel, where are you? Why does it have to be this way?

"Well," Oriana concludes, her focus back on the interloper, "I am sure that what you say has a kernel of truth. As for me, I had rather my first time been with a human being, someone that I actually care about." With that she swipes the panel to the most limited access setting, 'visibility only.' The woman's form immediately disappears.

Hearing Granddad open the front porch door, Oriana turns on the house speakers and raises her voice.

"For this, my dear Granddad," she says, the words carried into every room, "I will never, ever forgive you!"

INTERLUDE

Oriana awakens from a dream without images, only the rhythmic, pleading moan of a woman in fear and distress.

"Oriana! Oriana! Oriana!"

Just as well, she thinks, since this restless sleep can do nothing to restore her. The voice grows louder, and she notices it is coming not from inside her head but from somewhere in the room.

"Oriana! Oriana! Oriana!" The quiet is disturbed by the persistence of the cry.

"Hello?" Is someone here?" Oriana asks. She receives no reply. Groggy and disoriented, she sits upright, rubbing her hand over her shoulder until the blood returns to the tingling arm. In a daze, she strains to rise, and the child in her womb sinks further towards its opening to the outside world. The whitewashed walls of the Meeting House appear to shift from two dimensions to three, the wooden benches shimmering as if engulfed in waves of heat. Darkness has deepened, and the objects in the room are now shadowy silhouettes. The moon, beginning its descent towards the horizon, has withdrawn its illumination of the ceiling and walls.

Oriana steps slowly and deliberately to the front of the stark room, holding onto the edge of each pew, careful not to bump into them. When she reaches the facing bench, she stops, remembering that this is where the esteemed Quakers elders would sit. She imagines herself as one of them, three hundred years ago, delivering a Spirit-moved message:

"It is my distinct responsibility," she hears herself utter, "as an elder of this Meeting, to hold up the Light as it moves in me, and to speak out on an occasion such as this. Our Meeting is faced with a terribly weighty decision about what should be done with this former slave girl, Sadie Lee, who has chosen to marry a Man of the World."

Here Oriana languishes, lost in her imagination, unaware of the flow of fluid trickling down the inside of her thighs, or of the faint figure hovering over her head.

GOODBYE

Rocking forward and back, forward and back, Oriana glides on the front porch couch. With one foot tucked under her thigh, and the other pushing against the porch floor, the force of her effort provides a smooth, steady motion. She slouches, her head just high enough to see up, down, and across Broad Street. All is silent and still. Her mind drifts aimlessly from one thought to another.

These cobblestones of Broad Street are wearing away. What happened to the stone that was once there? Did it dissipate into the air? Or did it get packed down, so that the molecules themselves are closer together, but still there . . .

The bump on the end of my tongue is annoying . . .

Getting stung by a bee must really hurt. What does a bee actually look like? I like to eat honey, though Papa says ours isn't real . . .

I hope the beds in the Facility are comfortable. Papa's back gets so sore . . .

Did Grandma fall in love with Granddad, or was their union obligatory? I wonder if she would have liked me . . .

The moonless sky is nearly black. Former storefronts, a few houses, and the flat gray stones of the road are barely visible under the dim street lamps. Drying leaves, orange, yellow and maroon in the light of day, but black now to Oriana's eyes, rustle softly in the autumn night.

"Oriana!" calls a voice from an approaching figure. *How did I not see anyone coming in this direction?* Oriana sits upright, placing both feet down flat. Her mind races with confusion and delight, and she hardly dares to hope for something she fears may not be. *But who else could be coming?*

"Emmanuel?" she replies as his piercing blue eyes appear out of the blackness, illuminated by the light from a nearby lamppost.

"It's me," he offers weakly.

The tall figure climbs up the steps and onto the porch, and takes a seat by Oriana's side. It is really Emmanuel, though Oriana can scarcely believe it, sitting right beside her in the flesh. A tear comes to her eye as his hand touches hers. She can hardly speak.

"I'm so happy to see you, Oriana." Emmanuel speaks, ever so gently. He wraps his arm around her shoulder and pulls her against his chest. She leans into his embrace, breathing in the musky, familiar scent. Several minutes pass before either says a word.

"Where have you been, Emmanuel?" Oriana asks. He strokes her hair, and kisses the top of her head.

"They kept me locked inside, with no access to my Hood."

"Inside where?"

"The Facility."

"Emmanuel, what are you saying? I don't understand."

"It got really ugly between mother and me. My parents kept me inside the house, as if I were a criminal, with no access to any other people or to the outside world. They told me it was for my own good, that I'd be horribly mistreated and misunderstood out here. When I was finally disconnected entirely from VISHNEW, my mind exploded.

"I barely knew who I was anymore. I would lose control of my words and of my hands, hurting myself and fighting mother wildly. So my father escorted me from our home to the Facility. It was the middle of the night, and he gave me no explanation at all. He didn't tell me where we were going until I was all the way inside, and then he said goodbye. I have been inside ever since. For almost seven years I've been there, until today."

"So that explains why I couldn't find you," Oriana replies. "I thought it was because of me, that I had done something to offend you or was no longer significant to you." Oriana smiles at his glance of reassurance, her eyes alight with possibilities, as the realization dawns that she is not as unworthy as she feared.

"And now you're free and an independent like me!"

"In that way, yes, I am like you."

"Can you tell me anything about Papa?"

"I saw him shortly after I arrived. He asked about you. We talked about you whenever we were together."

"In what way were you two together?" Oriana asks.

"During treatment," Emmanuel explains.

"What's that?"

"I'd rather not talk about it," Emmanuel states.

Oriana lays her head on Emmanuel's shoulder. Tenderly and carefully, she strokes his cheek.

"Is Papa alive still?" she asks him.

"As far as I know, yes. The last time I saw him, though, they had him under long-term sedation."

"But why?'

"To ease his suffering and to increase their control over him. They maintain him in a satisfied state, feeding pleasant dreams into his brain."

"I am so confused."

"He asked me to tell you to wait here for him."

"Here at Granddad's house? Where else would I go? What else would I do?"

"He asked you to wait here on Nantucket until he is released and can take you off the island," Emmanuel relays.

"I think Papa is confused. No one leaves this island. He knows that perfectly well."

Emmanuel kisses her forehead. "You've been on my mind," he breathes into her ear, his kiss lingering on her earlobe. An undulating wave, unfamiliar to Oriana, moves from her navel to a place deep inside her womb.

"I came to tell you goodbye," Emmanuel says in a faint voice. Oriana has to ask him to repeat what he's said. "Now that I am out, I have to go somewhere else, away from my parents, and this island, and VISHNEW."

Oriana lurches backwards, grabbing her thighs. Feelings she never realized she had for him rush to the surface of her heart, crowding into her throat, bursting forth as a shriek.

"No! No one leaves. And if they do, they can never come back again. Everyone on Nantucket knows this."

"There are certain things you don't know."

"Things? What things?" Oriana queries.

"Not now, Oriana. I'm preoccupied with the fact that I have to leave here in the morning," Emmanuel explains.

Tears stream down her cheeks and under her chin. She folds her arms across her chest. Emmanuel kisses her wet face once, then again, and again.

"Please, don't go," she whispers. "You're the only friend I have, and now I realize probably the only boyfriend I'll ever have, Emmanuel. I thought I'd lost you forever. Now you've come back, just to say goodbye? That's so mean. Why didn't you simply leave? Why bother coming to me like this?"

"Because of our connection, that's why."

"Connection? I'm not connected to VISHNEW anymore, except very minimally."

"VISHNEW has nothing to do with our connection, Oriana. I've always been with you, ever since we were kids, since the day we went together to the tree. Even in the Facility, I was never gone from you. I just couldn't reach you. I could watch you, though. I had Hood privileges, but for observation only.

"Every day I watched you eat your meals, talk with your grandfather, bathe your beautiful body, put on your clothing, and drink hot tea in the afternoon. I didn't know what it meant back then, but from the time we sat on the front steps of your father's house drinking lemonade, I felt what I now know to be love. Maybe the only reason I loved you then was because I didn't have any other friends. But now, you're the woman of my deepest desires, Oriana. I came back to let you know that I love you."

Oriana gasps.

"Maybe you're right," Emmanuel continues, stroking her cheek with his fingers. "Maybe it's selfish part of me, but I couldn't leave without seeing you and letting you know how I feel."

Oriana, feeling the smooth skin of his palm on her face, takes Emmanuel's hand into hers and studies it carefully. She places her palms against his.

"You're right about us. Now it's we who are connected."

She leans in closer, looking into his eyes. This is not the Emmanuel she once knew, not the withdrawn boy whose voice was crippled when he was in his mother's presence, not the arrogant youth who mocked her lack of VISHNEW-enhanced faculties. This is a mature man with a clear head, a strong voice, and soft lips, a VISHNEW-independent like herself.

Oriana's brow begins to perspire. Her thigh and stomach muscles tighten as a wave of awareness washes over her brain, sinking into her lungs. Her breathing increases.

"Wow, geez, oh my goodness . . ." she says as she struggles to identify her feelings. Emmanuel pulls her to his chest, stroking her hair with his fingertips. Now she knows how he feels. Agony pushes down hard on her gut.

"I am so alone," she confesses. "Granddad is here, and he takes good care of me. But the inside of me is like a dark cave filled with a motionless body of cold water. I feel as if I am inside it, standing on a thin ledge. At any moment it will crack, and I'll fall in and drown, and no one will be able to save me." Emmanuel strokes her cheek, wiping away a single tear.

"I try to be strong," she continues, "for Granddad, so he won't worry about me, and because I can't disappoint Mama, even though she's never even known me. The least I can do for her is be grateful and content, and to live as though life matters to me."

Emmanuel stands, pacing the porch without a word. Then he stops and turns toward Oriana.

"I was a fright in my parents' eyes, a genetic mistake. They looked at me in disgust, seeing only their own disappointment. Losing their trust in VISHNEW, they turned against me instead of against the actual cause of their anger. Do you want to know how I feel? Like an unretrieved fetus imprisoned in an inhospitable womb."

Oriana jumps to her feet. She wraps her arms around Emmanuel's shoulders, pulling his body against hers, thinking that if she holds him tight enough, perhaps they can fold one body into the other and meld their insides so that neither will feel so isolated.

"Let's go for a walk," Emmanuel suggests. "To someplace we can be alone."

"Where would that be? It's not even possible," Oriana insists. "Every place on this island, within the borders at least, is completely VISHNEW-connected. Anyone can see us at any time."

"Not quite," he corrects. Emmanuel steps off the porch, illuminated by a wrought-iron lamp at the curb. Oriana follows. He picks up a stick and scratches onto the cobblestones in very small letters, as she watches. 'Friends Meeting House, 11 pm,' he writes, then smears the words out with his shoe.

"See you there, ok?" he says, and walks away.

Granddad tells her goodnight at about 10 pm. When he is clearly asleep, she heads out the door. Fearful, she walks to #7 Fair Street to meet Emmanuel. But once there, shielded within the unconnected meetinghouse from prying eyes, the two affirm their passion for each other. For the first time, the pangs of love stir, churn, and warm the deep well within her.

Returning to Granddad's house and settling onto bed, Oriana finds every cell in her body infused with a joyful alertness, the lingering sensations of her physical union with Emmanuel; sleep eludes her. The tenderness of his hands as he placed her on the Meeting House bench, the gentle strength of his arms under her back as he entered her welcoming loins, are still with her. But her mind, the merciless torturer, reminds her with unrelenting persistence that his touch, his love, is something she can never hold. Emmanuel is leaving Nantucket. Now, the fragile cliff breaks.

At 3:00 am, a ringing sounds from the receiver implanted in her ears.

"Can you hear me, Oriana?"

"Is that you, Emmanuel?"

"I am at my parent's house gathering up some of my belongings. My Hood is working for me. Can you get under yours right now?"

She moves stealthily down the staircase and into the parlor where her Hood is installed. Once inside the visualization program, she adorns herself with a flowing gown and the majestic head wrapping of an elegant Somalia princess.

"I'm glad you came," Emmanuel remarks. He switches from a 1980's pinstriped business suit to the tights, boots, and gown of a Russian prince. They go into a North African desert palace and are entertained by live musicians, magicians, poets, and tribal dancers.

"One more fantasy, okay?" Oriana requests. "I just can't bring myself to say goodbye again, at least not yet."

A moment later, Emmanuel re-appears wearing vintage 1960's bell-bottom blue jeans. Reddish-blond locks emerge from under a tie-dyed bandana and lie long and thick against his shoulders.

Oriana wears handmade silk dance attire from 16th century Persia, her face partially obscured under a sheer red cloth, her feet and hands covered in jewels. Emmanuel finds her hauntingly beautiful, and alluring beyond words. This time they stay close to home, sailing a small sloop along the Charles River.

"It's time for me to leave now," Emmanuel says. He pulls up the rigging, and the scene begins to fade.

"No, not now," Oriana pleads. "Just one more, and then I promise I'll let you go." Emmanuel agrees to one more fantasy when she agrees that it will be the last.

For their final encounter under the Hood in the predawn hours of the morning that Emmanuel will leave Nantucket, and in a completely un-orchestrated coincidence, they both re-enter the program as white wolves. When she spots Emmanuel in his male wolf form, Oriana the she-wolf takes off running into the scenery that forms in her mind. The program responds immediately. Emmanuel's imagination adds a surging river, a flower-covered meadow, and a densely overcast sky.

The male wolf chases her over the meadow, across a stream, and into a deep forest, until he finally corners her at the entrance to a dark cave. She runs inside, only to find herself facing a wall of stone. Swiftly, from behind, Emmanuel mounts his mate.

When he releases her, Oriana turns and backs out, her howls bouncing against the walls of the dripping cave. Emmanuel follows her out to a clearing under the trees, his canine cries echoing into the forest. They say their final goodbyes.

THE MATCH

Oriana waits in the foyer with anticipation, anxious even before the house signals the man's approach. Emmanuel is gone, and she must move on. She knows he will never be allowed to return to the island. Perhaps, when Papa gets out of the Facility, he'll take her to find Emmanuel. Of course, this is not very likely. Granddad has issued an ultimatum: Oriana must find a mate, as he will no longer provide her a home with him on Broad Street. Other than the suitor she expects momentarily, who seems genuinely interested in getting to know her in person, she has no other options.

Connor Murphy arrives seven minutes before she expects him.

"Such a stunning woman as you could only be Oriana Rotch," Connor says when the front door opens. His hazel eyes twinkle as he places a bouquet of sunflowers in Oriana's hands.

"Wow," she says, smiling at the gold and orange blossoms. "How did you know?"

Connor's pursed lips break into a playful grin.

"These are amazing," she says, delighted. She blushes.

"Who's that out there?" Granddad calls from the rear of the house. He knows very well who it is.

"Come inside, Connor. It's chilly out there," Oriana says, taking his arm and leading him into the parlor.

Conner takes inventory of the sparsely furnished room. An oval blue and gold braided rug, a ladder-back pine rocker, and a small square end table sit inside the broad bay window on the side of the room that looks out on the street. A side chair and footstool flank the fireplace, another braided rug underneath them. Hanging over the couch he sees a wide, pine mirror flanked by antique gas lanterns. Yellowing wallpaper, curling at the edges, sports a nautical motif of ships bows and billowing sails. The furnishings, not much different than they might have been a hundred years ago, belie the sophistication of the embedded sensors, cameras, speakers, and probes hidden throughout the room.

Oriana places her hand on Conner's elbow and escorts him to the couch. His skin, covered with fine strawberry-blond hair, feels soft to her touch. His eyes are cornflower blue and round, with curled lashes that enhance their sparkle. Red ringlets, parted on one side, hang just below his ears.

Connor smiles as his glance moves from her face to the form-fitting dress that reveals the curvature of her breasts, hips, and waist. He looks pleased.

"I take it this is the young man who is interested in the most fertile gal on the whole island!" Granddad exclaims, stepping through the French doors and into the parlor.

Connor turns to greet him with an outstretched hand. Granddad fails to return the gesture. Instead, his fingers comb the white strands of his beard, his eyes fixed on Connor's face.

"Mr. Rotch, I presume," Connor offers. "How ya' doin, sir?"

"You're a lot older than I expected," Granddad replies.

"Granddad, meet Connor," says Oriana.

"Well, I suppose you'll do," Granddad barks. "It's about god-damned time you showed up. What took you so long?" With that, he takes his leave as abruptly as he came in.

"Don't pay any attention to him," Oriana advises Connor as she closes the doors behind Granddad. Connor takes a handkerchief from his pocket and wipes away droplets of perspiration from his brow. He despises it when people comment on his looks. He has done all he can about the appearance of his aging, but the treatments don't work well on thin skin. Furthermore, his receding hairline is a genetic trait that cannot be altered due to its dominance.

Oriana doesn't care about these characteristics. She finds Conner attractive enough, and his bright-eyed feistiness and steady gaze appeal to her.

Connor steps across the room toward the framed images perched along the mantle.

"You've kept printed photographs? Geez, why would you do that?"

"My grandfather likes having them around, and that he can pick them up in his hands," Oriana returns. "They were made specially for him a long time ago."

"Who is that gorgeous woman?" Connor asks, pointing to one of the pictures and stroking his chin with intrigue. Oriana is pleased that he has noticed the picture, although his brashness is off-putting.

"That's Mama. Everyone always says how pretty she was."

"Was? No treatments to maintain her beauty?"

"Something like that. May I offer you a mug of hot cider?" she asks, moving away from the subject of her mother. "The apple pulp was freshly reconstituted this morning."

"Smells great," he says. "Thank you."

As he takes the mug into both hands, Oriana's ambivalence warms to willing curiosity. He seems nice enough, and respectful. They sit down together on the couch.

"I have to tell you, Oriana, that you're even more beautiful in person than in the holograph!"

Connor proceeds to explain to Oriana that he insisted each and every one of his mating criteria be met. He does not want a woman with mental anomalies. High intelligence is critically important. Her skin color is unimportant to him, but he requires certain body proportions. A strong woman with a narrow waist but with wide hips for in-utero childbearing is ideal, and these are qualities Oriana possesses. And he certainly prefers that his mate still have her original organs and most of her original skin.

His smiling eyes and broad grin give way to a mischievous chuckle.

"We could have a great time together," he says, raising an eyebrow. Oriana looks away in embarrassment.

What am I doing? This is a nightmare. How can this be happening?

Connor puts down the mug and reaches for Oriana's hair, pulling a cluster of curls to his nostrils.

"So gorgeous you are," he says, allowing the locks to slip through his fingers as Oriana relaxes her back against the couch.

"That's velvet you're sittin' on ya' know, not the fake foundry stuff. I'm telling ya, it's the real thing! So try not to mess it up, would ya?" Granddad yells over the house speakers. Apparently he's been watching from under his Hood.

Oriana stands up and adjusts the settings on the control panel from two- to one-way.

"As I said, it's best we ignore him," she reminds the man who is now grimacing beside her. "He's sweeter than caramel and grumpier than a whaler gone a month without a catch."

Connor sinks further into the softness of the down cushions.

"What do I care if he hears us or not? I have nothing to hide from anyone," Connor exclaims.

Oriana tells him she'll be right back, and then leaves the room. After a brief, quiet confrontation with Granddad about his behavior, she returns with a plate of warm oatmeal raisin cookies made with Foundry-fresh walnuts. Connor eagerly bites into one, speaking confidently with his mouth half full.

"The old man should be grateful I'm willing to take you off his hands."

Oriana's stomach tightens. She's not sure if this is a criticism of her or a roundabout offer to be her mate.

And you should be grateful to be here at all. It's not as if I need a mate. What I need is a place to live and some means of support, since independents are no longer hirable on the island.

"I will introduce you and Granddad properly as soon as he's accepted you a little more," Oriana offers. "He's pretty attached to me, despite what he says about it being time for me to 'get a mate and get out.'"

"Call me old-fashioned," Connor says to Oriana as he finishes the cookie, "but the most important mating criteria of all to me is that I will be your first. Can you confirm that?"

Oriana feels no obligation to provide Connor with her sexual history.

I'll confirm nothing of the sort.

Connor takes Oriana's hands into his, waiting for an answer to his question. Oriana holds her breath, uncertain what his reaction will be. He looks down at her palms.

"Oh my," he says, gasping. "You have no VISHNEW markings."

What can she say? After what Papa did, the neurological damage was too extensive for the technicians to make a full repair.

"I assumed you knew."

"I've never met an independent before," Connor gawks. He pushes Oriana's hair back to expose the skin of her temples and sees the scars at the original VISHNEW connection sites.

"I had heard there were a few remaining on the island. I was not expecting that you would be one of them."

"I still have some access, you know," she says, placing one of her hands on his.

"Oh?" he questions. "By all means, tell me about yourself." He reaches for a second cookie.

Oriana notices that he smacks his lips as he chews, and the sight and sound makes her cringe. She also notices that, while he's attractive enough, nothing about Connor Murphy appeals strongly to her. She wishes she felt even a little bit of excitement or intrigue.

"Well," she replies, trying to ignore the smacking, "I was raised mostly by my father. We live up in an old place at the top of Copper Lane."

"Not anymore, I don't think," Connor interjects.

"I did live there," she returns. "I still consider it my home. No one lives there now. When Papa left, and I moved here to Broad Street with Granddad . . ."

"After your Papa's internment in the Facility, you mean."

She pretends not to hear the remark.

"I'd sort of like to go back to Copper Lane, you know, to fix it up and live there. Maybe someday," she continues.

Granddad has never mentioned anything about her original home, the one where Mama and Papa lived before Mama died, and where Oriana lived with Papa until the day they went to the beach for a swim to celebrate her Retrieval Day.

On the day that she was discharged from the Critical Care Unit, she and Granddad drove past Copper Lane before heading for his house. She asked him when she'd be able to return to her home. He told her to forget that she ever lived there, that her home was with him now. He has said nothing about it since.

"I have a surprise for you," Connor exclaims.

"Oh?"

"It's mine now. Soon it will be ours."

"What will be ours?"

"Your old house, girl. I bought it, the one at the end of Copper Lane." A clump of cookie falls from the corner of his mouth. Oriana brushes it off of the couch.

"What are you talking about?" she asks, more annoyed than surprised.

"Isn't it great? We can go live there as mates!"

Oriana wants to say something appreciative, because Connor seems so pleased with himself, but she is in shock. She did not know that her childhood home was even on the market, and now she wonders where Papa will live when they release him from the Facility. She feels loss over the realization that she will never be able to live there with her father again, and despair at the thought of living next door to the place that was once home to Emmanuel.

"Well," she manages to say, "that was very thoughtful of you."

"I noticed there's an old flower garden at the house," he continues excitedly. "It needs some fixing up. It could be a sweet spot. Do you remember it from when you lived there?"

"Yes, there is a flower garden," Oriana repeats. "That was Mama's garden."

Connor leans toward her, placing his lips against her forehead, his arms around her back. It feels nothing like the touch of Emmanuel, or the sweetness of his embrace. It feels more like being possessed.

Connor leans back.

"When I requested a detailed report on your puberty extraction, there were not as many superior eggs as were originally predicted. However, I'm still pleased with the overall status of your fertility. I'm prepared to take you as my mate. I am asking for your decision."

I still have a choice about this, despite what Granddad says. Can I find a way to take care of myself, to earn my own living, to live on my own despite being an independent? My eggs and the fertility they make possible are not who I am, but are only a means to an end. Right?

"Oh my! I don't know what to say," Oriana replies.

"Then take a moment to give it some thought," he offers. "That will give us a chance to get our secrets out on the table. If you're concealing any insidious feelings or acts, they will fester into ugliness and spoil the integrity of our companionship."

"Insidious? You're kidding, right?" Oriana wonders where he got the idea. It sounds like a line from an old film.

"Nope, not kidding. Now, what do you have to tell me?" he asks earnestly, his lips forming a tight broad line across his wide jaw.

Wanting to share openly with Connor, Oriana tells him about what her father did, why he is no longer in her life, and how much she misses him. And although she does not consider it a secret, she also tells him that she feels responsible for her mother's expiration.

Connor questions her about whether it was actually Oriana's retrieval that led to the tragic loss of her mother, or if something else may have caused her death, and then vows to look into the matter. He says he wants to get all the facts straight so that Oriana can be freed of the guilt that could come from possible misinformation. Moreover, he tells her, he wants to assuage any fears she might have about VISHNEW's protocol for pregnancy.

Oriana also tells him about how she'd been schooled for a while under her Hood, just like everyone else, until the disconnection to VISHNEW disrupted the transmissions of knowledge. She explains to him that she had been excited about learning, but then had to go back to her childhood tutors, the Starbuck sisters.

"Thank you for sharing. Are you ready to hear my secrets?" Connor offers in return.

"Fire away," Oriana replies, withholding the biggest secret of all, her love for a man she will never see again. She knows she will have to put aside her feelings for Emmanuel if she is to mate with Connor.

Connor shares that he was conceived and gestated ex-utero, the product of the donated ovum of an Irish woman and the sperm of a Scottish man, gametes that were selected for their robustness and other excellent qualities. His genetic mother, he explains, is unknown to anyone besides the TEMPLE technician who catalogued the extracted her eggs.

"Is she still alive?" Oriana wants to know.

"It doesn't matter to me if she is or isn't. The two men who raised me are the only parents I have ever known."

"So one thing we have in common is that neither of us knew our mother," Oriana offers.

"Well, I wouldn't exactly call the donor my mother. As far as I'm concerned I never had a mother, Oriana. You did."

Oriana feels sorry for him in spite of herself. Or perhaps it's herself she pities. She had a mother, it's true, one who carried her and wanted more than anything to know her.

"So, is there anything else you want to tell me?" she asks. "Something . . . insidious, perhaps?"

Without hesitation, Connor tells her in detail about his sexual exploits under his Hood, with men and women and with other creatures. Oriana imagines the various scenarios as he speaks: Connor running naked with a man up the slope of an active volcano in Guatemala; Connor copulating in a mud bath with a youth-restored woman triple his age; Connor mounting a bottle-nosed dolphin in waters where Harbor Island, Bahamas used to be.

I can't even imagine what it would be like to live with someone like this.
Connor pauses.

"Has hearing about my experiences spoiled your attraction to me? Am I weird to you now?" he asks.

Not really. What attraction? I haven't yet felt an attraction.

Caught up in the spirit of mutual sharing, Oriana almost mentions Mammal, and then catches herself, thinking it better to keep quiet about it.

It was a private matter, an unnecessary detail of my life that he has no need to know. I hope that he wasn't watching me from under his Hood when Mammal was in my bedroom.

"No, please, tell me more," she replies, trying to determine what she actually feels about him. As he continues to recount his sexual adventures, Oriana finds that her muscles relax, her strained breath eases. His concern seems genuine. His voice is light and energetic.

"I will take good care of you, Oriana. There's nothing for you or your grandfather to worry about. With me you will have a good home and the care and support of a mate who wants only your well-being."

Not to mention my robust eggs.

"We will have incredible offspring, talented, attractive and smart, ideal in every way.

Clearly a major motive in all of this.

"Of course, first we'll need to get you reconnected to VISHEW, at least partially, you know, whatever they are able to do so you'll have the benefits of full health and safety throughout pregnancy. Cost is not a factor. To me you are worth every penny it takes."

He's actually sort of appealing.

Connor reaches for Oriana's neck and slides his hand down to the center of her chest. His touch is tender, and he radiates a soft yet commanding quality that reassures her. Her heart opens a little bit.

"Yes, Connor. I will."

She accepts his offer of mate-hood. Loneliness is a powerful motivator.

Oriana goes to the kitchen to tell Granddad about the proposal and finds him sitting in the dark, mumbling to his long-dead mate.

"I did the best I could, ya know. Ma, try to understand. The girl has no mother. She barely has a father. What else was I supposed to do? Seeing as how her life was going nowhere, and she'd given up on herself, the poor girl didn't stand a chance of finding a mate on her own. They'd have put all her eggs on the market if I didn't do something soon. And besides, I won't be around too much longer. Who will take care of her when I am gone? I didn't mean any harm, Ma. Tell me, what else was I to do?"

The ceremony is simple and quick. Oriana and Connor go together under his Hood and stand upon a lovely scalloped beach at dawn. A golden sun rises in the blue sky as soft warm breezes blow. Oriana wears her mother's gown, Connor a white tuxedo. Granddad is there along with the Starbuck sisters and a few of Connor's friends to witness the event. Oriana would have liked to invite Mrs. Wyatt, but the old woman doesn't use a Hood. The pair exchanges the conventional vows:

"We agree to mate, and then to procreate."

CONCEPTION

Oriana and Connor wind their way through the stark white corridors of the Laboratory for Controlled Conception. He is excited and intent, and she finds herself moving from ambivalence to acceptance. The pair takes a seat in the waiting room. Connor chatters on about nothing of importance, while Oriana listens for their names to be called.

Two holographic forms float towards them. Connor chuckles with delight, clapping his hands together and cheering. To Oriana, the images are haunting: one is a man with round blue eyes who looks a lot like Connor, and the other a woman, the image of Oriana, holding a bald, hazel-eyed baby boy.

"Go away and leave me alone," she exclaims, throwing her hands in the air.

The image fades into a smoky haze. She closes her eyes, placing her face in cupped hands.

"Well, come on already," Connor says after the receptionist requests their iris signatures for the procedure. Oriana goes first, placing her nose at the designated point between the lenses.

"To the left, please," the clerk instructs. "Try to get the cylinders evenly spaced over both eyes."

When the couple has finished the identification process, the clerk registers their obligation to adhere to the VISHNEW pregnancy protocol.

"Hi, I'm El," greets a lanky techno-medical assistant, whose parents apparently opted for their progeny to be intersexed. "I'll be assisting you with the procedure today."

Connor appears to take great interest in El. He's seen a few such intersexuals before, so he's not at all surprised, though he can't help wonder what has been done about the genitals.

With a flat chest, slight facial hair, firm belly, and rounded buttocks and hips, the body offers no clear indication of a particular gender, and the voice, pitched within a mid-range octave, provides no further clue.

"The first phase of conception involves documentation of your genetic markers," El says as they follow him/her into the implantation room. "Next comes the implantation of your selected eggs, fertilized with the genetic material you have requested."

Oriana asks about any possible discomfort or pain.

"You won't feel a thing," El assures her.

Oriana studies the assistant closely, marveling at his/her eyes.

"Why the purple iris pigmentation?" she asks.

"Because it's my favorite color," El says brightly. "Sort of an adolescent rebellion, I suppose, an alteration to my parent's original design."

The procedure room itself is small, with just enough space for an examination table, one chair, and a counter for holding the instruments.

"Slip off your underwear and climb on," El requests. He/she places a sterile drape over Oriana's body. Connor settles into the chair.

Why did I get myself into this? How do I get out of this situation? I've been in some kind of haze. I could care less about what Connor wants. It must be Granddad I am still aiming to please.

El leaves the room, wishing them luck. The obstetrical engineer enters the room shortly after.

"Hello, young lady," he greets Oriana with a perky voice. His expression is devoid of affect. Oriana lifts herself up on her elbows.

"My name is Dr. Chung," he says, patting Oriana on the top of her head before shaking Connor's hand.

"Well, now," he announces, with a cursory glance at the holographic image of Oriana's genitals floating a few inches above her stomach. "I say we get started. Everything looks normal and healthy to me."

"I'd like to help," Connor announces, standing.

"Your help will be welcome in a moment," instructs Chung. "For now, take a seat and relax."

Chung holds up a sealed vial containing the zygote suppository.

"This material has had all known genetic markers screened carefully for disease, deformity, and dullness of mind," he explains, placing it onto a glass dish by his side.

"We have a whole tray, hundreds more of your eggs, screened and ready for fertilization for you or other women on the island who may need them," he goes on. "Oriana, do you realize that you are one of the primary sources of genetic material for our community? It is an honor to work with you. What a generous contribution you have made."

"Wait," Oriana says, sitting up and pulling her knees together. "I'm not so sure about this."

"Come again, Oriana?" Connor asks, rising once again. "What are you doing, darling?"

"Try to relax. It's a simple procedure," Dr. Chung assures her, nudging Oriana's shoulder until she is lying down again.

"No, really. I want to go home. I need more time to think this through."

Dr. Chung removes a cloth from the counter and swipes it swiftly under Oriana's nose. She quiets immediately. Then Chung addresses Connor.

"Your turn now," he instructs, handing him a tube of cream. "This will dilate the cervix and nourish the uterus, establishing an optimal environment for embedding the zygote."

Connor squeezes some cream onto his gloved finger and coats Oriana's cervix with it as Dr. Chung directs.

"Excellent," Chung says. "That part is done."

He removes the suppository from the plate and inserts the frozen lump into a golden rod, leaving only the blue bio-string attached to its end visible.

"This gets a bit more complicated. Use the holographic image to guide you. It's simply a lever. Insert the rod through the cervical opening, and then press this release, right here."

"What about her?" Connor inquires as he runs his fingers along the shiny object, awestruck at the thought that he is about to create new life. "Is she going to be all right?"

The engineer explains that the sedation is short acting, and that Oriana will be back to normal within a few minutes. He urges Connor to work quickly.

Connor kisses his mate's forehead. Oriana's eyes drift aimlessly, but she can feel Connor insert the implement and release the suppository, which appears in the holographic image as it slips into the breeding ground of her body.

"Wow! That's great," Connor says excitedly.

Oriana, returning to full consciousness, stares at the holograph above her. Her vagina is wet and her uterus cramping, but somehow she can't quite reconcile what she sees in the holograph with what she feels in her body. The cognitive dissonance makes the experience seem surreal.

"Why don't you two take a few minutes alone?" Dr. Chung offers, switching off the observation lenses that have been transmitting the session to the clinic's control room.

Connor turns his back on Oriana and goes to the sink to wash his hands.

Oriana quickly puts her hand under the drape and reaches inside of her vagina, thumb and forefinger grabbing the string of the suppository. She pulls the slippery nugget out and slips it into the adjacent orifice before its contents can make their way into her womb.

The reinsertion goes unnoticed. Connor turns around, beaming with pride and feeling very connected to his mate. He embraces her tenderly and tells her how much it pleases him that in a few hours, a zygote of their combined genetic material will burrow its way into the soft flesh of her womb.

"Good job, folks," Dr. Chung states as he and his gangly, purple-eyed assistant re-enter the room. A quick look reveals to the obstetrical engineer that the remnants of the suppository are lying on the cloth by Oriana's crotch.

"I see that the string has already fallen off. This means the suppository has worked its way into the uterus and is beginning to dissolve. Now we can seal off the cervix."

Carefully avoiding the urethra to assure the unobstructed flow of urine, Dr. Chung covers Oriana's vaginal area with an impenetrable seal, measuring a mere 80 nanometers thick.

"VISHNEW is great!" he exclaims, affixing the soft shield that will eventually dissolve.

The assistant leads Oriana to the washroom and gives her instructions on how to clean herself without disturbing the seal. The melting suppository begins to seep out, its viscous liquid seeping down between her thighs. If she doesn't get to the washroom quickly, her transgression will be revealed.

"In there," El instructs. "That's the washroom."

Closing the door behind her, Oriana lifts the gown and squats over the porcelain waste tube, pushing with enough force to squeeze the suppository out of her rectum. She wipes herself dry as the white glob slides down the slippery surface of the commode.

"Oriana," the assistant calls, knocking on the door.

"I'm coming," she replies hastily, and presses the 'evacuate' lever. The waste disposal apparatus makes a sudden 'whoosh', and the bundle of molecules that was meant to become her perfect son decomposes into dry dust and disappears down the tube.

"It's important now that you lie quietly and rest," El explains as he/she leads Oriana into the relaxation chamber.

Oriana enters the dimly lit room and finds herself alone. The sound of singing whales fills the space, and images of fetuses in wombs float overhead in a variety of formations.

She lies down on a deep, soft mattress that molds itself to her body, and brings her knees to her chest in a fetal position. Closing her eyes, she sighs with relief at the thought that she has ruined the entire inception. An image of Emmanuel forms in her mind's eye, a creation that delights and comforts her.

PREGNANT

E ventually she'll have to tell Connor what she's done. And then they'll have to decide whether to continue as mates. He will be furious. What was the point of their union, he'll want to know, if her heart wasn't in it and she had no intention of fulfilling her promise to him?

"Oriana, are you awake?" Connor asks, tapping her on the shoulder.

"I can't believe you're waking me up when it's not even light outside yet."

"Sorry, it's important," he explains. "The color in the toilet bowl . . . you must have peed during the night and forgotten to flush," he explains, stroking her matted hair.

"I never flush in the middle of the night," she returns. "Call it consideration for the fact that you're sleeping and I don't want to wake you, or I'm groggy and I want to get back in bed -- whatever. Can you let me finish my night's sleep?" She buries her head under the blanket.

Oriana benefits from having her body wired with a plethora of techno-medical diagnostics, although these are limited since she is a partial-connect. A 'lab on a chip' is embedded beneath her tongue, and dye-releasing sensors in her bladder indicate the state of her physical condition: brown urine indicates insufficient iron, orange means her blood sugar is high or low, and black, always startling, lets her know that her energy expenditure is low relative to her caloric intake.

"No, Oriana. We need to talk," Connor insists, pulling at the blanket to uncover her face and neck.

"Why are you studying my pee?"

"You know why. It's time, isn't it?"

"Time for what, Connor?"

"Don't play games with me, Oriana. You know exactly what. Let's get going."

She burrows back under the pillow.

"Go take a look in the toilet for yourself if you don't believe me," Connor suggests.

Oriana sighs, stands, and shuffles to the bathroom, scratching at her itching scalp through her matted hair.

I need to take a shower, is what I need to do.

She stops, looking into the waste tube. Her face suddenly flushes.

"Well? Do you see it or not?" Conner shouts.

"How in the hell?" Oriana whispers. The bright blue residue is unmistakable. Oriana's heart rate increases. She shuts the bathroom door, leans her weight against it, and slides down to the floor.

How can this possibly be?

She has no eggs in her womb. They were all extracted and stored in the gamete bank when she was fourteen. And she knows she averted the insemination in the clinic.

I really don't understand.

Connor knocks lightly at the door.

Trying to remain calm, and stalling for time to think, Oriana gets to her feet, strips off her night clothes, and slips her naked body under the falling hot water of the shower, her mind racing as she considers the possible explanations.

Could the insemination have actually worked? But it's not possible! I saw the suppository in the waste tube . . .

Maybe the sensors in my bladder are malfunctioning? Honestly, there's no telling how long my pee's been that color. I've never monitored my urine like I should . . .

Connor bangs lightly on the door again.

"You saw it, right?" he asks. "So come on, we have to get ready to go."

If the sensors are wrong, and I'm not pregnant, there will be questions about the insemination. But if the insemination worked after all, there'll be interventions . . . either way, no good can come of going to the clinic now.

Connor pushes on the door and finds it locked. He flips the camera setting to 'washroom.'

"Oriana, what are you doing just standing there under the shower like that?"

Oriana ignores his question.

"The only way to guarantee our child will be born perfect is to get to the clinic right away." He pounds harder on the door.

"Stop it," she snaps as she gets out of the shower. She wraps a towel around her and looks at her belly.

Sort of like a kangaroo pouch, only inside.

"Leave me alone. I'm not going in for any interventions." Oriana turns the knob, unlocking the bathroom door to let him in, and turns to face the mirror over the sink.

"What's going on with you, Oriana?" Connor asks, stepping into the bathroom with her. "I have explained this to you so many times. We've discussed it over and over again."

She pats her skin dry with a soft hand towel, looking into the mirror as Connor's reflection looks back from the doorway.

Oriana makes her way out of the bathroom and back onto the bed. She lies down. Connor follows closely behind and sits down next to her. She reaches for his hands, but he pulls away and folds his arms tightly across his chest.

"You're pregnant. I'm right about that, am I not?" he demands. Oriana's golden brown locks are arrayed against a crimson pillowcase. She places the other bed pillow over her face.

"That's what I thought," Connor scolds her. "There's nothing to discuss, and nothing for you to say on the subject. We've made our commitment, so let's go." He tosses the pillow off of Oriana's face and takes her chin in his hand.

Oriana throws herself at Connor's chest. Her palms push against his ribs in a futile attempt to push him over.

"No, damn it. Listen to me!" she screams.

He lunges to his feet, pressing wildly against the dial pad embedded in his palm.

"That's it. I'm turning you in," he announces. The sensors in his hand establish a connection.

"My mate is pregnant," he shouts. The speaker inside his cheek transmits his words to the clinic.

"Then congratulations are in order. You don't have to shout, if you don't mind," a voice replies in his inner ear.

Oriana slips onto the bedroom floor, buries her head between her knees, and hugs her legs. Moaning, she rocks back and forth.

What is going on with my body?

"She's refusing to come in for the assessment and intervention," Connor complains. "I want Island Security here right away to take her into the clinic. Murphy, yes, Connor Murphy and Oriana Rotch," he shouts.

Oriana gets up slowly and walks across the room. She looks out the window. The predawn light of the setting moon makes the ice-coated limbs of the bare trees shine.

Next-door Emmanuel's childhood home stands dim, still, and sad. The flower garden below lays fallow and bare.

What is happening to me?

"Yes," Connor replies to the disembodied voice. "It was blue . . . deep blue, in fact."

Oriana sighs.

"Okay, Connor, okay. I'll go with you," she interrupts. "Disconnect, would you please?"

It's obvious where this is going, and the last thing I want is a formal complaint.

Oriana opens her arms in a gesture of conciliation. Connor measures the sincerity in her eyes.

"Never mind," he says to the voice on the other end of the connection, and brushes one palm over the other to end the transmission.

He walks over to the bedroom closet and takes out his favorite of Oriana's dresses.

"Now stop being foolish," he cautions. "The procedure was done nearly three days ago. You're pregnant as planned. Get dressed. You know what is required of us."

Oriana snatches the dress from his hands and tosses it across the bed.

"We can't go through with the interventions. Please, Conner, we can't."

Oriana pulls on a clean pair of panties and bra, reaching to the floor for the lounging pants she had taken off the night before.

Connor walks calmly to the bed and picks up the dress.

"The VISHNEW connection to your womb will be made today. Our growing son will be monitored from this day on, and when needed, interventions will be made."

He hands the garment to Oriana.

"It's your father who's corrupted you," he says with a patronizing nod of his head.

Oriana looks at the dress in her hands and the eager expression on Connor's face. A well of emotion surges inside her. Her nostrils flare as her eyes fill with rage.

"I think I may actually hate you," she says quietly.

"I never should have brought you back to this house," Connor shouts. Oriana begins to shake.

"Time to get over your complexes, little girl," he sneers, pushing on her upper back. "It's time to get on with your life."

Oriana starts to laugh, nervously and a little too loudly. The staccato outburst is very different from her usual smooth chuckle. Laughing at Connor himself rather than at what he has said. Laughing because crying will only hurt more.

"We're going to get you some help, Oriana," Connor says as he reconnects to the techno-medical urgency line.

Oriana collapses on the floor.

"Come home, Papa!" she cries. "I need you!"

The radiant lights embedded in the ceiling begin to dim as daybreak returns to Nantucket.

THE VOICE

"It's almost time."

The voice is soft and kind and barely perceptible, but she can't tell where it is coming from.

Is someone here? Who is speaking to me?

Oriana sits up, her back rigid against the pew, and pulls the chameleon coat around her shoulders. Her fear grows as she considers the legal ramifications of having disconnected herself from the VISHNEW network and left her marital home. She looks behind her and all around the room, finding no one. Perhaps what she heard was her own voice, calling to her from deep inside her own mind.

"I'll be with you again soon," the voice says.

Oriana ignores it. The words make no sense. She distracts herself by shifting her attention to the pressure on her groin, the hunger in her belly, and her desperate need to sleep.

"I'm so close now, Oriana. But I have never been very far."

My name has been spoken. My mind is compromised by thirst, hunger, cold, and a full-term pregnancy. Was the disconnection incomplete? Maybe someone is trying to reach me though my inner ear.

"Hello?" she replies. "Who's there?"

No one answers. Oriana remains very still, trying to anticipate nothing and yet hopeful for much. In this way, she resembles the Quakers who sat here each First Day for over two hundred years.

THUMP.

A thud draws Oriana's attention, and she raises her eyes to find that a cat has perched on the inside ledge of a window. Its wide eyes stare at her, round and penetrating, and she cries out in panic.

"Get the hell away from me!"

PART THREE.
GESTATION

DIAGNOSIS

Connor rushes Oriana out of the house and into his hover. Within minutes, they arrive at the offices of Dr. Chung and his associates.

A blood test confirms the pregnancy.

"My heartfelt congratulations to you both," Dr. Chung offers, shaking Connor's hand vigorously. The obstetrical engineer smiles broadly.

Oriana's chest muscles tighten. She doesn't know what to say.

I don't understand. The insemination must have worked after all. How is that possible?

"Oh no, Doctor, all the congratulations go to you," Connor returns. "It's because of the fine work of your clinic that Oriana and I are on our way to becoming parents!"

Connor reaches for his mate's hand. He glances at her quizzically, searching for some indication of excitement or joy.

Oriana looks away.

"Doctor Chung?" Connor says to the man who will now make it his professional commitment to see that their child is born healthy and free of defects.

"I understand there are many decisions still to be made about our personal specifications for the baby. Is there any information about our child you can give us at this point?"

"Absolutely," he returns.

Dr. Chung positions Oriana on the examination table, then sets the imagery control on 'holographic projection'.

"Take a look," he says, gesturing toward the image floating just above Oriana's abdomen. "Notice the shadow on the upper left corner of Oriana's uterus. That's the implantation."

"Amazing," Connor replies, squeezing the sweating palm of his mate.

"Our task now is to perfect hematopoiesis," Chung continues.

"What does that mean?" Oriana asks.

Dr. Chung puts a hand on Oriana's back to support her as she sits up.

"Hematopoiesis is the formation of blood cells," he explains.

Connor scratches at his scruffy chin, noting that he forgot to shave.

Oriana furrows her brow. Dr. Chung places his hand on her back again and nudges her off the table.

"Oriana, would you come with me, please? I have a few further assessments to make."

Connor gets up to follow.

"I only need Oriana right now," Chung instructs, raising a hand in the air. "Please make yourself comfortable in my office."

Dr. Chung pushes Oriana firmly out of the examination room and down the corridor.

"Stop it. That hurts," Oriana complains.

"I have the authority of VISHNEW to question you," Chung tells her. "Right now, you are coming with me."

With Oriana in tow, Dr. Chung weaves through the turns of the corridor, past the Clinic for Controlled Conception, beyond the Relaxation Room and the Fetal Retrieval Center, out the rear exit of the building.

"Climb in," Chung demands as they arrive at a hover parked just outside the building's rear door.

Oriana turns to leave.

"Oh, no you don't," Dr. Chung warns, grasping her elbow in his hand.

"Where are we going?" she asks, her eyes darting in search of a place to run. The hover doors open and the seats swing out.

Oriana climbs into the hover, and Chung takes a seat facing her.

"You and I need to work this out in private," he explains, setting the controls to 'lift'.

"I see," Oriana replies, wondering if she has any choice.

"We've got to get out of the range of the frequencies," he explains. "That means going out over where S'conset used to be."

Oriana's lips twist into a pained smile.

Oh yes, how well I know that place.

The obstetrical engineer and his pregnant patient rise up over the pavement, headed for Milestone Road. Dr. Chung checks the coordinates and scans the sky for monitors.

"We haven't a moment to waste," he says. "It will be no time at all before a VISHNEW probe apprehends us. So talk to me, Oriana. What's going on here?"

"I don't know. You say that I'm pregnant. But I pulled out the fertilization suppository, so I don't know how this happened . . ."

"Well, it didn't happen as a result of my treatment, that's for sure. I don't know how I missed it three days ago during the procedure, but you are nearly two months pregnant," Dr. Chung tells her. "How did this happen?"

Oriana is stunned.

Two months? How? They extracted all of my eggs at TEMPLE. I don't understand.

"I have no idea," she whispers.

Dr. Chung rubs a hand across his sweat-drenched forehead. His wrinkled brow belies the air of dignified composure he struggles to maintain.

"Oriana, we may be able to find a way around what you have done, although I can't promise that. The baby you are carrying is a female, which is not what VISHNEW decreed."

A daughter? Oriana can't believe her ears. The whisper of a hope begins to take shape in her mind.

Could it be true?

"You may not believe this," she tells Dr. Chung. "I am in shock. But I think something wonderful and amazing has happened."

"Late last night," she continues, "I had a very unusual dream. Not the kind that goes on and on, with distinct characters and images of strange and unfamiliar scenes, but a different kind of dream. Everything was gray, except for a beautiful baby girl."

"Stop, Oriana," Dr. Chung interrupts. Being fully connected since retrieval, he has never dreamed.

"No, let me finish, okay?" she persists. "She was gleeful, this baby, laughing as if she were delighting in simply being alive. Seeing her made me feel alive, too, in a wonderful way I can't quite describe. The baby in my dream wasn't a VISHNEW-connect, a feat of technology, or the result of a clinical procedure."

Oriana keeps talking, hoping that if only she can finish explaining, Dr. Chung will come to appreciate the quandary she's in.

"I can't explain why I'm pregnant, except that the dream leads me to believe that Connor and I are going to have a daughter, completely on our own."

Dr. Chung looks at Oriana sympathetically.

"What you need to understand," he explains, "is that there is absolutely no leeway for the monitoring and treatments you and the baby are going to receive during this pregnancy. My hands are tied, and so are yours. At some point we are going to have to explain this situation to Connor."

"But I don't want to participate in the standard protocols," Oriana explains, "either for my sake or for my daughter's. Plus, I'm only a partial-connect."

"Your VISHNEW status is irrelevant to the interests of society," Dr. Chung continues. "The rights of your child supersede any rights you have as an individual."

Dr. Chung reaches into the pocket of his lab coat and pulls out a silicon film document.

"I don't suppose you're familiar with this, are you?" he asks, placing the object in her hands. Oriana shakes her head no.

"Well, time for a lesson in the law," he continues. "Read it out loud, Oriana. Read every word very carefully."

Oriana clears her throat and focuses her eyes on the tiny lettering. She reads aloud:

"The town of Nantucket, in promoting its interest in the potential of each fertile human egg, mandates the extraction of all viable eggs from every female resident at or around the onset of puberty, but no later than by the age of fourteen. Furthermore, the law expressly forbids any action or judgment that interferes with the optimal gestation of an embryo from the moment of fertilization to retrieval. Once a licensed obstetrical engineer confirms uterine implantation, optimization, enhancements, and interventions will be implemented to assure the favorable development, perfection, and protection of the fetus."

Oriana lays the document in her lap.

"I don't understand," she says, her breathing becoming rapid and shallow.

What am I going to do?

Dr. Chung sighs deeply.

Oriana looks out over the water as the hover makes a wide turn. Her lips begin to quiver.

"What am I going to do?" she says aloud.

The hover touches ground. Oriana begins to panic, confused and perplexed about the fate of the new life forming in her womb.

"Please help me," Oriana implores, as Dr. Chung stares at her face. "I have no idea at all how this happened."

The obstetrical engineer bows his head in silence, studying the palms of his hands. He closes his fingers and then releases them. He puts one hand to his face.

"Well, then, we do have a serious problem," he says, rubbing his chin. "At least for the time being, I suggest that you tell everyone, including Connor, that your child was conceived in the clinic. And that you proceed with treatments per protocol."

WARNING

The baby presses against Oriana's rib, stretching inside the cocoon-like space.

"Ow, that hurts, little one," she grumbles. With some effort, she sits up and reaches for the blanket folded across the back of the couch. She wraps it around her shoulders. Although she's not cold, the covering brings her a sense of comfort.

Placing her forefingers against her temples, she massages them in slow circles to ease the pain. A low groan of which she is barely aware moves through her throat.

"Are you all right?" Connor asks, poking his head into the living room.

"Sure, other than my aching head, sore ribs, and squeezed bladder," she retorts. "Other than that, I feel fine."

"I'm worried about you," he replies. "Can I get you anything?"

She shakes her head no.

"It's late, and I'm tired," he says.

He reaches for her hands and pulls her up, then helps her up the stairs and into bed. He lies down next to her and strokes her head until he falls asleep.

Oriana, wide awake, removes his limp hand from her face and turns over onto her side. She tries to curl up; knees to chest, but can only manage to get her knees to the bottom of her belly.

For a few hours she dozes on and off. Shortly after midnight, her eyes open wide, and she becomes aware of a bewildering glow. As her eyes adjust to the dim light, she notices a figure standing at the foot of her bed. She gazes at it, intrigued, and suddenly gasps.

"Papa? Is that you?"

The shadowy figure puts an index finger to his lips in the shushing gesture Oriana knows so well.

Oriana turns to Connor, his thick mop of hair sticking out from under the spread. He remains sound asleep.

"You've come home!" she whispers to the figure. She strains to sit up, but the man gestures for her to lie back down.

"What are you doing here?" she asks out loud.

Connor moves in the bed.

"What's wrong, Oriana?" he mumbles, but a snore supplants his attempt to communicate.

She has missed Papa more than she realized. Granddad had explained to Oriana that many years of correctional treatment would transpire before Papa would be released, and it was possible that she might never see him again. But she remembers that before he left, Emmanuel had told her that he'd talked to Papa in the Facility and that Papa had asked her to wait for him.

"I thought you were still in the Facility," she says.

Oriana reaches behind her to swipe her hand over the sensors on the wall panel, wanting the room a little brighter so she can get a better look at him. The figure shakes his head, warning her not to bring the light up any further.

Oriana looks at him more carefully. Even though the bedroom is dark, a glow around the figure outlines the man well enough for her to see that he is indeed Papa.

Her father staggers to the window, and then wanders toward the bathroom before shuffling back to the foot of the bed again.

Is he drunk? she wonders.

Oriana pulls back the covers and starts to climb out of bed, wanting to take hold of her Papa and help him to sit down. Once again, he gestures emphatically.

"Okay, Papa, fine. Come and sit down beside me," she pleads. "You look like you need to sleep."

"Sleep? No," he replies, his body seeming to float slightly above the floor.

"Ori," he says softly, "I've come to speak with you. But I don't have very long."

"What about, Papa?" she asks too loudly. Connor rolls over, scratching his crotch.

"About this pregnancy. About VISHNEW, and about your child."

"Go on."

"Ori, try to find a way to fully disconnect. Then, find somewhere to go where you can stay out of view."

Oriana bristles.

Papa moves closer. Oriana reaches out to touch him, but he moves away.

"Oriana, listen to me. I know you better than anyone else."

On this point he's absolutely right.

"You need time and space to sort things out," he continues in a raspy voice. "You can't trust anyone around you. Everyone, including those who supposedly care about you, has motives that have nothing to do with you."

Papa's eyes grow heavy, and his head falls against his chest.

"Papa?"

"There is a presence here with you," he says, raising his head and gazing around the room.

"What are you talking about?" she asks.

"Go into a place of isolation, Ori, where you can be entirely alone. The help you need, will find you. Go into the silence and wait there."

Papa's voice trails off, and his body begins to fade.

"So sorry, Ori. VISHNEW is pulling me away. I have to go back under sedation now."

"No, Papa. Please don't leave me again. No, don't go. I need you," she pleads. She reaches frantically into the empty space.

"Come back, Papa, come back. Hold me!"

Papa disappears.

"Of course I'll hold you," Connor mumbles, reaching a sleepy arm around Oriana's waist.

"Papa?" she whimpers.

"Oh, you're missing your father," Connor surmises as he pulls her more tightly into his embrace. "You must have had a bad dream."

A stream of tears falls over Connor's arm.

"Don't cry, babe. It confuses me. Sorry we couldn't get that fixed."

Oriana raises her arm and swipes the light panel behind her head. A warm yellow glow begins to spread across the ceiling, mimicking the rising sun.

"Papa was here," she sobs, wiping away the tears on her face. "He came back to me. He's come home."

Connor places a hand on her forehead, checking to see if Oriana is feverish.

She is surprised that he doubts the efficacy of the sensors that monitor her health.

"No, he didn't come back. That would be impossible," he assures her. "At least I hope not. That man is the last thing you need right now."

Oriana removes Connor's hand from her waist and turns away from him.

"Oriana," Connor says softly, "this experience you had is no more than a symptom of your pregnancy. Hormones can cause such delusions. Go back to sleep now, and remember that I'm here for you."

Connor swipes the panel behind his side of the bed, dimming the room from deep orange to brown, and finally to a nearly impenetrable black.

"Connor, who am I to you?" Oriana whispers into the dark.

"You shouldn't have to ask me that question."

"How about our child? What does our child mean to you?"

"Oriana, I am alerting the techno-medics to order a remote treatment for calming you back into sleep."

"I'd rather you not, really," she requests, staring into the darkness. "The thing is, Papa seemed really tired. What have they done to him, Connor? What have they done?"

"You know the answer to that question. That's what happens during cognitive rehabilitation. They put him into a state that mimics deep sleep. You have a vivid imagination Oriana. He couldn't have been here tonight, and he's not likely to come back for years. He may never come back. It's time for you to accept that."

BRAIN CHEMICAL IMBALANCE

On an afternoon in early September, Mrs. Wyatt bicycles over to Oriana and Connor's home. Oriana, sitting on the front steps, waves to greet her.

The old woman's sandaled feet push back against the pedals of her bike. She slows to a stop.

"Well, well! How-do, Miss Oriana?" she calls out. Her cataracts are white in the midday sun, her grin dark from the absence of numerous teeth.

"I'm fine, what about you?" Oriana yells back.

Mrs. Wyatt pats her own stomach and smiles to indicate her joy over Oriana's pregnancy.

Many islanders laugh at Mrs. Wyatt when they see her. Her wrinkled skin, shapeless black dress, and wild, gravity-defying gray hair make her an entertaining sight. Few islanders understand her decision to age. At eighty-eight, she could look much better. Most of the women her age do.

The island children, especially, find Mrs. Wyatt's appearance frightful. Her bent-over hobble, slumped shoulders, and arthritic limp make her appear monstrous to the young ones, sending them running in shrieks and giggles.

No one bothers to whisper anymore. They gossip openly about Mrs. Wyatt in her presence, shocked that she has allowed the aging process to get the best of her when VISHNEW could have kept her young. The techno-medics could still so easily extend her life, restore her youth, and minimize her bodily aches and pain. But because she has steadfastly continued to refuse connection, any remnants of compassion folks may have once had for her is gone, and zealous adherents of VISHNEW have unseated her from her coveted position at TEMPLE. Most have come to see Mrs. Wyatt as the island heretic.

Even though Oriana can't help but chuckle a bit at the sight of her, she feels sorry for Mrs. Wyatt, who has no mate or family and appears to have no friends at all. Moreover, she feels compassion for her because she was her Mama's friend.

"What a surprise and a treat to see you, Mrs. Wyatt," Oriana exclaims. Then her smile fades.

"Oh no!" she yells. From out of nowhere, a hovercraft appears over Mrs. Wyatt. A barely visible thread drops down and hangs about an inch above her head. Mrs. Wyatt looks up, sees the thread, and shakes her fist in the air.

"You People of the World, get away from me!"

The protest is in vain. The craft lowers to the ground between the home of Connor and Oriana and the home that was once Emmanuel's. Connor steps out of the house and into the side yard to see what's going on.

Out of the hover climbs a young woman, dressed in gray clinical pants and top, a gray cap covering most of her forehead. She approaches Mrs. Wyatt.

"I am obliged to tell you that your condition has been evaluated and is now registered in Nantucket's Citizen Assessment files," she explains coldly.

"And what, pray tell, is your finding, my dear?" Mrs. Wyatt asks.

"BCI, which means Brain Chemical Imbalance, is the official rendering, Mrs. Wyatt."

Mrs. Wyatt climbs off her bike, lowers herself to the ground, and clasps her palms together in prayer. Oriana approaches her, wanting to help in some way.

A threesome of adolescent boys whizzes by on air skimmers.

"They've got that wrinkled old sack now!" shouts one of them. "Wrinkled old sack, don't fight back!" the others chime in.

"We can take care of this right away," the techno-medic says as Mrs. Wyatt struggles to stand up. Oriana helps the old woman to her feet. Mrs. Wyatt puts her index finger out in front of her nose and hisses.

"You'll take care of nothing, you hear me!"

A capsule containing a tiny cutaneous penetrator slides between the techno-medic's fingertips.

"You won't even know what's happened, only that you'll feel much better immediately," she reassures, as she reaches for Mrs. Wyatt's head.

Mrs. Wyatt grabs a stick from the ground and raises it to smack the woman's hand. She misses. The woman grabs Mrs. Wyatt's shoulder, pulling her head towards her chest.

"Leave her alone!" Oriana gasps.

Connor grabs her.

"Stay out of this," he warns, holding her tight.

"All I'm going to do is stimulate the pleasure center," the techno-medic explains as she immobilizes Mrs. Wyatt and penetrates the skin on the back of her neck.

"And even out your behavior," she adds. "Trust VISHNEW. You'll see how much better life can be."

Mrs. Wyatt, stumbling around and mumbling about 'walking in the Way of the Light' and 'living my Truth,' totters over to her bike and gets on it.

The wind is high, and it seems to Oriana that one hard gust could knock the elderly lady down. She hopes the old woman won't suffer this further humiliation.

Connor heads back into the house.

"Show's over," he announces.

Oriana heads into the flower garden. Mrs. Wyatt leans forward over her handlebars, watching her.

"I have something to say to you about the baby you're growing," she says, shaking a finger at Oriana.

"Oh?" Oriana returns. "And you rode all the way over here on your bike to do that?"

"You'd better keep vigilant. They'll be after you before too long, mark my words," Mrs. Wyatt declares.

"I'm not sure I understand what you mean, Mrs. Wyatt."

"I mean, now that your mate has the right to claim your eggs, and I mean all of your eggs, he doesn't care what happens to you. It's how they make their money, you know, these People of the World. How else do you think this island keeps thriving? It can hardly keep up with the global market for eggs."

"The baby and I will be fine," Oriana reassures Mrs. Wyatt. But something inside her grows cold and scared at the old woman's words.

"You still don't know who you are, do you Oriana?" Mrs. Wyatt returns.

"Of course I know. I am Oriana Rotch, sole progeny of mates Rebecca and Gardiner, partially-connected descendant of the Nantucket Quakers, with a mixture of Semitic, African, Wampanoag, and Anglo-Saxon blood running through my veins," she announces, chuckling. "And I'm proud of it all!"

Oriana reaches for the bucket of fertilizer, scooping out a cupful and tossing it over the blooms.

"Thanks for dropping by, okay?" she says, trying to politely end the conversation.

Most people on Nantucket don't bother to try holding a conversation with Mrs. Wyatt. They see her as an old fool who makes no sense anymore. She chose to age, and to remain independent, even when the opportunity for connection was offered to her at no cost. Because of that, most islanders scorn Mrs. Wyatt. But Oriana appreciates the apparently genuine concern the old woman seems to have for her and her unborn child.

"Well, now, I don't suppose you have any idea who that is in your womb?" Mrs. Wyatt persists.

"That would be my child," she asserts. "Sure as the sky is blue."

"Oh, is that so?" Mrs. Wyatt says, laughing. Not a smug laugh, but rather a knowing one, as though she understands something no one else does.

"You are a lot like those sunflowers you are tending to, young lady."

"Really? How is that?" Oriana asks.

"Stretching, reaching, and bending toward the light, that's how. Which is why she's around you all the time. And why you are the one she's chosen as her mother."

"She who?" Oriana inquires nonchalantly, not paying much attention to the woman. Down on her knees, she works the dirt with bare hands, kneading in the nano-composite mineral supplement and the rotting Foundry compost.

Mrs. Wyatt appears lost in thought.

"Can you explain who you think has chosen me?" she asks again as she spreads the nutrients over the base of the plants.

"The sunflower is a very important flower, metaphorically speaking," Mrs. Wyatt continues, changing the subject. "The strong, cultivated annual grows only for one season. Yet it provides nourishment for many creatures.

"At sunrise, most cultivated sunflowers face the east, as if greeting the new dawn. Over the course of the day, they track the sun across its arc to the west, moving along with it. At night, they face the east again and wait for morning to come again. They do this every day until the bud stage ends, and then the stem stiffens and the flower blooms."

Oriana lifts her face and smiles, impressed by her friend's knowledge.

"However, my dear," Mrs. Wyatt continues, "you are most like the wild sunflower, which typically does not turn toward the sun. Its flowering head may face any direction when it is full-grown. Beautiful and mature, you take in the light no matter which way you turn."

Oriana leans back and lets her bottom rest on the ground. Reaching for the closest sunflower, she cuts it off near the ground, stands, and carries it over to Mrs. Wyatt.

The old woman takes the bright wide bloom into her hands and places it carefully in the handlebar basket on top of three zucchinis, a perfectly ripe cantaloupe, and a loaf of Foundry-fresh bread. She grins broadly.

"Thank you, Sunshine," she says, balancing her bike and riding away.

DEPRESSION

Autumn descends on the island, stirring in many of its residents a sense of wonder and ease. The low arc of the sun causes its rays to cast golden hues across the shoreline and to turn the water a softer shade of blue. The island trees prepare to release their leaves, the strong green of summer fading to gold. The algae begin to disappear, and the powerful odor of its summer bloom abates.

Connor stands rigidly, staring through the geometric array of stained glass panes in the front door of their home. His hands press deep into his pockets, and his narrow nose turns upward in dismay. Despite his coldness, Oriana tries to engage him in conversation.

"Connor, come on. Don't take it so hard. It's going to be okay, really it will."

His head remains stiff, as if locked into place. He ignores her pleas. Oriana yanks his coat collar down from around his face. His eyes, fixed onto hers but appearing to see nothing, make no acknowledgement of her presence.

She reaches into his mound of matted hair, rubbing hard on his scalp, as she knows he likes. He flinches.

"Connor, how can you stand that ringing inside your ear?" she asks. "Your alarm has been sounding for over two minutes now. Give me your hand and I'll shut it off."

Oriana takes hold of Connor's elbow, and his arm goes limp at her touch. She lifts his hand from the pocket and holds it, palm up, in hers. The controls glow under his skin. A matrix of intersecting lines, circles, and dots indicates full connectivity. She locates the small green star at the base of his thumb and presses it to disengage the alarm.

The beeping stops and Connor's face softens somewhat.

"You'll be late if you don't get going," she suggests. He groans.

"Move away from the door and go back to your Hood," she implores of her mate. Connor is among the most skillful security-team members assigned to monitor the island for intruders. This week they are on high alert, and Connor is on twenty-four-hour call because someone reported seeing an enclave of Seekers trying to enter VISHNEW territory.

"It's time for you to sign in at work," she insists.

Firmly and deliberately, he pushes her aside.

"Leave me alone," he answers. "I have to think." His tone is harsh yet barely audible.

"Fine, then stand there all day," she admonishes as she walks away. "You're not the only one who is upset about our situation."

A peculiar sound comes from Connor's throat.

"Connor, what is it?" she asks, returning to his side.

"Go away," he chokes out.

In almost no time, two techno-medics and a security-bot arrive at the front door. Four minutes, to be exact. Connor has moved to a chair in the living room.

"What seems to have caused Connor's distress this morning?" one of the medics inquires brusquely, brushing past her.

"He didn't tell me," she replies. "Maybe you should ask him."

"How would you describe his condition?" asks the second techno-medic, following behind the first.

"You sound like you are accusing me of something," Oriana remarks.

"We will be preparing a full report, for which your testimony is required," the pair says, nearly in unison.

"It looks to me as if he's sad," Oriana offers.

"Are you being sarcastic?"

"Not really. I thought I was answering your question."

"Why is he sad?" one returns.

"Hmmm. Because of a deep sense of loss, I would guess," Oriana surmises.

"Loss over what?" the other demands. "VISHNEW records list no expiration of a loved one, nor dismissal from employment, recent financial setback, or other likely cause. So tell us, Oriana, what could it be?"

Oriana plops onto the stool in front of Papa's favorite chair. She crosses her arms over her chest.

"I beat him at poker last night," she scowls.

Connor sneers. Yes, they played a game of poker last night; it's true. And yes, he was quite upset at the game's conclusion. Losing to Oriana was not the problem, however.

"When he woke up this morning, he realized how badly he had lost to me," she continues. "It was a terrible devastation. He has hardly said a word to me since."

The female of the techno-medic pair unlatches a transparent black box and removes a shiny sphere. She places it against Oriana's forehead.

"Oriana Rotch, I am authorized to detain you for non-compliance," the bot declares.

Oriana slumps unconscious into the security-bot's arm-extensions. Thoughts of regret fill her mind in the last few seconds of awareness.

I should have heeded Papa's warning. It was clearly a mistake to share the truth with Connor last night. I took a calculated risk on gaining or breaking his trust, and I lost.

Connor would have learned the truth eventually anyway; that the child she is carrying is not the one they chose at insemination. Her deception would have been exposed when Oriana delivered a girl, rather than the boy VISHNEW had decreed, and no amount of help from Dr. Chung could hide that truth for long. But she had hoped she could gain forgiveness and support from Connor and that together they would face any repercussions that might ensue from the larger island community.

"Connor, I have something very important to tell you," she said. "This baby that I'm carrying did not come from clinical procedures. It came from our union, Connor. I don't understand how, but I am pregnant with a daughter, and it's ours."

Initially, Connor was dismissive. Assessments had been made. Interventions had been performed. Dr. Chung had assured him all was well.

"No, Connor," Oriana said. "The fertilization procedure at the clinic did not take. I dislodged and disposed of the suppository before it had a chance to implant. Dr. Chung knows."

Connor was incensed.

"Why would you do such a thing?" he demanded. "You know that VISHNEW cannot guarantee the perfection of our progeny if we do not follow established protocols."

Oriana tried to explain about her dream of a laughing baby girl. The more she spoke, the more pitiful she sounded. Connor turned away from her in disgust.

"At least look at me, will you?" Oriana begged. "Do you not trust me at all? I'm talking about a child, our daughter, who I saw in a dream. It's a mystery how it happened, Connor."

Connor winced.

"Oh come on!" he said. "Do you not hear how ridiculous you sound?"

The more Oriana talked, the more confused she became, until she was completely befuddled.

"I beg you, Connor. Hear me out," she said, kneeling at his feet, angry at her desperation.

Connor lifted one eyebrow, raising it into a high arch. He threw up his hands.

"Go on, I'm listening," he said.

But he didn't listen. He refused to accept Oriana's claims. He looked at her as though she had lost her mind.

VERDICT

"Straight ahead, Oriana. Keep going," the bot commands.

Oriana looks up into the V-shaped sensors that serve as the ears and eyes of the machine looming over her. How has it come to this? She never expected things to go this far wrong.

"Back off of me, you imbecile," she hisses. At six foot three inches tall, the human replica hovers far too close for comfort.

"Keep going, Oriana," it instructs, pushing her toward the double doors leading into the Court for Obstetrical Compliance. Oriana imagines shoving the thing aside as she steps at a defiantly slow pace.

What am I doing here?

The bot follows close at her heels, its stride clumsy and un-graceful. It shoves a sharp digit between two vertebrae in her neck.

Oriana shrieks, her voice echoing against the white-paneled walls of the nearly empty room. The air outside is bitter, and gray clouds hang dense and low. Most islanders are home watching the hearing from under their Hoods. Oriana passes row after row of empty chairs.

"Sit here," the bot demands as she reaches the row directly in front of the judge's dais. Stopping to attend to an itch on the bottom of her foot, she slips off her left shoe and, with her right toenails, scratches the irritated spot. She takes a seat at the end of an empty row.

On her shoulder hangs the bag she inherited from her grandmother, which Granddad gave her when she was mated. She reaches inside, finding a shawl that Mrs. Wyatt had given her as a gift. Taking it in her hands, she drapes it across her shoulders and over her head

"Where the hell is Connor?" she says.

The bot pats her head with its long digits.

"No talking," it replies, pressing into her scalp almost hard enough to break the skin.

Oriana fights back tears. She turns her head and sees a few familiar faces.

"Granddad!" she cries out.

"ALL RISE!" bellows a disembodied voice, reverberating through the tiny speakers spread invisibly throughout the ceiling and walls.

As Oriana stands, Connor slips in through the courtroom doors, his eyes darting around the room. She turns, smiling hopefully at him, and his blue eyes make direct contact. Scowling, he looks away.

"THE HONORABLE JUDGE FARADAY PRESIDING!" declares the disembodied voice.

Oriana grimaces, slipping her fingers under the shawl and rubbing her temples gently. These days, the piercing pain is almost always present.

The judge takes a seat at the dais and places her hands on the smooth surface of the command panel in front of her. Its colorful transmission lights illuminate her face, the restored skin clear, tight, and the color of cream, and accentuate the hint of blush-pink dyed into the cheeks. Plump lips, long brown eyelashes, and cat-like eyes tinted gray give the judge an alluring charisma in spite of her years. VISHNEW has provided generously for her old age, islanders say.

"Be seated," Faraday says blankly, covering a yawn with her hand.

Connor slips into an empty chair on the far side of Oriana's row.

"Techno-medic to the bench," Faraday commands, as she removes a piece of grime from under her fingernail.

Carrying a small black box, the medic moves to the front of the courtroom and waits for further instructions.

Faraday looks out over the near-empty courtroom.

"Let's see if we can wrap this up quickly and get out of here sooner rather than later," she says. She smiles forgivingly at Granddad, who is slumped over and snoozing in a chair near the rear.

"Before making my opening remarks," she says, "I call Lilly Apashamen to the bench. Our island Wampanoag descendent has been invited here to conduct a 'traditional opening.'"

The public hearing process on Nantucket incorporates protocols and customs that are largely based on Anglo-American heritage. By adding a 'traditional opening', the community acknowledges the importance and historic significance of the Wampanoag people, who were the first to call the island their home many hundreds of years ago. Oriana finds it a patronizing custom, belonging as it does to a people who have all but disappeared.

"Thank you, Judge Faraday," Lilly replies as she takes her place at the front of the courtroom. Like nearly everyone else on the island, Lilly is VISHNEW-connected. Her youthful appearance, glowing eyes, and shimmering palms give that away. Around here, connection is considered a profound privilege and a source of island pride.

With arms raised upward, Lilly opens her hands toward the ceiling as if reaching for the sky.

"Let us give thanks for the dawn of this new day, for the Foundry which supports us, and for VISHNEW which sustains us. And let us be thankful for the wisdom of this honorable judge."

Lilly's straight brown hair falls across her face as she moves her head for emphasis. Her bracelets tinkle as she claps her hands together.

The side door of the courtroom opens and then closes, catching Oriana's attention. A man enters and stands against the back wall. He wears a simple black cap and a long dark coat, and nods slightly at Oriana. She returns a tentative nod to the stranger.

Distracted by the man, Oriana doesn't respond when the judge beckons her.

"Oriana, come forward, please," Faraday says with a tap of her fingers on the dais. "

Who is he?

"I am summoning you to the bench, Oriana," the judge repeats.

Why doesn't he just use his Hood?

"I mean NOW, Oriana!"

Oriana, startled, turns her attention to the front of the courtroom.

"So sorry, Judge Faraday. Are you calling for me?"

"Yes, young lady. I am asking you to approach the bench."

Oriana steps away from her chair. The security-bot glides behind her as Oriana takes her place in front of the judge's dais.

Faraday lifts an eyebrow, rolls her eyes, and proceeds.

"Obviously, you folks know why we are all here today."

Oriana sighs and presses her hands into her aching back, rubbing on both sides of her spine. It dawns on her that Judge Faraday might give Connor full custody of the fetus, or sentence her to time in the Facility. A sudden feeling of terror comes over her. She spreads her fingers and covers her abdomen with her hands. The judge continues.

"Aside from the deception and broken trust you have inflicted on your mate -- which are not so much illegal as they are an affront to our community -- you allowed yourself to be impregnated outside of standard protocols, which puts your child at risk for random, uncontrolled genomic characteristics." Faraday perches her chin on her palm.

Oriana continues holding her belly.

"Tell me Oriana, what were you thinking?" the judge asks. "Why would you ever want to be impregnated at such risk?"

A sneeze rips through Oriana's lips. She should have covered her mouth. The judge's fingers move quickly across the console.

The lights on the control panel flicker as the micro-org vacuum drops from the ceiling. Spreading its tentacles around Oriana's head and chest, its suction absorbs the spewed droplets. Almost as quickly, it retracts.

"Oh come on, now!" Oriana rants, running her hand through her hair to neaten the muss made by the vacuum. "What the hell? It's not as if I'm contagious. If I was harboring germs, I'd not have gotten through those courtroom doors!"

She points behind her at the entryway for emphasis.

Faraday ignores the diatribe and continues.

"Secondly, you refused the monitoring and interventions that assure optimal development of the fetus."

Oriana curls her lips in disgust.

"And thirdly, the most egregious of your misdeeds, Ms. Oriana Rotch, was the theft of impounded eggs, as well as of Connor's sperm. You stole genetic material."

With that, Faraday folds her hands behind her head.

"I didn't steal anything," Oriana retorts.

"I beg your pardon?" Faraday says.

"Please, Your Honor," Oriana returns. "There's been a big mistake."

Faraday leans back in her chair.

"Well, somehow a gestating, fertilized ovum is nearly fully grown in your womb. It apparently didn't get there through standard clinical procedures, Oriana. Who, besides you, could have done that?"

Oriana hunches her shoulders in a gesture of innocence.

"You tell me, because I have no idea how I can be pregnant. All of my eggs were extracted."

"Exactly the point," returns Faraday. "And you also removed the gamete suppository placed in your uterus by Dr. Chung. This leaves us with only one plausible explanation. Theft. I need not say it again."

The judge signals the techno-medic, who approaches Oriana with a small black container. The bot removes a sensor from the box and attaches it to Oriana's scalp.

"Your response now to the charges against you, Oriana?"

"I have no idea how this could have happened."

The sensor on Oriana's head relays the neurological patterns of lying to the control panel in front of the judge. Faraday's eyes narrow and her lips pull taut. The apparent untruth of Oriana's claim angers her even more than the girl's blatant disregard for the court.

"A stinking lie!" she screeches, tapping her re-calcified fingernails on the hard surface of the dais.

Oriana cringes at the sound.

Connor lunges from his chair.

"I knew it. I knew it!"

Oriana looks back at her mate, wishing she could explain. The judge instructs Connor to sit back down.

Oriana shakes her head.

"I already told you. I don't know how this happened," she mumbles. Her heart rate increases to 128.5 beats per minute, a pounding pressure mounting inside her chest. The lenses of five thousand miniscule cameras, which are spread out across the room, zoom in, capturing the baffled expression on her face. Islanders watch closely under their Hoods, intrigued by her despair.

Oriana's elevated heart rate is detected through her scalp and relayed to the control panel. As the indicator light on Faraday's dais glows purple, the judge becomes further incensed.

"Get control of yourself, before I do it for you," she scolds.

Oriana crosses her arms over her chest, closes her eyes, and takes a deep breath.

"I am telling you, these charges are entirely spurious!" Oriana blurts out.

And with that, the judge reigns in hard, nodding at the waiting security-bot.

"No! I don't need that!" Oriana protests, as the bot reaches for her forehead. It grabs a wad of her thick hair, securing the back of her head against its chest.

The techno-medic lifts a mask from her black box and places it over Oriana's face. The quieting pulses move through the thin skin of her eyelids, penetrate her irises, and flow into her brain. Her pursed lips relax, her eyebrows unfurrow, and her chin drops to her neck. The bot removes the mask from her face and returns it to its container, then lowers her eyes in abeyance.

Oriana lifts her head. Calm, conscious, placid, yet only vaguely aware of her surroundings, she offers Faraday a smile.

"Do you understand the charges against you?" the judge asks her.

"Forgive me, Your Honor. I am afraid I do not," Oriana says, her eyes soft with the pleasure of a simulated nirvana.

"What's not to understand?" Faraday explains. "We are among the very few in the entire world fortunate enough to have been chosen by VISHNEW. It's one thing to decide for your self not to take advantage of the opportunities it affords. No one is forcing your participation. But as long as you are a member of this community, you are expected to abide by its ordinances and laws, the primary of which pertain to the perfection and enhancement of human life."

Faraday involuntarily snorts as she takes in her next breath.

"There is confusion over the origins of the child in your womb. Because of that, your mate is charging you with the theft of his genetic material, which is why we are here today. However, now that you have come to the attention of this court, your obstinate neglect, your refusal to be monitored, and your rejection of any interventions lead me to be concerned over the quality of the baby's growth and development. The question now is whether the baby's well-being has been compromised." The judge makes a tsk-tsk sound.

"How sad, Oriana, how sad."

As Faraday continues to scold her, Oriana enjoys the bliss pervading her head.

"We need to do everything possible to assure that the child is optimally healthy and perfect," Faraday says. "I only hope we're not too late."

She pauses to accentuate the gravity of her words.

"You've eluded your maternal duties for nearly the entire pregnancy. The day is fast approaching when your fetus will be developed enough to be retrieved. At that point, its genetic qualities, physical capabilities, and personal attributes will be assessed. If anything at all is wrong with this child, you will lose your maternal rights to it and any further access to the material of your fertility."

"What do you mean?" Oriana asks, her knees weakening and her stomach beginning to feel queasy. The brain intervention has begun to nauseate her.

The judge leans in, her artificially plump breasts perched against the console. The flickering lights of the panel reflect off of her face, accentuating the beady look of her eyes.

Oriana, momentarily distracted by Faraday's lizard-like glare, frowns in curiosity and stares at her. The judge continues.

"I am ordering that the remainder of your pregnancy be VISHNEW-monitored, and that the fetus be connected immediately. That way, there will still be some opportunity to correct any anomalies, and, if we're in time, to correct any defects and enhance its form. And I order this be done right away."

Oriana's chokes on her words, and her face flushes with frustration.

"No, I don't think so," she manages to say.

"No?" Faraday throws back.

Oriana nervously scratches her arm. She stands resolute before the authority of the judge, holding fiercely to her dream of a beaming baby girl.

How good can VISHNEW be?

"Obviously, you don't understand what this means," the judge says, clicking her nails against the dais. "So let me put it a little differently. At the retrieval of your full-term fetus, a techno-medical assessment will be made. If anything is wrong or even less than perfect with the specimen, then you will be deemed a neglectful gestator, and you will lose your fertility rights, as well as the right to mother your child. Your womb will be immobilized and your remaining eggs made available on the open market."

"Immobilize my womb?" she stammers. "Really? Why? I never did anything to hurt my baby."

Faraday shudders over the sacrilege of the statement.

"I'm sorry. I have to go," Oriana says, turning to leave the courtroom.

"Well, I am not quite finished!" the judge bites back. The bot moves to obstruct Oriana's path, turning her body around to face the judge. Its strength surprises Oriana, and she freezes under the discomfort of its tight grip.

"You realize, of course," Judge Faraday continues, "that your behavior has cost you your eligibility for FVRP."

"I don't know what that is." Oriana replies.

"The Feminine Vitality Restoration Program. It's a true gift of VISHNEW to our womanhood," Faraday explains. "It would be quite a loss for you."

Oriana chuckles at the ridiculousness of this idea.

Faraday's fingers move across the panel, rendering her final decision into the records of the court.

"Why am I being punished?" Oriana shouts. "I've caused no one any harm!"

Faraday looks up from the console and waves a dismissive hand in the air.

"Do you not see the harm in using genetic material against the owner's will?" she asks. "Your mate had no intention of having his offspring gestated without proper techno-medical protocols."

"I am trying to tell you, that is not what happened," Oriana replies.

Connor lurches toward her, yelling.

"Why don't you admit it, you whore!"

Granddad stands, hollering from the rear.

"Don't you go near her, g'd damn it!"

Faraday takes out a shield, slips it over her head, and swipes her hand across the panel. Atomic stun aerosols spray through the air. Everyone in the courtroom becomes docile and calm. Even the bot responds, its shoulders hunched over, hanging low.

Faraday removes the shield, satisfied that she has regained control of her court. Clearing her throat, her head taut, with nose pointed up in the air, she continues.

"We will see what has to be done as soon as we get the fetal specimen retrieved and connected," she declares.

Oriana releases a breath of exasperation.

"Such a selfish woman you are," the judge barks, "to disrespect the desire of a mate who wants nothing other than a viable specimen, one, by the way, otherwise incapable of determining for itself whether or not to be born perfect, healthy, and well. How dare you!"

Oriana becomes quietly resolute; her brain now recovered from the stun waves.

"I'm a VISHNEW-independent, only partially connected," she announces. "And that is through no choice of my own."

Faraday nods. Everyone knows what Oriana's father did.

"I imagine you all despise me for it," Oriana continues, addressing the islanders she knows are watching closely from underneath their Hoods.

"My computational capacities may be slower, my memory duller, and my body more vulnerable to viruses, bacteria, parasites, and radiation than yours. Sometimes it feels as if you see some kind of horror when you look at me."

The black-cloaked man standing at the back of the courtroom wipes a tear from his eye. No one notices. A VISHNEW-connect doesn't cry, and an independent that does so elicits nothing but scorn.

"You have a lot to be grateful for," Faraday says. "To begin with, you were perfectly formed at retrieval. If only your father had made a different choice for you at that time."

"Oh, you mean to have me fully connected?" Oriana says, raising two fingers to her temples, rubbing to rid herself of the recurring pain.

"We can make that better, you know," Faraday offers.

"No thank you," Oriana mumbles. She smiles faintly.

"Please, Your Honor," she says in a quiet voice. I have made a promise to my baby."

Faraday glares.

"I have no interest in hearing such nonsense. What I am asking for is your decision. Now, what's it going to be?"

Oriana rubs her eyes as the last of the quieting pulses sent into her brain subside. She asks for further clarification.

"If I give VISHNEW immediate access to my womb today, allowing full connection of my baby, then I can keep the child as my own, correct? And I would retain the right to maintain a viable womb and future access to my eggs?"

Faraday nods.

"As long as the infant is a perfect specimen at retrieval," Faraday clarifies, "then your womb and the baby will be yours to keep. If not, then the specimen will be decomposed."

"How could I survive such a horrible thing?"

"Part of the procedure involves memory suspension, so there will be no sense of loss for you or your mate after it and your womb are gone."

"Oh, please, no, Your Honor," Oriana interjects.

"No more from you," the judge exclaims, putting her hand in the air to indicate she has heard enough.

"Connor Murphy, please approach the bench."

"Yes, Your Honor," Connor says, taking his place next to Oriana.

"Am I to understand that you have no interest in committing to the parenting of a defective or otherwise imperfect specimen?"

"Yes, that's absolutely true."

"And that you are asking this court to authorize decomposition of such at the time of retrieval?"

"Exactly, Your Honor."

"And to relieve you of your rights and duties as the mate of Oriana Rotch under those circumstances?"

"Absolutely, without question."

"Of course, you still have full rights to the ova which were retrieved from her."

"Yes, thank you, Judge Faraday, for clarifying that."

"And if, however, the assessments indicate a wholly healthy, robust, optimally-developed infant at, or close to, techno-medical perfection, you will maintain your mating responsibilities for the purpose of raising the child?"

"It would be my pleasure to do so, Your Honor."

"Well then," Faraday continues. "Let's assume the best outcome. In that case, immediately after retrieval the standard post-natal protocol will provide the child with sensory enhancement, automatic brain chemical balancing, an internally driven, intra-island communication link, and direct access to other VISHNEW-connects worldwide. Tumor blocks, immune boosters, muscle builders, rapid information processors, memory and other vital brain enhancements and, of course, location indicators and safety sensors will also be installed in-corpus. The child will benefit from internally-activated, biochemically–specific nutritional enrichments and from anti-oxidant, anti-viral, and antibacterial releases on an as-needed basis."

"Oh my," Oriana says. "That's not at all what I want for my child."

"Excellent," Connor exclaims.

Faraday shifts position, leaning back in her chair.

"Well then. We are clear. Have we heard your final decision, Oriana?" she asks.

"I've not agreed to any of this. Plus, I have made a promise to my daughter."

"What's wrong with you?" Connor shouts.

"Nothing at all," Oriana returns.

"What about my rights?" Connor yells, flailing his arms. Oriana pushes her hands against her ears to dull the sound of his shrill, penetrating voice. A chill seizes her shoulders and causes her to shudder.

"I am the source of the genetic material you threw away," Connor exclaims, pounding a fist into his palm.

The sound of a slamming gavel startles everyone in the room.

"Mr. Murphy!" Faraday says, piercing Connor's eyes with her authority. "I will give you only one warning. Keep control of your mind and of your mouth."

Oriana, crouching now on the floor, clutches her head in her hands.

"Get up right now, Oriana, and listen to me. This decision is one you may regret for life." The judge's eyes turn topaz yellow as they bring into ultra-focus the details of everyone and everything in the room. She observes the beads of sweat forming on the forehead of the obstetrical engineer seated in one of the middle rows.

"Come forward, Dr. Chung," she demands.

Dr. Chung walks to the front of the courtroom, reaching down to assist Oriana back to her chair on the way.

"Come on, Oriana. Stand up now. This whole ordeal will be over soon," he assures her.

Faraday turns her attention to the engineer.

"We will deal with your role in this travesty later. For now, what, in your expert, techno-medical judgment, would be the optimal day for retrieval of the specimen from this woman's womb, Dr. Chung?"

He turns to look at his patient, and finds her eyes filled with tears. He takes her elbow firmly in his grip and pulls her close to his side. The fatherly, protective gesture unexpectedly reminds Oriana of Papa.

"My calculation of complete gestation would place the preferred retrieval date at one month from today, Your Honor."

"Be specific!" she demands.

"Monday, December 13," he says.

"Well then, Dr. Chung, by the authority of this court, I order you to schedule retrieval for the morning of December 13. You are to notify me immediately after the successful completion of the procedure. Assessments are to be made right away. Uterine suppression is to begin if indications suggest any irremediable imperfections."

Dr. Chung releases Oriana. She stands with her head down and her arms folded firmly across her chest.

Papa, can you hear me? Maybe this connection can reach you where you are. Papa, I am afraid and confused. My life is a mess, and I don't know what to do.

Connor turns to his estranged mate, raising a fingernail to her nose and pressing in hard.

"You'd better hope my child is perfect."

Oriana grabs the offending digit and bites down on it, nearly breaking the skin.

"Damn you!" Connor yells.

"Get away from my granddaughter," Granddad calls out. He gets up from his seat and moves into the aisle.

Oriana gulps in horror as the old man begins to stagger.

"Granddad!" she says as she heads toward him.

He steps back and leans against the jamb of the courtroom doors.

"Don't upset yourself this way," Oriana pleads as she approaches her beloved grandfather.

His knees buckle beneath him.

"No!" Oriana shouts, as if her outcry could prevent the imminent slide.

Granddad's head slams down hard against the floor, and the man in the black cap slips out of the courtroom through a side door.

NOVEMBER 21

Nestled between the soft bed sheets, Oriana stares over at the bedroom window and notices the frost on the edges of the panes. The winter sky is gray, the outside air temperature uncomfortably frigid, and Oriana feels there is no place to be but inside. She settles into the billowy warmth of the comforter, which feels wonderful against her bare skin. Yet discomfort tugs at her mind.

"I've got to get out of here," she whispers to herself as she closes her eyes more tightly to fend off the increasing daylight.

She lies motionless for a while, and then begins to squirm. Finally, giving up on further sleep, Oriana opens her eyes.

She tosses the covers aside and sits up, her naked body exposed to the cold, dank air of the room. The house-warming process that kicks in at this time of day is only now just beginning.

Oriana lowers her feet to the wide boards of the cold floor. Feeling for the slippers she's so fond of, she slides her feet inside and grabs the bathrobe lying across the foot of her bed. Standing, she pulls its belt across her pregnant waist and shuffles down the steps to the kitchen.

"I hate winter," Oriana announces as she takes a seat at the table. The melancholy on her face is unmistakable.

Connor looks up from his morning meal.

"I can understand that," he replies. "How about a nice trip to Hawaii?" Oriana has no interest in going anywhere under her Hood. She decides instead on storytelling night at the Whaling Museum.

An uneventful afternoon passes slowly, much of which Oriana spends considering what to prepare as her contribution to the evening's community gathering. She decides on a dessert and mixes one up quickly.

"Are you coming with me, Connor?" Oriana calls from the kitchen as she packs up the sweet treat and heads into the entry hall.

"Go ahead to the ultra-light. I'll be right there."

"I'd rather walk, if you don't mind."

Oriana reaches for her coat, taking it down from the peg mounted on the foyer wall. Covered dish in hand, she steps outside, bracing herself for what folks might say or do when they see her in person. The cold catches her off-guard and causes her to wince. The frigid air shocks her lungs. Under normal circumstances the chill would cause her to quicken her gait, but tonight Oriana's steps are hesitant and slow in anticipation of community rejection.

When she arrives at #13 Broad Street, an odd shadow from the rooftop catwalk of the museum catches her attention.

"I thought I saw someone up there, moving past those windows," she says to Connor as he steps up over the curb and crosses the sidewalk. He links elbows with her. Oriana pulls away.

"What'd you bring?" he asks, sniffing at the lid of her potluck contribution.

"Did you see that?" she asks, gesturing with her chin towards the roof. "Something was moving up there. I think it was a person."

"Maybe one of the famed ghosts of Nantucket," Connor offers wryly. "Come on, let's get inside. It's cold out here."

"What are we doing here?" Oriana asks, peering through the opening of the museum door. "We never should have come."

"Don't worry, it will be okay," Connor returns, his hand pressed against her back as he reaches to open the museum door. "You look tired. Are you all right?"

He puts an arm around her waist. The unwanted affection taunts Oriana. *He acts as if he's actually concerned.*

The mates step inside just as a person rushes out, brushing against Oriana's arm.

"Hey, watch where you're going, would you?" Connor says, scowling. He turns to Oriana.

"Who the hell does he think he is?"

Oriana turns to catch a glimpse of the man's face, but all she sees is the back of his head, which is covered in a tight black cap. She notices the scarf wrapped around his neck.

Connor heads back out the door to follow after him. The figure turns quickly down South Beach Street, crossing it. When Connor reaches the corner, the man has disappeared.

"Did you see who it was?" Oriana asks as she catches up.

"Just one of the island jerks, probably," Connor says. "I didn't see enough of his face to recognize him."

"There's no harm done, really, Connor," she says. "It's not as if the man hurt me or anything. He seemed preoccupied, that's all."

Connor follows Oriana back inside the building, which was originally a candle factory and was erected in 1848.

"I think he may have been the person who was up there on the catwalk when I first got here," she explains as they walk together across the museum foyer.

Oriana takes inventory of the people gathered in the main gallery, about twenty-five folks in all. Most seem to take no particular notice of her arrival as they begin to arrange the chairs in a circle.

Granddad waves an excited hello to her from the other side of the room. A handful of people remain in the foyer, sipping on warm cranberry juice.

Connor greets a few acquaintances as they make their way to the refreshment table. He takes the lid off of her potluck dish and teases her.

"Well, that almost looks edible."

"Never mind," she says, laughing. "There's nothing wrong with the cobbler. It looks a little odd, that's all."

Connor fixes a Foundry fresh cracker with cheesy spread for Oriana.

"Here, eat one of these," he offers as he turns to speak to a childhood friend. Perhaps he didn't notice the pale green tint of the spread, which would have signaled him that bacteria had begun to grow. Oriana hands the cracker back to Connor.

"No thanks from the baby and me," she says. Connor pops the rejected treat into his mouth.

"Absolutely delicious," he says as he heads for the gallery.

Hovering in the corner is a holograph of a crusty old sea captain, his piercing blue eyes staring down at the assembled group. With blood- stained hands, the menacing figure trembles, his leathery arms reaching out into the room. Oriana has never seen this image before, and finds it hideous and distracting, and much more haunting than the museum's other historic projections.

"This has got to go," she says, making her way to the control panel on the back wall. One swipe across 'Figure #17—OFF' and the captain disappears. With another swipe, a round-bodied man with a gloating smile floats up into the corner of the room. The tattered whaler holds a three-foot tusk triumphantly in his hands. The pungent odor from his blubber-smeared hands wafts over the room and then subsides.

Oriana and Connor take their seats in the circle next to the Starbuck sisters. Storytelling night is an island tradition. Islanders look forward to hearing the stories the Starbuck sisters tell about the early days of Quaker living on Nantucket, and about their time as schoolteachers in the late twentieth and early twenty-first centuries, when most children still walked to school buildings where they were taught in non-virtual classrooms.

A man named Frank stands up and tells a story about a lone sperm whale calf he sighted under his Hood last week while monitoring Brandt Point. The moment he finishes the tale and sits down, Freda Starbuck stands up, her eyes sparkling with the joy of being the center of attention. She launches into a soliloquy.

"Everyone listen careful now to what I have to tell you. In the early 1770's, membership in the Nantucket Society of Friends was over 2,200. Back then, Nantucket was in its whaling heyday and Quakers were the most prominent and influential people on the island. Uh huh. That's right.

Her voice shakes, a sign of untreatable age. But she continues talking with passion.

"They had quite a hefty hand, hefty, ah yep, in the prosperity of the whaling enterprise. Many of those there whaling boats were captained and crewed by Quaker men, whose wives were left behind sometimes for many months and even years at a time to manage their homes and also the affairs of the community. Uh huh. It's the truth.

"By the year 1783, in the aftermath of the American Revolution, only twenty four of the 158 whaling ships that were based on Nantucket remained under island control. The fishery lost nearly a million Pounds Sterling and more than one hundred Quaker seamen were imprisoned for opposing the war, opposing it, a-yep, uh huh.

"Of the eight hundred households on Nantucket at the time, two hundred were headed by widows and there were 340 orphaned children," Freda explains. "The Quaker women held fast, yep they did. Uh huh. They became the stronghold of Nantucket life, leading efforts to resist the war, working to maintain the spiritual integrity of the Friends Community, lending support to the growing number of widows, feeding their families, and educating the island's children. Even with the inevitable collapse of Quakerism, a-yep, uh huh, they did indeed collapse on the island in the next century, the women remained leaders in the faith.

"Back when most of the women on this island would have worn cotton undergarments, the Quaker woman refused to do so. As the product of slave labor, cotton was considered to be a symbol of human suffering. Uh huh. Let me tell you that the Quakers believed purchasing cotton would perpetuate the system that kept enslaved people from freedom. A Quaker woman of clear moral convictions would never have worn cotton. Instead, her cloak would have been hand-woven wool. To Meeting for Worship she'd have worn a lightly colored linen bonnet on her head, tied under her chin with a simple bow, and a gray linen dress.

"In cooler weather she would wear a dress made of wool, and cover her legs with wool stockings, all these clothes dyed to a rich, simple black. And when these garments were soiled, she would scrub them with her own hands in warm water and lye, then hang them out under a low winter sun, on the hope they'd be dry enough to wear again soon. It was a matter of principle, such simple attire."

Oriana leans forward and puts her elbows on her knees, opening her thighs to accommodate her huge abdomen. She is eager to hear more about her island history.

"Of course, most of us in this room are familiar with the well-known early Quaker women on Nantucket, like Sarah Barney and Margaret Folger Swain. Then there was Mary Coffin Starbuck, who Alice and I believe to be a distant ancestor. Uh huh. That's right, an ancestor. Anyway, I am almost certain that other than Oriana, no one here tonight is related to the free slave Sadie Lee Gardiner, the unsung heroine of Nantucket Quaker faith, until, that is, she lost her way and her community."

Oriana drops her eyes, not wanting to become the focus of attention.

Freda continues on.

"Our Oriana is a direct descendant of Sadie Lee."

Oh no! I should never have come out tonight.

"And just like Sadie Lee, Oriana is unfit to carry new life in her womb."

"Leave her alone, Freda!" Granddad yells across the circle.

Oriana moves a hand over her pregnant belly as all eyes turn to her. Sighing, she begins to feel like the holographic sea captain who greeted them tonight, curious yet repulsive to behold.

"Connor," she whispers. "Can we go back home? I really don't want to be here."

Connor leans close to her ear and reminds her that the chance to enjoy the company of the townspeople in person only happens once in a while.

"I'm leaving whether you come with me or not," she whispers. Since VISHNEW full-connects are extremely sensitive to sound and to displays of emotion in particular, the rest of the room hears every word of the argument. Freda ignores her, as does everyone else, as the story continues.

"For centuries, the Indians of Nantucket thrived as a vibrant, healthy community. With the arrival of the English, and their domination of the island, there would be drastic changes for the native peoples. Uh huh. Eventually, you know, they would be entirely wiped off of the island, weakened by debt, servitude, disease, alcohol, and starvation. It's true."

Granddad, sitting across the circle, raises his hand and speaks slowly, some of his words a jumble of barely audible murmurings.

"This is a solemn tale, don't ya know. The Nantucket Indians, who in the year 1659 were three thousand members strong, dwindled to five hundred by the year 1750, and down to a mere 146 by the year 1767.

"Over and over again they tried but failed to appeal to the ruling whites in Nantucket Town, attending town meetings to ask that their rights be observed, including the right to maintain their lands for their own personal use. The powerful men who owned and controlled the island's resources denied their requests. The only efforts that would be put into sustaining the Wampanoag, was for those Indians who had skills to share with the fishing industry. It was such a shame. Those Indians sure were used for their sea hunting knowledge, teaching the whites their harpooning skills. "

Oriana adjusts her position for better comfort, making a pillow of her personal bag. Her mind's eye creates visual details of the story as it unfolds.

Freda continues where Granddad leaves off.

"Uh huh. That's right. As for those who sought to adhere to their native ways and remain in isolation in the villages, their ongoing pleas to the white men and women of Nantucket continued to fall on deaf ears. Instead of the recognition they sought of their inalienable rights to the resources of their land, what they got was more visits from Quakers, Methodists, and other missionaries who sought to convert their 'wild ways' to those of the Christian God.

"Listen carefully to what I am about to tell you. In 1848, only a handful of the Indians remained alive in Miacomet."

Oriana stretches her legs, then her aching back.

"You know Oriana," says the woman beside her, "I knew your father when he was a boy. He was always different. Even so, he grew up to be the best animal techno-medic on the island. He was a partial-connect, your dad, not like the rest of us. But he was once a good person. We all liked him a lot until he changed. I guess losing Rebecca was too much for him to bear. Now, she was an incredible woman."

"Who?" Oriana asks.

"Rebecca, your mother, of course."

"You knew my Mama?" Oriana persists.

"Sure did," she replies.

The room begins to murmur, then swells of laughter rise.

"May I put my hand on your belly?" the woman asks. "My child gestated in an ex-utero womb at TEMPLE, so I never got to feel it under my skin."

Oriana scoots her chair back to avoid the reach of the woman's hand.

The woman leans in closer.

"Such a brave girl you are," she whispers, "stealing sperm and taking a chance with an in-utero pregnancy."

Before Oriana has a chance to stop her, the woman's hand presses against her protruding midsection, frantically rubbing up, down, and around.

"This is amazing. It's so taut, not at all what I imagined!" she remarks. Putting her face to Oriana's belly, her mouth practically touching Oriana's shirt, she calls out.

"Hello in there!"

"Really, please don't . . ." Oriana asks.

Suddenly, three pairs of hands assault her abdomen.

"What does an illegal conception feel like?" says a voice from behind her.

"I had my child ex-utero. Let me touch, too. I want a chance!" demands another, pressing on Oriana's stomach where she can find space.

"Me too," another woman proclaims. "I never got to feel a pregnant uterus."

A hand slips nonchalantly under Oriana's shirt, and all of the women are giggling. Now Oriana realizes what is happening. It's a CSI, and these are always unpredictable. Community Social Intoxications are a VISHNEW manipulation designed to give the fully connected a rush of stimulation to the pleasure center of the brain.

Giggling and touching, the women fondle, rub, grab and delight in the orgiastic bliss of Oriana's pregnant body.

"Get away from me!" she yells, trying without success to push them away.

Most of the men in the storytelling circle stand, staggering and laughing, a few dancing to the music that streams into their inner ears. More hands make unwanted contact with Oriana's back and shoulders. One moves down under her shirt and over her breasts, another one lands on her thighs, and yet another touches her waist. Faces press against her face. A woman's hair falls over Oriana's head and neck.

"Papa," she whimpers, tears streaming down her face. The group draws back, horrified over the emotional display.

Connor, who had staggered out of the room singing an old Irish ballad, returns to find the curious mob around his mate.

"For the love of VISHNEW! Leave her alone!" he cries, lunging across the room. Wrapping his arm around Oriana's shoulders, he leads her out.

"I am taking you home," he tells her.

MEETING FOR WORSHIP

"You can still change your mind," the voice says.

Judge Faraday startles Oriana out of the meditative state a warm bath has caused her to slip into. The words echo through her auditory implant.

"My original offer stands."

Oriana finds this neither helpful nor encouraging. She reaches for the sponge and squeezes the oil-drenched water over her shoulders and back.

Connor bursts into the bathroom.

"Did you hear that? Is your speaker turned up?" he asks.

"Leave me alone," Oriana implores him.

"That's fine," Connor remarks. "You're selfish, you know." He opens the curtains and lifts the blinds.

"Me?" she asks.

"Who do you think? Did you ask me if it would be okay for you to decide on your own how to create our child?"

Oriana strains under the weight of her midriff as she climbs out of the bath. Connor sits down on the waste tube, his eyes wide, staring at her belly.

"Connor, what is my womb to you?" she asks, placing one hand on the tub edge and the other on her abdomen.

"If you have to ask that question, you'll never appreciate the answer," he says.

"That's what I was afraid of," she retorts. Oriana wraps a towel around her body and leaves the bathroom, slamming the door behind her.

Connor enters their bedroom and lies down on the bed facing the ceiling, his arms propped under his neck.

"Pregnancy causes rapid mood changes. Don't worry. I understand."

A second relay comes through the house speakers.

"Good morning, Oriana. It's Freda."

"And Alice, too!"

"How about joining us for a cup of tea?" say the cheerful siblings, practically in unison.

"How kind of you to call," she replies wearily.

"Come along, my friend, and don't be too long," Alice says.

"Oh, go, why don't you?" Connor encourages.

Oriana adjusts the setting to one-way receiving.

"Okay," she says. "Come along if you want to."

Connor passes on the offer.

Oriana bundles up for the cold. As she steps out onto the pavement, she notices Emmanuel's mother peering through her front door. Oriana waves, and the door abruptly shuts.

It's been nearly nine months since Emmanuel left. Oriana misses him, thinks of him nearly every day, and anguishes over his mysterious disappearance.

She makes her way over to India Street. The red painted door swings open on her arrival at the Starbuck home. Alice, dressed neck to calves in dark gray, greets her.

"So, you've decided to join us! What a delight," she says. "Welcome to our home."

"Thank you, Alice," Oriana says as she makes her way up the wooden steps to the saltbox home. "I'm glad to be invited."

Alice reaches out and grips Oriana's hand.

"Come on in from the cold and join us in the kitchen where it's warm," she offers.

Oriana steps into the parlor. The smell of fresh baked muffins blends oddly with the musty air. Three Nantucket lighthouse baskets of varying sizes are perched on an old pine table. Mounted on the wall above it is a whale tusk with scrimshaw-carved words lettered in black. Mesmerized, she reads the words over and over:

'Remember me when far away,
from thee on the stormy sea.
For whatever course I'm steering,
my heart still points to thee.'

"Would you like to take off your coat?" Alice asks, pointing to the peg rack on the back of the door and breaking Oriana's reverie. Oriana hangs her coat and follows Alice into the kitchen.

"Look who's here," Alice announces to her sister.

Freda smiles warmly and offers Oriana a chair. Oriana sits down.

"We hope you'll join us for some Quaker style worship," Freda says.

"I've never done that before, but I don't mind trying," Oriana answers.

"Just settle into the quiet with us and turn your attention inside. In the silence you may sense the still, small voice."

Oriana bristles.

All I know is what I see, feel, and have been taught to be true, which includes nothing about this voice. I see what makes it through the filters of my corneas: the devastation of this island, VISHNEW's watchful hovercraft floating silently over our town, the hopeful roundness of my body, and the disappointment on your faces when you look at me. I feel Connor's tentative touch, and the baby's twists and turns underneath my stretched skin. I feel sorrow because I don't know what I actually believe, or see, or feel anymore. I don't expect to hear any still, quiet voice this morning. That receiver seems to be out of whack.

To Oriana, the Starbuck sisters are throwbacks to Nantucket's past, except, of course, for the fact that both are VISHNEW-connects. They are the only Quakers still alive on the island other than Granddad, who doesn't identify himself that way any longer. They, on the other hand, continue to maintain a strong identity with the history of Nantucket and its friendly people, even without a formal Meeting for Worship.

Facing one another across a square pine table, the three women sit perched on ladder-back, cane-bottom chairs. The sisters close their eyes, and Freda encourages Oriana to do so as well. Oriana looks around the room and then down at her thighs, out the window, and up at the ceiling, before finally closing her eyes.

Thirty-three wordless minutes pass. Alice clears her throat and clasps her hands together loosely. Freda clears her throat, too, as though answering her sister. Freda's smooth white hair is pulled back so tightly that it gives her eyes a slight slant. Alice's hangs short in a precisely cut bob.

Both sisters' eyes remain closed. Alice's head hangs low. Freda scowls. The soporific silence continues.

Oriana fights sleep, fidgeting, pulling at the cuticles around her fingernails, and biting the loose pieces of skin.

"Damn it," she whispers as a drop of blood forms at the base of her thumb. It hurts.

Twelve more minutes pass.

What am I doing here? Oriana considers that she has far too much to worry about to justify spending the morning this way. *I simply should not have come.*

Alice takes a long, deep breath, then stands slowly and with deliberation at her place by the kitchen table, her brown eyes opening round, cow-like.

"The island's children have been abandoned," she says. "They need the care and attention of real teachers. VISHNEW cannot replace the effects of direct, face-to-face instruction. Children have always needed the intervention of adults to guide and discipline them. They simply cannot do for themselves, which is essentially what we ask of them with VISHNEW's educational program. There, they may learn their facts and figures, but what do they learn about trust, compassion, and peace unless they interact with one another and with teachers in person?"

She sits back down in her chair. Neither Alice nor Freda says another word for fifteen grueling minutes, until Freda reaches for Alice's hand. Each clasps one of Oriana's hands and squeezes at nearly the same time.

"Good morning!" Alice says to signal the end of Worship.

"Good morning," Freda repeats, turning to Oriana with a firm nod. The sisters break into song.

'Tis the gift to be simple, 'tis the gift to be free
'Tis the gift to come down where we ought to be,
And when we find ourselves in the place just right,
'Twill be in the valley of love and delight.
When true simplicity is gain'd,
To bow and to bend we shan't be asham'd,
To turn, turn will be our delight,
Till by turning, turning we come 'round right.

Alice's raspy alto voice strains at the high notes. Freda's effort at harmony is probably not as pleasing as she believes it to be. As the last stanza ends, Alice clears her throat, wipes her brow, and speaks with a glimmer of reproach.

"You know, back when I was a young child, Friends used to gather together in the Meeting House."

She grows more somber as she continues to speak.

"Though there weren't too many of us even then, we gathered in the silence every First Day over on Fair Street, and waited to be moved by the Light."

"Oh yes, I know that building," declares Oriana, who catches herself before saying too much.

"For many folks," Alice continues ruefully, "the direct religious experience available under the Hood became more personally satisfying than the actual Meeting. Friends stopped feeling the spirit move at Meetings for Worship, and the religious gatherings of Quakers turned more to expressing concerns over what folks were seeing under their Hoods of the lives of others, than about listening for the voice of God."

Freda grimaces.

"Ya huh, so true, Alice, you and I will never let the tradition die, not as long as we are alive. Right, Sister?" she declares plaintively.

Alice pats Freda on the hand, stands up from the creaky chair, and walks over to the food production center to remove the fresh Foundry muffins from the oven.

Oriana raises her eyebrows, remembering the times she had direct religious experiences under her Hood. The tutor had encouraged it in order for her to better understand the history of human religiosity. Oriana made a pilgrimage to the Holy Ka'bah, delighted in walking on hot coals among worshipping Hindus, and was blessed by the Pope on a visit to the Vatican. She was amazed by her experience in Scotland, chanting with men and women in Celtic prayers.

Above all, however, talking in tongues among snake-handling Holy Rollers of the Appalachian Mountains left her completely spellbound. Nothing could have convinced Oriana that God himself wasn't inside of her as she shook in a feverish dance. And since the Hood connectors provide direct endorphin flow inducers to the brain, she felt a head to toe rush of pure ecstasy during the simulated service. For Oriana, today's Meeting for Worship pales in comparison to spiritual experiences she has had under her Hood.

Alice returns to the table, carrying a plate of apple butter and pumpkin muffins. Oriana reaches with gratitude for the treat, and takes a bite too big for her mouth.

Freda picks up her teacup, sips from it, and then speaks softly.

"Friends, let us hold Albert Rotch in the Light."

"My Granddad?" Oriana replies.

"He is suffering over the very difficult decision he had to make." Oriana's spirit is lifted, her entire being alert, as Freda continues.

"A caring man he is, and so wise to have gifted the house to Connor."

Oriana's jaw drops.

"What house?" Oriana bursts out. "Freda, what house are you speaking of? I don't get it, about a gift."

"Now, calm down," Alice scolds. "Don't get yourself all out of whack."

"What do you mean, 'calm down?' I'll do no such thing until you explain what this is all about," Oriana persists.

"Come now, Oriana," Freda replies. "The poor man struggled terribly with the decision, and even now he is in pain over it, not knowing whether it was the right thing to do after all. Yet his heart was in the right place, and in the end, I do believe that what he did has led to good for all concerned. Here you are as the evidence, a beautiful woman who is finally mated, and just in the nick of time, with a child on the way."

"What has my status got to do with a house, and what house are you talking about?" Oriana asks in a much louder voice.

Freda stands behind Oriana and places her hands on her shoulders.

"The house you are living in, where you grew up. Your father's house, of course. It was given to Connor on the agreement that he would take you as his mate, provide you with a home, and care for you and your progeny."

Oriana pushes Freda's hands away, stands, and steps away from the table.

"May I use the bathroom?" she says stiffly.

Freda brushes her hands down along her apron to neaten it.

"Why, of course," she says.

After a few minutes, Oriana returns. It's obvious that she's been crying.

"I have to leave," she explains, walking into the parlor and taking her coat off of the peg.

"Slow down, Oriana. There's no emergency here," Alice says, following behind her.

"You don't understand," Oriana continues. "His voice is coming into my receiver."

Oriana whispers into the tiny receiver wired through her nostril, placing her hand alongside her face for privacy.

"I'm on my way, okay?"

A shaken Oriana walks to the front door of the Starbuck sisters' home.

"Goodbye, Friends," she says. "Thank you both so much for inviting me to join your worship this morning, and especially for the muffins and tea."

Alice, with a broad smile, reaches past Oriana and opens the door for her. Freda, standing behind Alice, pulls her sweater closed to shield herself from the brisk winter air and peers around her sister's head.

As Oriana walks out onto the landing, Alice's smile vanishes, her lips pinch together tightly, and then she speaks.

"Her child's impending retrieval should be cause for joy, not the deep disappointment it has meant for us, for her sweet mate, and especially for her lovely grandfather."

"Uh huh . . . that's the truth," Freda remarks.

"It would do the child good to follow her Inner Light," adds Alice.

Slowed in her gait by the hurtful gossiping, clearly intended to reach her ears, Oriana stops on the lowest tread. She grips her hand hard around the wrought iron railing along the steps.

"Maybe that Inner Light you speak of is precisely what is leading me to do as I am for my child." She lifts her head, releases the rail, and makes her way down the street. The sisters watch her as she walks away.

Alice turns to Freda.

"Whatever happened to the sweet little Oriana we islanders so adored?" she asks.

Oriana begins to walk more briskly. *What have you done, Granddad? How could you deceive me this way?*

PART FOUR.
MOTHERHOOD

DISCONNECTION

"I'm coming right now, Granddad," Oriana replies to the voice inside her ears.

"Granddad?" she calls as she steps inside his front door. Oriana steps back, recoiling from the smell of silver-titanium dioxide disinfectant.

"Granddad?" she shouts louder, covering her nose with her sleeve. An odd agitation washes over her as she makes her way down the dimly lit hallway of the place she once knew as home.

"'Bout time you showed up." His tone is emphatic, his voice hushed yet urgent as it wafts through the French doors of the parlor.

Oriana finds her grandfather settled into his favorite upholstered chair, staring into an empty fireplace. He doesn't look at her when she arrives by his side. His eyes are transfixed and shadowy.

"Hey there, Granddad," she chirps. "It looks like you've finally found something to do besides go under your Hood." Hoping for a cheerful response, Oriana instead gets no response at all.

Straining to bend because of her enlarged midriff, Oriana places a kiss on Granddad's cheek.

"You have some explaining to do, old man." Suddenly she notices the fresh blood pooling inside his ear. She gasps.

"Hold on, Granddad. I'll get something to fix you right up."

Oriana tries to keep her voice chipper and light in order to keep from alarming him. Her stomach turns, as she grows more anxious. Why has his tissue self-repair failed to activate around the wound?

She scurries into the hallway and up the stairs. The weight of her full-term pregnancy makes her ascent much more difficult than the last time she was here.

The shadows are particularly distracting because Granddad's house still gets its illumination from light bulbs screwed into the sockets of fixtures on the walls, and at night the bulbs cast an unpleasant gloom. Oriana prefers the light at her own house, which comes down evenly from organic LED panels across the entire ceiling. There, in her childhood home, being inside at night is much like being outside in the day.

Oriana reaches the top of the landing and walks past the bedroom that was her own less than a year ago. Everything is exactly the same. In the bathroom, Granddad's medicine cabinet is unchanged, stocked with the same toiletries and pharmaceuticals that have been there for years: Gum Strengthening paste, Plaque-Away nanospray, an expired tube of Anal Fissure Instant Repair gel, Wipe-On Radiation Neutralizer in individually wrapped packages pressed neatly into the lower shelf (very potent stuff, able to penetrate the skin into all the tissues of the body), and a barely used carton of nano-bands that are starting to disintegrate around the edges.

This is what I am looking for, Swipe-n-Seal. I hope it's not too old for use. She takes the tube from the shelf and heads back down the staircase.

Blood is now oozing from inside Granddad's ear and from a tear duct, too, dripping over his nose and across his lips.

"What the bajeezers, Granddad," she exclaims. "What is going on here?"

The bright red blood drips onto his shirt and onto the floor covering. Opening a Swipe-n-Seal pack, Oriana smears the impregnated cloth inside his ear and across his eyes, desperate to stop the bleeding.

"This stuff should help a laceration heal over quickly," she assures him as she looks at the red soaked swab. "So don't you worry at all." She strokes Granddad's snow-white hair. *Why are the techno-medics not here yet? The sensors should have triggered them minutes ago.*

Granddad's breathing diminishes, and he seems unaware of his compromised condition.

"Are you feeling okay?" Oriana inquires. Without replying, he turns to look at the empty fireplace at the corner of the room.

"I think you miss watching the flames dance," she suggests, seeing the direction of his gaze.

'Studying the dance of the flames'. That was how Granddad once described to her the hearth-front experience of his childhood, before tree-grown hardwood logs became unavailable.

"Foundry-manufactured wood doesn't burn very warm, and casts off a sickly dull light," he told her, and that was why Granddad stopped using his fireplace.

Oriana places a hand on her Grandfather's shoulder. Together they watch the empty hearth, scrutinizing the cracks of its old brick lining. She wonders what it actually felt like to sit in front of a fire's warmth, to hear and see the burning of wood. She knows what it feels like to be warm, but wonders if the experience would be different if she could see the source of the heat and feel it radiating against her skin.

Granddad turns his head towards Oriana, his eyes drawn to her rotund belly. He glares at its firm plumpness and then up into her eyes.

"Sit," he says gruffly, pulling on her arm.

She reaches for the needlepointed footstool that has been in the family since the 1940's, the one Papa and Granddad say belonged to her grandmother's great-great-grandfather. Sliding the faded, well-worn antique in front of Granddad's chair, she starts to lower herself down onto it.

"You're too big for that now," Granddad snaps.

Oriana eases onto the floor instead, trying to keep her balance. Granddad drums his fingers against his knees. She plants a kiss on his ruddy hand and he, in turn, snatches hold of her ear and twists it, rebuffing her attempt at affection.

"Ow, Granddad," she says, her face wan. "That really hurts. Let go of me."

"What are you complaining about?" he barks. "That's nothing. You can't begin to know what real pain feels like."

Oriana notices the swelling around Granddad's calves and lifts the pant leg to his knee. Carefully, she peels away the pliable layer of warming cream that has adhered to his skin. She massages Granddad's limb in the way she did when she was a little girl, hoping to ease the stiffness around his nano-gel knee cartilage and titanium ankle joints.

Her touch fails to soothe the old man. He leans his head forward.

Her back stiffens in anticipation of what she knows is about to come.

Granddad's cerulean eyes pierce hers and his brow begins to furrow.

"Enough!" he bellows. His stale breath drifts around her nose and cheek. It smells of soured milk, not its usual sassafras.

She lets go of his calf and leans back.

"What Granddad? What are you saying?" Oriana asks.

His head tilts back and eyes fall closed, shutting her out of his view.

"What a pigheaded Yankee you are," she says.

"What's gotten into you, girl?" he demands, suddenly alert again.

"Me?" she returns. "How about you? I just learned you gave Papa's house to Connor, trading it for me!"

"Damn it all," he cries out, his eyes clenched shut as he grimaces in pain. It's been awhile since he's been so animated, his fiery eyes bulging, his taut pink lips quivering as he speaks. But before long, he falls quiet again.

Winter's bleak stillness seeps through the crevices of the antique home. Oriana and Granddad sit together wordlessly, each keenly aware of the other's torment and pain. Other than the VISHNEW implant pulsing in her inner ear and the occasional slap of Granddad's hand against his thigh, Oriana doesn't hear a sound.

She remembers the early days when she used to sit with him in this same spot. He'd tell her about how the waters started rising and the land became salt-saturated when the Great Storms hit, and mainlander tourists forgot all about their beloved Nantucket because they were too busy tending to their own struggles back home.

"Used to be our Gray Lady was a hustle-bustle kind of place. Until she decided to pull away from the world," Granddad had said.

Oriana inspects his ears and eyes and is relieved to see the bleeding has stopped.

According to Granddad, Nantucket has been through cycles of isolation at least three times before VISHNEW came into being. The first was when the whaling industry went bust during the Revolutionary War in the 1700's, and the second was because of the Great Fire of 1846. The last happened in the 1860's, when the whaling industry failed because of the rush for gold in California and the opening of the petroleum fields in Pennsylvania.

The Great Storms devastated Nantucket, but Nantucket found new prosperity in the wake of VISHNEW's emergence.

"Who would have thought that our connection would attract so much interest and wealth to our forgotten home?" Granddad had explained. "If not for the wisdom provided us by VISHNEW, the island would no longer be habitable."

Oriana looks at Granddad, his hands folded in his lap. She notices the signs of untreatable aging.

"You've still got time," Granddad says, disturbing the quiet.

"I suppose you're talking about this pregnancy," she responds.

"Retrieval is tomorrow, Oriana. Make the right choice for yourself and that baby you are carrying. Stop this foolishness."

Oriana slides closer, placing her head in his lap.

"We're all vulnerable to the whims of nature," he goes on. "She's a harsh and heartless mother, that one. Don't fall weak to her."

Oriana rests one arm on his thigh and wraps the other around his calf.

"Look around this island of ours," Granddad continues, placing a hand on her back, "and see for yourself; she is also a vindictive one, that nature mother. If not for VISHNEW, I don't know . . . "

"Granddad, please don't," Oriana begs, interrupting him.

"Now you hear me out!" he presses on. "Put your trust in something powerful that can offer you some security and control. That's what your Mama wanted for you when she agreed to have you connected."

"No. Mama never agreed to that. You're wrong, Granddad," she tells him, lifting her face towards his.

"Sure she did. Before you were even retrieved. But VISHNEW went down, Oriana. That's all. VISHNEW simply went down. No one could have saved your Mama. Even without VISHNEW to support her through your retrieval, she'd have died anyway, with the placenta pulling away as fast as it did."

Granddad leans forward and takes his granddaughter into his arms.

"Oriana," he says, tightening his embrace. "You're a good girl. Be a smart one, too. Go on now and accept the judge's offer. It's not too late. Do it, dear. Call Judge Faraday and tell her you will comply."

She looks back at the empty fireplace.

"You don't have to be this brave," he declares. "Put your trust in VISHNEW."

Oriana's shoulders begin to shake.

"Why did you give him the house, Granddad? You could have just given it to me! I can't believe you bartered my life with him." Her pregnant belly quivers under the pressure of the mounting sobs. The child in her womb rotates, head moving down and flattening her bladder.

"There you are, little one," she whispers to herself.

"Now, now, Oriana," he offers.

"I don't know what's what anymore, Granddad."

"Sure ya do. Use that fine mind of yours," he throws back.

"I don't trust Judge Faraday and I certainly don't have faith in VISHNEW, not at all. And now, I can't even trust Connor. It's just like Papa said." Oriana leans into Granddad's chest, holding onto the arms he has wrapped around her.

"What does it matter anyway? Tomorrow my child is scheduled for retrieval. Connor will see to it that this baby is fully connected, regardless of any decision I make. And then they'll immobilize my womb to punish me for my obstinacy. Granddad, this baby already belongs to the World's People."

"'The World's People'," he repeats, chuckling over the expression used by the Nantucket Quakers of the 1700's to refer to non-Quaker islanders.

"Where did you come up with that?" he asks, releasing his hold on her and sitting back.

"What are you talking about, Granddad? I got it straight from you," she reminds him as she stands.

Granddad would often refer to folks as the 'World's People' when he was angry over a business transaction gone bad, or an unjust ordinance, or an unfair taxation from Nantucket Town, or any other attitude or action with which he disagreed. The expression has been in the family for centuries.

Granddad's laughter subsides, his eyelids fall shut, and his head drops down against his chest. Oriana, arms across her bosom, watches his face relax into an expression that she finds unfamiliar. She studies him closely, thinking about how well he's treated her over the years, regretting being such a disappointment to him in recent months, trying to forgive him for what he's done, and trying to forgive herself as well. She never meant to hurt anyone, especially not Granddad. *Look what I have done to him, breaking his heart by following my own.*

"Granddad, are you awake?" she asks softly, tapping lightly on his shoulder. Puffs of air exit his throat with an odd, scratchy noise.

"I'll get you something to drink," she offers.

Oriana walks into the kitchen and pours Granddad a tumbler of Foundry Fresh de-sal. Taking a sip, she finds the cool water soothing to her sticky mouth. She returns to his side and places the glass on the table by Granddad's chair, watching him closely.

His jowls vibrate violently under the force of another exhalation. Oriana feels a burning sensation in her heart. Panic begins to rise.

"Hello?" A man's voice calls from inside the foyer.

"Who's there? May I help you?" Oriana responds, stepping into the foyer. Three techno-medics are standing there.

"What took you so long?" she asks them. "He's not well."

"Will you confirm that you are Oriana Rotch, granddaughter of Albert H. Rotch?" one demands.

"Yes, that's me. Granddad's right in here," she says, pointing into the parlor. All three look at the activity on their palms.

"We know exactly where he is," one returns, holding up his hand with authority.

"We are here to confirm his expiration," another says, her tone of voice matter-of-fact.

"His what?" Oriana asks with a whimper.

"Albert H. Rotch notified VISHNEW at 8:00 p.m. last night of his desire to terminate his connection. That decision was registered and approved at 8:32 p.m. He was disconnected at midnight, except for the sensors that register his vital signs. Those sensors indicate expiration at 2:34 p.m., exactly two minutes ago."

"I don't understand," Oriana protests, stepping through the parlor's French doors. "I was just talking to him!" She approaches her grandfather.

"We need to get to his body immediately. So please, Oriana, move out of our way."

"I still don't know what you're talking about!" Oriana shouts.

"All we have to do is confirm his status and prepare his carcass for removal."

Oriana places a palm on her Grandfather's forehead.

"Granddad is asleep, don't disturb him," she says, shoving away the techno-medic who attempts to touch him. "He has always been a bit of a prankster. That's all this is, you'll see." She takes her grandfather's hand.

Oriana lowers herself onto the stool in front of Granddad's knees and gently strokes his arm.

"Wake up Granddad, you have visitors," she declares. "And will you ever get a kick out of why they're here!"

Granddad slumps over. A techno-medic grabs his head, pulls it back, and opens the lid of one eye.

"You g'd-damned People of the World," Oriana screams at the top of her lungs. "Just get away from him!" She climbs onto Granddad's lap and presses her shoulder under his chest, attempting to prop him up. Throwing her arms around his neck, she holds on to him for her own dear life.

"Granddad, why now?" she whispers, the reality of his condition beginning to dawn on her. "You had so many more years authorized to live!"

MATERNITY

Uncertain if she is asleep, awake, or somewhere in between, Oriana begins to stir. She clamps her upper teeth hard over her bottom lip. Gnawing against its tender flesh, she feels the immediacy of the pain. But the effort fails to clarify her state of mind.

One possibility is that she is sedated, in which case the movements of her mind are beyond her control. She grows increasingly anxious as her hold on reality becomes more tenuous.

Maybe I am in limbo, she considers, an irrational thought that causes panic to rise in her chest, *or somewhere under sedation, like Papa.* Her heart feels jumpy and erratic, her breath constricted and tight.

She struggles against the wanderings of her mind and gradually comes to realize she is in the Retrieval Preparation Cell, a sensory-enhanced space designed to put the pregnant woman in a state of emotional readiness for the retrieval procedure by inducing tranquility and complacency. Measurements are taken and assessments made without the woman even knowing. All she is to feel is bliss.

The underground space, tight and door-less, mimics the in-utero experience and thereby increases the woman's sense of unity with her baby; the design is especially helpful to those with exo-uterine pregnancies.

Oriana, however, feels more trapped here than relaxed, more disorientated than enthused. Haunted and tormented by anxiety and fear, she preoccupies herself not with the details of the re-trieval procedure, but rather with concerns about her child's fate and her own. Her fully developed fetus will be retrieved tomorrow.

Soft vibrations course through her head. Her rhythmic vascu-lar flows are deep and soporific, singing an intimate song of her own self. Oriana closes her eyes.

Stark, vivid images appear behind her eyelids, bringing back the horrid memory of Papa's fingers moving furtively along her forehead, pulling at her temples and probing for the wires buried inside her ears. She sees it vividly, as if the incident were happen-ing right here and now, and this adds to her confusion.

"Papa, what are you doing to me?" she had tried to ask him as he worked. Twinges of pain seared her skull. But the words never reached her tongue.

I love you deeply, she thought she heard him say as he yanked out the last of the nano-fiber threads.

"I am doing this for you, my beloved daughter," he said when the thin cord came out of her ears.

"This is what Mama would have wanted."

With a trembling hand she places three fingers against her tem-ple, an almost unconscious gesture, tenderly rubbing the laboratory grown skin used to repair the damage. Shifting her hand to the back of her neck, she touches the knobby wound, callous, rough, and bumpy to the touch, that never quite healed after Papa's extractions.

Oriana lifts heavy eyelids and gazes across the dimly lit room. Across from her, a woman in a white hat sits motionless, her hands across her pregnant belly.

"Do I know you?" Oriana asks. Waves of color course subtly through the air along with controlled emissions of ozone and oxygen and the soothing sounds of low-timbered chimes, singing whales, and woodwinds.

The woman smiles at her, and Oriana smiles back. But the image is blurred. Oriana squints to bring the woman into clearer focus. Now she notices her almond skin and the wavy hair that lies long around her shoulders and chest. Oriana leans forward and rests her elbows on her knees.

"Who are you?" Oriana asks. "You don't look familiar."

The woman looks away, her hat slipping down to obscure her eyes.

My heart is beating, air is moving into and out of my nostrils. I feel pressure against my groin. And, yet, I don't know what I am seeing. Like a dream, the woman begins to quiver and then to fade. Oriana shudders, questioning whether she was ever there at all.

Oriana touches her pregnant belly, and the baby shifts position under her palms.

"Hello little one," she whispers. "I can feel you moving in your secret place. Is this a foot against my palm? Wow, you're strong. I push and you push back hard."

Oriana pats a hand against what she guesses to be the baby's bottom. The child recoils, leaving a hard little elbow just under her abdomen.

"You sure are a mystery in there," Oriana continues. "Which is exactly why I am in such trouble." Oriana begins to sing, her voice carrying softly through the stark room.

"And when we find ourselves in the place just right,
we will be in the valley of love and delight.
When true simplicity is gain'd,
to bow and to bend we shan't be asham'd,
to turn, turn will be our delight,
till by turning, turning we come 'round right."

When Oriana looks up again, the woman has returned, her image clear and strong now. A delicate hand lifts the hat from her head. Her eyes are wide, soft, and sea green. Her lips begin to part.

"Go into the silence," she seems to say, reaching her unenhanced palms toward Oriana.

"How? Where?" Oriana replies. Only, the woman has vanished.

DECEMBER 12

The night before the scheduled retrieval, Oriana makes her way down the staircase to the front door of her home. Her thoughts are anxious and chaotic. Papa's warnings haunt her. An image of Granddad comes to her mind, causing her throat to tighten, and her chest to sting with anguish. The light fixture mounted above the entry door slowly brightens as the sensors pick up the onset of dusk. *I need fresh air. I've got to get out of here.*

Oriana opens the door to the control room and stares at the motherboard, an intricate grid of flashing colors and gyrating command cells, on the wall across from her. . Baffled and overwhelmed, she tries to activate it with a simple voice command.

"Disconnect me," she orders.

There is no response. Hopefully, she can figure out how to access a VISHNEW protocol that will guide her through the disconnection process.

"Disconnect command needed, please."

"Are you asking to deactivate your connection, Oriana?" replies a voice, remarkably similar to Connor's that reverberates between the four walls.

"Yes, I am," she responds.

"Kindly swipe hand to confirm," the voice instructs, flashing a blinking green light on the translucent panel in front of her.

Oriana passes a hand over the communication pad.

"Signal unreadable. Iris imprint, please," the voice requests.

Oriana opens her eyes wide and places them over the blinking blue panel.

"Personal settings locked!" the voice declares. An image of Oriana's irises appears on the panel. A red light flashes three times.

"Disconnection denied. Unauthorized command from Oriana Rotch."

"How could I be so stupid?" Oriana exclaims. Judge Faraday would never allow her to terminate her VISHNEW connection, minimal though it might be. Flustered, Oriana scrambles desperately to override the command, but to no avail. She ponders other options for disconnection, knowing that even a small error could put her in jeopardy.

Breathing in deeply and slowly, she reaches into the back of her throat and searches for the ends of the nano-wire thread woven through her gums. Finding her fingers too bulky for the operation, she reaches for the tweezers hanging on the wall, the same ones Connor uses for replacing hydrogen cells.

"These should work fine," she whispers, taking them down from their hook.

Oriana removes an antimicrobial wipe from the drawer under the control panel, cleans the tweezers, and grips the wire inside her mouth firmly, tugging on the knotted end of the miniscule cable that connects the transmitters and receivers from her mouth to her inner ear.

"Damn," she utters over the stinging, which shortly fades to a tingling sensation under her tongue.

She lifts off the casing that fits tightly over her rear molars, yanks the implant out from underneath, forcing herself to muffle the sudden gasp that passes from her stomach into her throat. The searing pain lasts for a moment and then begins to subside.

"Personal connection compromised. Alert! Personal connection compromised," an adamant voice relays.

This is not good at all. She's got to act immediately or VISHNEW will notify Connor, and her escape will be thwarted before it even begins.

"Thank you. Alert acknowledged," Oriana utters quickly, enunciating as clearly as she can. To her amazement, the voice alarm quiets and the motherboard stops flashing. She backs out of the control room and reaches for the front door, bumping into Connor.

Hands on hips, he gawks at her, and she wonders if he knows she has disconnected herself. She waits for an indication, trying to interpret the fretful, annoyed expression on his mouth. She's in deep trouble if he's figured out what she's done.

"Do you really think you should be going out right now?" he asks.

Pulling out the wires has left her light-headed and queasy. Saved by an empty stomach, she offers a convenient truth.

"Actually, Connor, I feel a bit nauseous. I think what I need is a quiet walk in the fresh evening air."

Connor reaches for his mate.

"I insist on going with you," he says.

Oriana steps aside, trying to make clear that she wants to be alone.

"Please Connor, don't do this," she replies. She takes her coat off the wall hook and nudges Connor out of her way.

"If you're nauseous, then medicate," he suggests.

"No, fresh air is the best medicine for me right now," she says with determination, careful not to give away the desperation she feels.

Connor turns away and walks into the living room, plops down on his personal chair, and pulls the Hood over his head.

How can I be so insensitive, leaving him alone on the night before such an important day? The self-scolding leaves her feeling oddly indifferent, and she resolves to put her mate out of her mind.

She pulls the chameleon coat over her shoulders, slides her arms into the sleeves, and presses the front flaps together with a light pressure to engage the seal. Oriana looks down at her feet.

"Oh no," she whispers, realizing that she's wearing obstetrical shoes which contain sensors that press against the bottom of the wearer's feet and alert VISHNEW to her location and condition if something unusual or threatening happens.

I can't wear these. They've got to come off quickly.

Sitting on the bench by the door, Oriana peels off one shoe after the other, tosses them inside the coat closet, and grabs her personal bag. Heading out of her home, barefoot and alone, free from monitoring or observation, the only remaining Rotch on the island of Nantucket steps outside into the last night her baby will be protected in her womb.

A RETRIEVAL

I n a windowless room, warm, oxygenated air drifts through the soft porous walls. Connor stands by Oriana's side, stroking his fingertips across her head. She watches his palms with curiosity. The blue, yellow, red, and green lights of the VISHNEW connection twinkle like tiny stars under the surface of his skin. He asks her how she's feeling.

Oriana is too sedated to respond. The techno-medics enter. The realization of where she is hits her.

This is a retrieval room. Her back tightens in anticipation.

"I never wanted to do it this way," she pleads as a medic places electrodes against her head.

"Shh, relax now," Connor whispers, kissing her on the mouth.

The cool fluid dripping into her vein chills her forearm. The retrieval machine drops from the ceiling, and its tentacle-like arms slip under her knees. The apparatus widens and lifts until her legs and thighs are vertical to the table, her calves suspended in the air. A sharp pinching in her groin causes her toes to twitch and curl.

One techno-medic speaks to the other and then to the machine. Calculating, discerning, and calibrating, the mechanism informs the pair how and when to proceed. Connor is escorted out of the room by a security-bot. He looks back over his shoulder and grins.

A techno-medic reaches for the harnesses and puts Oriana's arms inside. Gently he clamps her head down. The materna-bot leans over her face, smiling knowingly and kindly. A shiny sphere is lowered onto her forehead, gelatinous and cold against her skin. Its long, hair-like strands penetrate her temples.

"Don't worry," the bot says softly in her ear. "The procedure is nearly complete." The bot's voice sounds familiar, yet causes Oriana distress.

"It was a mistake to replicate her mother's voice. Another would have been much better," one techno-medic says to the other. The medic adjusts the pitch and timbre controls, and the materna-bot speaks again to Oriana.

"I am so proud of you, Ori. You are doing great," it says in a timbre and tone indistinguishable from Papa's. The familiar voice activates the pleasure and security centers of her brain. Neurotransmitters stimulate the limbic region, which lulls her into a state of serenity.

"I missed you, Papa," she says.

"Now," a techno-medic commands the materna-bot, signaling the assessment to begin. Ten thousand tiny needles slide through the pores of Oriana's skin and into the amniotic fluid. A holographic image floats in the corner, displaying the needles as they meet the warm fluids of Oriana's womb.

Reaching the fetus, the probes soften into flowing white fibrous tendrils. Passing over and around the baby's body, they read her condition. The tendrils sweep over her genitals, into her vagina and rectum, along her back, and into each vertebra of her spine. They insert themselves gently into her lymph nodes and probe each nostril and ear. They enter her brain from beneath the occipital ridge. Gently, softly, persistently, they work to gauge the quality of her cells to determine the characteristics of her physiology and to assess the cognitive abilities of her mind.

Oriana begins to tremble. Sweat drips from her brow.

"Please stop," she mumbles, almost in a stupor from the drugs.

The examination is complete. The tendrils break off under the skin of Oriana's belly, disintegrating into simple proteins.

"We have the information we need," one of the techno-medics says. "The specimen is ready to be retrieved."

The maternal-bot reaches its mechanical extension into the birth canal and quickly pulls the baby out. Immediately, its other extension slides a golden rod through Oriana's cervix and sucks the placenta into a white ceramic bowl. Brown particles of nano-gold flow back through the tube and coat her uterine wall.

Oriana touches her face, feeling the sweat drip from her brow to her neck. Her eyelashes are thick with the crust of sleep.

It was only a dream, though the taste of fear remains on her tongue.

VISITORS

"Oriana."

"What?" she replies.

"I am with you."

There it goes again, probably my imagination. I suppose the time has come to go back home. Nothing's been accomplished. Nothing has changed.

"You will be responsible for anything that is wrong with our child," Connor threatened yesterday after she'd returned from Granddad's house. He didn't know what had happened or why she had been out for so long.

"That includes any kind of physical defect, genetic disorder, tumors, impaired vision or hearing, neural tube defect, and anything at all that might have been detected, treated, and cured while she was still in that precious womb of yours!"

Oriana covered her ears, stood up, and tried to walk away.

Connor followed close behind her, shrieking, his temper rising.

"How do you not get it? Why are you acting as if you don't understand what will happen when our child becomes a VISHNEW reject?"

"Granddad died, you jerk!" she screamed. But he had continued to yell about her obstinacy, to insist that she go to the Retrieval Preparation Center.

She collects herself to leave the Meeting House. *They'll soon find me anyway. Even disconnected, the homing system will eventually pick up my scent.* She gathers up her coat and bag and steps carefully through the dark sanctuary, past row after row of benches, until she reaches the front door.

She turns the knob and opens the heavy, creaking door. A dense fog has moved in. Oriana pulls the door closed and retreats to the shelter of the Meeting House.

Not yet. I'll go home soon, just not yet. She finds her way to a nearby pew and sits down. She closes her eyes and bows her head.

"Mama," Oriana whispers, uttering a name she knows well but has never before this moment used as an address. She holds her face in her clammy hands.

"Why did you leave me that way?" she says, as if someone could hear.

"Why did you leave me that way!" she repeats, her voice ringing out against the stark walls, heard by no one.

Sobs overcome her. The moon has set, but the sun has not yet risen, so the Meeting House is almost pitch black, unknowable and frightful. Oriana slides down onto the floor and rocks side to side with her arms wrapped around her chest.

A hand takes hold of the latch on the Meeting House door. Creaking, it opens slowly. The same scratchy voice calls inside.

"Oriana?" the strange man from a few moments ago asks, ever so tenderly.

Oriana slides underneath the bench as far as she can manage.

"Oriana, I know you are here. Don't worry, I've come to help," the voice says, drawing nearer.

Oriana remains as still as possible, attempting to muffle the sound of her own panting breath, burying her mouth inside the sleeve of her coat. A light flashes along the aisle where she is laying. Oriana looks up into its glare, unable to speak from the horror that grips her. The stranger reaches for her hand.

"I've been watching out for you all night. They've been looking for you."

Oriana reaches back, allowing him to help her to standing.

"We are running out of time, so please listen," he pleads.

"What are you talking about?" she replies, as he helps her up onto the bench. She pants, trying to catch her breath.

"I don't even know who are you are," she says. Oriana brushes clumps of dust from her dress, coughing as the particles reach her throat.

"May I sit here beside you?" he asks. "You must be thirsty by now." He hands her a container from the large sack he carries with him. She smiles at him as she takes the container from his hands.

"Parched," she says, taking a few small sips of the warm liquid and tasting the flavor of cinnamon and apples.

"Thank you. I really needed this."

The man reaches under his scarf and disconnects from his throat a device that has altered the sound of his voice. Then he removes the scarf from his face and neck, takes the black cap off his head, and pulls off his gloves. He sets the articles to his side.

Oriana spews the drink from her lips.

"It can't be," she sputters, recognizing the same man who entered at the side of the courtroom on the day of her hearing a month ago.

"Maybe it's too much to ask," he says, "but I need for you to trust me." The voice is unmistakable. "Please forgive me for concealing my identity from you."

And the same man who was up on the catwalk and brushed past her at the Whaling Museum.

He reaches across her lap and takes her hand in his. She notices how calloused and rough it is, yet tender in its grip. He places her hand over his heart. She feels it beating under her palm, slow, rhythmic, and strong. A rush of emotion moves from her chest into her throat, releasing all she had forbidden herself to feel.

From his other hand he takes a flashlight and holds it up by his cheek. She sees his skin, its beautiful panther coloring, and his eyes, a soft, rich blue. She falls sobbing into his embrace.

"Why didn't you tell me back there that it was you?"

"Oriana," he implores, "we have very little time."

"Time for what?" she whimpers. "The retrieval is scheduled to begin within the hour. I will be found well before then."

"There are things I need to say to you, very important information you must have."

Oriana raises her head from his lap and sits upright against the back of the hard pew. Her pelvis burns, and strong cramps take hold of her back and hips. She moans with pain.

Emmanuel places his arm around her back and pulls her against his shoulder.

"I've got you. Now breathe slowly," he suggests.

"Where have you been?" she asks him.

" I've been living on Martha's Vineyard for just over nine months now," he explains.

That's impossible. The Vineyard has been uninhabitable since the Great Storms. She searches his eyes for signs that he is telling the truth, trying to figure out why he has come to her this way. Another cramp overcomes her. She cries out, grabbing her hair.

"It's natural to feel the pain. You can handle it, Oriana. Breathe more slowly and deeply if you can."

"I don't understand why you are here."

"You've not been told the truth," he tells her, stroking her head.

She remembers the night he came to say goodbye, the night they had walked together to this very place. She was consumed by a passion she did not understand and overwhelmed by the grief of his leaving. As he pressed through her widened and inviting legs, the two were united in heart and flesh. There was no fear of pregnancy, as her ova had been removed years before.

He had never intended to leave Oriana that way, never planned to lose control of his desire for her.   Holding Oriana in his arms that night and knowing that he would have to say goodbye to her, all he could do was to let her know how much she truly meant to him.

"You've come back for me now?" she asks, gripped by pain and the torment of her destiny. "It's too late for that. They'll be coming after me, so you get out of here. I have no choice other than to go back home."

Emmanuel gazes at her as she makes her way towards the Meeting House door. She turns back and waves a last goodbye. The faint form of a woman standing by Emmanuel's side raises her hand in response.

There, smiling, her head adorned with a broad hat, is the woman who was standing out in the cold last night under the lantern down the street.

"Mama?" Oriana whispers, immobilized and disoriented. Her knees buckle. She grabs hold of the closest bench. Her heart begins to pound, and she feels breathless and faint. The baby's skull, pressing against her pelvic floor, sends a sharp pain into her vagina. A contraction begins, stabbing sharply into her groin.

"No, not now!" she cries out.

"Exactly as scheduled," Emmanuel affirms. The techno-medical preparation treatments are timed to engage the onset of labor precisely one hour prior to the scheduled retrieval.

"How do you know my schedule?" she snaps, as Emmanuel reaches for her.

"Grace has kept me abreast of it all."

Jolted by another contraction, Oriana collapses. Emmanuel eases her onto the ground, and she clutches his knees. The warm fluids of her womb break free, flowing onto the filthy floor.

"Grace Wyatt? What's she got to do with this? I need you to help get me to the clinic," Oriana pleads.

"I don't think that's what you really want," Emmanuel suggests, rubbing his hand along her back.

The Meeting House door creeks open. Mrs. Wyatt, wearing a tan coat and a brown and yellow cap, a satchel hanging across her shoulder, enters the room.

"Finally!" Emmanuel exclaims frantically. "Not a moment too soon."

"We have very little time," Mrs. Wyatt says, kneeling over Oriana. "My, it's cold in here. And dark, too!" She draws a cloth from her bag, along with other supplies, and sets up a solar lantern no more than a foot high.

She spreads a blanket on the floor, and Emmanuel helps Oriana to position herself into a squat.

"Why this way?" Oriana asks.

"Trust us," Emmanuel returns.

The aging woman kneels down beside her. Oriana groans and strains, breaking into a sweat. Drawing another cloth out of her supply bag, Mrs. Wyatt wipes it over Oriana's brow. Moist and soft, impregnated with essential oils of lavender and vale-rian root, the poultice calms Oriana until another contraction overwhelms her.

She opens her mouth to cry out, but Mrs. Wyatt places her hand over Oriana's mouth.

"Oriana. No one can know that we are here."

"I am afraid," Oriana mumbles through the woman's firmly gripped fingers. "I don't know what to do." She whimpers with pain.

"You don't have to," Mrs. Wyatt woman responds. "Your body knows how to birth a baby, and your baby knows how to be born. So let go and trust. In your very cells is the wisdom of millions of generations of women who have given birth."

Oriana expels her breath, panting, gasping, and spitting with pain.

"That's not what I am talking about. I don't know what to do about Judge Faraday's decree. Retrieval is scheduled for this morning."

"What you are going to do," Emmanuel replies, "is give birth to our child."

"She's crowning. There's her head," Mrs. Wyatt says to Emmanuel. He grabs Oriana firmly from behind, bracing her shoulders and back to support her weight. Mrs. Wyatt fixes her eyes on the daughter of her closest friend. Oriana gazes blankly back.

"OUR child?" Oriana asks, groaning.

"Keep your focus on the release of your child," Mrs. Wyatt instructs.

"I don't want to let her go," Oriana admits. "She'll be made into a child of VISHNEW."

A torpid mass, wedged within a space that seems far too small to contain it, presses against her lumbar nerves, sending pains shooting through Oriana's rectum.

"No, I can't do this!" she shouts.

"Create a vision, Oriana, one that will help you to birth our daughter," Emmanuel speaks into her ear.

With a broad, toothless grin, Mrs. Wyatt commands Oriana in a clear, firm tone.

"Now push!"

BIRTH

In the shadows of early morning, the shrieks of new life fill the Meeting House as ancient spirits look on. Silent Friends nod austerely, acknowledging the glory of the occasion. Mrs. Wyatt places the infant on Oriana's chest. Streams of sunlight fall upon the child's face as she latches on to her mother's breast. The sweet union lasts only a few moments. As soon as the newborn releases her lips, Emmanuel reaches for the child.

"Sorry, but we've got to hurry," he says, taking the infant into his hands. He studies her with care as he wipes away the thick paste remaining from life inside Oriana's womb, and cleans out her nose, ears, and mouth. Then, with a cloth from Mrs. Wyatt's bag, he swaddles the child tightly.

Mrs. Wyatt presses down on Oriana's belly, rubbing vigorously. Then she takes the newborn into her arms. Emmanuel delivers the placenta and seals it tightly into a bio-bag. Mrs. Wyatt places the child back into Oriana's arms. She drinks into her heart the loveliness of the child.

"Congratulations," Mrs. Wyatt says.

"I can hardly fathom it. She's born now," Oriana replies.

"I have something for you," Mrs. Wyatt announces. "Consider it a gift from your Mama, one she could not give you herself."

Mrs. Wyatt pulls a hand-made quilt, one that is clearly quite old, out of a second bag.

"Rebecca's great-great-great-grandmother made this. It's been in your maternal family since the 1800's." She drapes the blanket around Oriana and their daughter, its colorful swatches surrounding them both.

"Listen carefully to me now," Mrs. Wyatt continues. "There are two things you need to know, and both are very, very important."

Oriana forces herself to look up from the child, gripped by the pangs of a mysterious love.

"As you may remember, Oriana," Mrs. Wyatt continues, "I was the matron on TEMPLE duty the day you came to deliver your eggs."

"Yes," Oriana replies. "I remember." She looks down serenely at the child in her arms.

"Oriana," Mrs. Wyatt says sternly. "I did not remove all of your eggs. I left over eight dozen inside your ovaries."

"What?" Oriana asks, incredulous.

"You got pregnant on your own, Oriana. Please forgive me. It was a promise I made to Rebecca."

Emmanuel strokes his hand across Oriana's cheek.

"But why did you leave eggs behind?'

"Because I promised your Mama, that's why."

"I believe that this is our child, Oriana," Emmanuel interjects as he stands to collect the birthing supplies. He places the items back in the satchel and then begins to clean himself up. "I've come to take you both back to the Vineyard with me. Mrs. Wyatt is coming too. The three of you will be safe with me in a community of independents," he explains.

Oriana puts the baby to her nipple once more. The baby's lips latch on again. It's painful at first, but the pain feels good, and tells Oriana that her body is working to keep her baby alive.

"Please eat," Emmanuel suggests, offering Oriana dried black-berries and muffins. She consumes the fruit eagerly, berry after berry, until only a handful remain. Then, in a few quick bites, she wolfs down a muffin as well.

"Where did those come from?" Oriana asks.

"The berries? We grow them on our land," Emmanuel says.

"You grow your own food? I don't get it. How? Where?"

"All of that will be explained in due time."

"Why do they taste this way?" Oriana asks, pining for more of the sweet fruit.

"It's the life force," he tells her.

"The what?" Oriana asks.

"The Foundry-produced food you are accustomed to eating has no life force. It's too far removed from the land. That's why you sometimes eat when you are not hungry, because you have had plenty of food but not enough life force."

Oriana wants to know more.

"Your body craves the life force, not simply the taste of the food or its chemical content," he says.

"Interesting, but implausible," Oriana remarks, furrowing her brow.

The newborn releases Oriana's nipple, drunk from the elixir that drips from her mouth. Oriana puts her index finger into the baby's tiny hand. The small fingers squeeze around it.

"And how in the world did you manage to cross over to Nantucket from Martha's Vineyard, and get past Island Security?" she asks

"Good question!" he replies. "I used a stealth hydro-huv."

Oriana chuckles nervously, never having heard of such a thing.

"It uses a photo-hydrolysis system. When it's under water, it runs on fuel cells so there's no combustion to create noise. When it's in the air, the solar propulsion system is pretty quiet, too."

"You own one of these hydro-huvs?" she questions.

"Actually, it's not mine alone. It belongs to our community. We use it for special occasions to go off-island on business or to visit family and friends on the mainland. Coming for you counts as a special case."

"Coming for me?" she asks.

Emmanuel takes a seat on the floor by Oriana's side and kisses Oriana on the cheek. His breath, which smells of honey-soaked squash, is moist and warm as it falls over her nostrils.

"Is no one living on the Vineyard VISHNEW-connected?" Oriana queries.

Emmanuel nods in affirmation. He watches her eyes. Clearly, she is troubled over why she has never been told about the sovereignty of the neighboring Martha's Vineyard, or of its VISHNEW-independent citizens.

Why was I never given a choice to go? Oriana suspects that the answers may have something to do with Granddad and what he did and did not want her to know. Her eyes grow wide and her face reddens.

"Damn him," she mumbles, nostrils flaring.

"Try not to be angry," Emmanuel counsels. "Those who leave here to live on Martha's Vineyard can never come back. It's a very serious decision to go. Maybe it's best that you never knew." Emmanuel wipes a tear from her face.

"We'll talk about that later, okay? Right now there's something more important that I think you may want to know."

"Oh? She replies. "What might that be?"

"There was a woman here." Emmanuel says quietly. "I saw her a few moments ago, standing by Mrs. Wyatt's side."

"May I?" he asks, reaching for the baby.

"This woman seems always to be with you," he tells her as he pulls the child close to his chest. "She was next to you in the courtroom during your hearing a few weeks ago. She followed behind you when you came through the Museum door at storytelling night. And she was there when we met on Main Street tonight. Oriana, she was here with you in the Meeting House when I arrived."

"I don't understand," Oriana replies, rubbing her fingers on her temples. "I've been here alone all night, until you came."

Oriana lays her head on her love's shoulder, her mind racing as she takes in the beauty of the newborn child asleep on Emmanuel's chest. After a moment she jerks her head up.

"Oh god, maybe I do understand!" she says, her eyes bulging. "It started with the woman in the pediatric emergency room, who stood at the foot of my bed when I was so sick as a little girl. Then there was the woman who passed by Granddad's house one summer evening. And I think that must be the woman who was sitting across from me in the retrieval preparation room yesterday. Oh! Oh! And the same woman whose image sat framed on Granddad's mantle!"

Oriana drops her head, crying quietly.

"It's my Mama," she whimpers. "But how?"

"Oriana," Emmanuel says quietly. "You've been deceived."

Oriana looks into his eyes and recognizes the boy who was her only childhood friend. She reaches up for his hair, slipping the blond strands through her fingers. She trusts him, and trusts her feelings for him.

"In what way, Emmanuel?" she asks.

"About your Mama."

"What's to know about her, other than that the system went down, and her life was unexpectedly and tragically cut short as a result of my birth?"

"Your mother loved you then, and she loves you still."

"Still?" she probes.

Emmanuel rubs his hand over his chin and cheeks, keenly aware of the passing time. He tries not to rush the words, despite his sense of urgency. He wants to keep Oriana calm and relaxed.

"Your Mama never died. She'd been sentenced for a crime and taken immediately from the retrieval table to the Facility. Even your Papa did not know they'd revived her. They kept that information from him. Once he was in the Facility, he spotted her. She'd been put into a state of suspended animation."

"Hurry, Oriana, you don't have much time," Mrs. Wyatt implores. "We've got to get going right now.

"No," Oriana answers slowly. "The baby and I won't be coming. It's best we stay right here. Papa will be looking for me."

"Listen to me, child, and listen well," Mrs. Wyatt relays. "I've been watching your daughter. The child is unable to see. Her eyes do not respond to light."

Oriana looks down at the bundle in her arms, noticing that the infant's eyes are wide open.

"Look at Mama," she says, and kisses the newborn's forehead. "Come, little one, look at your Mama now."

The baby's eyes are fixed and dilated. Oriana moves her head, but the baby's eyes don't follow. She moves her hand over the child's face. Still, there is no response.

"We have hardly any time left," Emmanuel says urgently.

A tear tumbles down Oriana's cheek. She realizes that she hasn't a choice. The child's fate is sealed. She reaches for Emmanuel's hand and squeezes it hard. "How do I know that we will be safe there?" she asks.

"Our sovereignty guarantees your right to live as a VISHNEW-independent, Oriana. Plus, we can offer you the support and care of a community of people who will welcome you and the baby as our own."

"What about the security-bots and their hovers, Emmanuel? It will take them no time at all to track us and bring us back."

"True, leaving with her puts you both in grave danger until we are back on the Vineyard and you and our baby are registered as members of the community. Once that happens, you will be under our jurisdiction. Then it will be within your rights to stay," Emmanuel explains, gathering the remainder of their belongings. "There's no hope for either of you unless we get going now." He glances at a gadget hanging from a cord around his waist.

"How did you gain re-entry onto Nantucket?" Oriana asks, "without Island Security detaining you?"

"It's because I left without actually leaving. Remember, I was once a full-connect," he explains. "The rest is too complicated to go into now. The indicator on my sensor is picking up an approaching security craft. We may already have run out of time."

Oriana hands the baby to Mrs. Wyatt, and Emmanuel helps them both up from the floor.

"We're coming, Emmanuel," Oriana says, taking the baby back into her arms.

The four step out into the cold December air, the rich blue sky strewn with thin white streaks of clouds. Everything shimmers: the branches on the trees, the roofs of the houses, the sidewalks, and the child's green eyes. The air, crisp and clear and fresh, is totally free of the putrid smell that permeates it most days. Oriana squints in the bright winter sunlight. The baby's eyes remain fixed, open wide. The frigid ground numbs Oriana's bare feet.

Emmanuel takes Oriana's elbow and guides her into the waiting craft. Mrs. Wyatt steps inside next to her as Emmanuel starts the soundless engine.

A security-hover glides over the rooftops and turns the corner of Fair Street and Main. Connor sits inside, wildly animated, pointing in their direction as the craft approaches.

"That's her! She's in there!" he yells.

Oriana hands the swaddled infant to Mrs. Wyatt.

"Her name is Zoe, meaning 'life'." With that, Oriana slides out of the craft.

"Get back in!" Emmanuel insists as he sets the controls to 'launch'.

Oriana's pulls away from the vehicle.

"I've got to get to Mama," she shouts. "Get out of here! Now!"

The hover door closes as the craft lifts swiftly from Fair Street. Within moments, Emmanuel and the baby and Mrs. Wyatt are out of sight.

The security-hover lands. Connor approaches with two techno-medics and a security-bot. Oriana hears the sound of a woman wailing, loon-like and sorrowful, but doesn't realize that the voice is her own. Less than half a mile away, the hydro-huv and its precious cargo slip under the swelling crests of Nantucket Sound.

ABOUT THE AUTHOR

As an Associate Professor of Engineering and Society at the University of Virginia, Rosalyn W. Berne teaches courses in "Science, Technology and Contemporary Issues: Science Fiction and The Future," and "Science, Fiction and the New Reproductive Technologies." She was a recipient of the National Science Foundation Career Award, which for five years supported her research in the ethics of nanotechnology development. Seeing the capacity of science fiction to provoke reflection about emerging technologies and their effects on humanity, and to stimulate the moral imagination, she both writes and teaches the genre.

Emerging from the author's scholarship, *Waiting in the Silence* explores human reproduction, privacy, aging and spirituality in a world where novel technologies have emerged from the convergences of nanotechnology, biotechnology, information, neuro- and cognitive sciences. The sequel, *Walking on the Sea* is underway.

Other books by Rosalyn Berne include:

Nanotalk: Conversations with scientists and engineers about ethics in the development of nanotechnology;

Creating Life from Life: Biotechnology and science Fiction; and

When the Horses Whisper: The wisdom of wise and sentient beings

61742831R00166